CHILD'S PREY
The Nanny Problem
Book 3

NOLON KING

LAUREN STREET

CHILD'S PREY

Prologue

I FLOATED ON MY BACK, staring up at the sky.

Then I rolled over and continued swimming. The warm water and cool night air felt like a cocoon, making me feel safe and protected.

I listened to the chirping crickets as palm fronds rustled overhead. It was dark and I felt like I was floating in space, a million miles away from Los Angeles. And the Marlowes. And any drama. For a moment in time, I was untouchable.

I took a deep breath and dove to the bottom, sitting cross-legged on the tiles, eyes closed, holding my breath. The water pressed against me from all sides, muffling any sound from the world above.

I heard a splash.

Dammit.

So much for this pool being "mine."

Alright, I'd been in Los Angeles far too long if I'd started thinking that way. Entitlement was too contagious in the Hollywood Hills.

I pushed off the bottom, surfacing. I took a breath and opened my eyes. Someone had joined me in the pool. They

1

probably hadn't seen me sitting on the bottom. I glided to the edge. "Hope I didn't scare you," I called out.

No response.

I gripped the deck and then hoisted myself out, water streaming down my skin. I walked over to one of the lounge chairs and grabbed my towel, wrapping it around my body. The night air felt like a kiss of cool against my wet skin.

I glanced back at the pool.

A man was floating face down, fully dressed. Dark liquid spread around him in the water like an oil slick.

"You spilled your wine," I added.

No response.

My stomach sank and something told me that wasn't wine surrounding him.

Oh God. He hadn't jumped in. He'd fallen in. Maybe he hit his head on the side of the pool.

I yanked my towel off and jumped back into the water, swimming over to him. Why was there so much blood? Much more than a simple head injury would cause.

I rolled him over onto his back.

His throat gaped open at me like a second mouth.

I screamed.

Chapter One

"Are you sure the Carlsons were okay with you borrowing their car?" I asked.

"Of course." Elsa braked for the red light. "Though I really wish I wasn't taking you to the airport."

Strapped in her car seat in the back, Kiersztyn gave a sharp *blat!*—she obviously agreed.

Outside, people hunched against the rain. Umbrellas everywhere. The usual blur of bodegas and laundromats streaked past.

I didn't know how I felt.

New York had been the home I chose. The one that had seemed to fit me best. And now I was leaving it. Albeit temporarily.

"I mean, I always knew we might not both be nannying in New York," Elsa said, gripping the steering wheel. "But Los Angeles seems like it's on the other side of the world."

"I know."

I glanced at my best friend. Her red curls stuck out everywhere. She hadn't been herself all day.

"I'll be back at Christmas," I said. "I made sure to get two weeks off written into my contract."

Elsa glanced at me. "I guess that'll be alright." She didn't sound convinced. "You hear from Frenchie?"

I flushed and shook my head. "No. But they were all off to Europe. Sailing, I think. He said communication might be spotty."

"Uh huh," Elsa said.

I glared at her. "He'll reach out when he can."

I wasn't sure who I was trying to convince. Her, or me. Part of me wondered if Frenchie was thinking about me as much as I was thinking about him. But I needed to be focused. No time for dwelling on that with another kid to look after.

Elsa hit the horn and cursed under her breath, accelerating through a stale yellow light. She was usually too careful when driving. And that never worked out in New York City.

"Alright, what's wrong?" I asked. "You don't seem like yourself."

Elsa sighed. "Nothing. The Carlsons have been arguing lately. It's starting to mess with my sleep."

"Do you want to find a different nanny position?" The tension in her jaw was obvious.

She shook her head, glancing over at me. "No. I like where I am."

"Are you sure?"

Elsa's cheeks flushed pink. "Yes."

I raised an eyebrow. "You're hiding something."

"I'm fine," she said, but the way she gripped the wheel said otherwise. "I'm just going to miss having my best friend so close."

I sighed. "Same. And just for the record, you're coming to visit me when you get time off. We can do whatever you want. Hit up the beach. Go shopping. Stalk your favorite actor."

Elsa's laugh came out wrong. Forced.

Kiersztyn let out a squeal from the backseat, and I turned to look at her. "Sorry, you can't come. I don't think your parents will go for it."

She laughed.

"Take care of Elsa for me, though. If anything happens to her, I'll hold you personally responsible."

Kiersztyn blew bubbles at me. I turned back to the front, blinking hard.

We lapsed into silence.

Elsa reached over and squeezed my hand at the next red light. I held on tight until the light turned green.

We hit traffic approaching the airport, cars packed bumper to bumper.

"You ready for the Marlowes?" Elsa asked.

"As ready as I'll ever be. Still can't believe I'm going to be nannying for Hollywood Royalty."

"Hopefully this time will be better," Elsa said.

I nodded.

We both knew she was referring to the Stockports. And the Mansfields. My nannying resume so far was starting to read like a true crime podcast lineup.

Elsa pulled up to the departures curb. My stomach tightened. This was it. I grabbed my carry-on from the footwell and met Elsa's eyes.

"You'll call when you land?" she asked.

"Wild actors couldn't keep me from that."

She laughed again.

We both got out of the car. I retrieved my suitcase from the trunk and Elsa met me on the curb. Neither of us moved.

"Take care of yourself, Zoe," she told me.

I nodded, not daring to speak. Then we hugged.

Other travelers walked past us with rolling luggage, saying their goodbyes to their friends and family, but we stayed there, unmoving.

Her eyes were as glassy as mine when we finally parted.

She opened her mouth, then closed it, waved, and dashed back to the car. She climbed into the driver's seat and pulled away into the stream of airport traffic. I watched until the Carlsons' car disappeared and then turned toward the terminal.

Time for another adventure.

I made my way inside, dragging my suitcase behind me and headed straight for the washroom. I made my way into the cubicle, crammed my luggage in, closed the door, and burst into tears.

I should call Madeline and tell her I couldn't do this. That I wasn't strong enough to leave New York. Or Elsa.

No.

That wasn't fair to the Marlowes.

Leaving shouldn't hurt this much. I wiped my tears on my sleeve, left the stall, and washed up at the sink. Then I made my way back out into the departures area, checked my bag, and joined the security line.

It took so long to be processed that I almost chickened out several times. But right when I was deciding that this was a bad idea and I should stay in New York, the TSA agent waved me through. I felt calmer on the other side.

I went to my gate and found a seat.

My phone rang as I sat. I dug it out of my pocket, expecting to see Elsa's name.

But the screen read: *unknown caller.*

I let it ring through to voicemail. They didn't leave a message.

And then it rang again.

My thumb hovered over the decline button. But what if it was Bella or the twins calling? I'd promised I'd always be there for them. Or maybe it was Frenchie? Or the Marlowes calling with an update? Madeline had given them my number.

"Hello?" I answered.

Silence. And then a male voice: "Zo?"

I froze. The airport around me faded to a dull roar.

"Zo?"

Was that my…dad?

I disconnected.

The phone rang again immediately.

I switched it off, my hands shaking, and stuffed the phone back into my pocket.

What the hell?

It would have been bad enough to hear from Toxic Tania, but my dad? I hadn't heard his voice in years.

I felt punched in the stomach. How did he get my number? Tania must have given it to him. Mom and him back in contact couldn't be good.

Maybe LA wasn't far enough.

I got up and walked to a café kiosk and ordered a tea, hoping it would help me feel less rattled. Why was he calling now? Was he out of prison? He had to be. There was no automated message announcing the correctional facility. Either that or he was using a burner.

What did he want?

Had to be the same thing he always wanted. Money.

This was the last thing I needed.

I was trying to move forward in mylife, not get dragged back into my past.

I got my tea and returned to the gate. Maybe it was a mistake. Maybe it wasn't him. But I knew that voice.

Stop it.

Don't think about him.

I didn't want to think about Elsa either. Or Frenchie. Because I missed them both.

Instead, I reviewed the meeting I'd had with Madeline a few days earlier.

Chapter Two

I STARED AT MADELINE. "Los Angeles? That's on the other side of the country."

Madeline smiled. "Your geography skills never cease to amaze me, Zoe."

I bristled. "I only meant that it's far away."

Her Cartier caught the light. "2800 miles."

I glared at her, leaning back in my chair. "That's not helping. What if I run into trouble?"

Madeline folded her perfectly manicured fingers and rested them on her desk. "You've proven yourself quite adept at handling trouble."

Images of a burning mansion flashed through my mind. The smell of smoke. Blood in the rain. Screams.

I pushed the memories away.

"Maybe. But I like knowing you're close by. Like my own personal Batman."

I swear to God something softened in her expression. "I could arrange a visit. Make sure you're settled in."

Yes, please.

But I didn't say that. I couldn't. Not when I'd spent so long pretending I didn't need anyone.

"No, it's fine. I'll be okay." Besides, I didn't want her to think I wasn't capable. "Now who is the exceptionally lucky kid who gets me as a nanny?"

Her lips pressed into a line. "I see your confidence has returned."

I grinned.

She opened a sleek leather portfolio and pushed it across the desk. A family photo stared up at me. Picture perfect smiles, designer clothes, and two familiar faces.

"Rose Marlowe and Caleb Penrose." Madeline tapped a crimson nail on the photo. "And their son."

I leaned forward, my jaw hanging open. "Wait. *The* Rose Marlowe?"

"I wasn't aware there were multiples."

"No, I mean. Rose Marlowe, the actress? As in my favorite actress since I was fifteen? The woman who made me cry through *Summer's Child* and laugh until my sides hurt in *Taxes, Tequila, and Trouble?*" My voice sounded embarrassingly starstruck even to my own ears.

"Well, I don't know about that," Madeline said. "We've never discussed favorite anythings before."

I grunted and picked up the photo to study it.

She continued. "She and her husband need a nanny for their thirteen-year-old son, Talon."

The boy was as tall as both of his parents and had his father's jaw and his mother's dark eyes, hidden behind the kind of glasses one might call spectacles.

I looked at her. "Why does a thirteen-year-old need a nanny?"

Madeline's mouth curved ever so slightly. "Why does any child need a nanny?"

I blinked. "Good point."

After all, every situation was different.

Madeline slid another document toward me. "The house is located in the Hollywood Hills. Rose, Caleb, and Talon live with her father."

"The legendary producer Maxwell 'Smokey' Marlowe?"

"I'm sure I can't say."

"They call him Smokey because of all the cigarettes he used to smoke."

She raised a sculpted eyebrow.

I bared my teeth. "Or at least that's what I read in one of Rose Marlowe's interviews."

Her eyes lingered on me. "I do hope you'll be able to manage the stars in your eyes upon arrival."

"You mean I can't even ask Rose for an autograph?"

She inhaled, looking horrified.

I grinned. "I'm just kidding, Madeline. Relax."

"Same contract as usual. Monday to Friday, weekends off. However, they've asked you to sign an additional NDA."

Madeline presented another document, this one thicker than the one I'd signed when she hired me. You know the kind. Promising not to share any secrets of the rich and wretched. My name was already printed at the bottom, awaiting my signature.

I hesitated. There was a lot of fine print.

"I had the lawyers personally vet it," she said. "Basically don't talk to anyone about the family or you'll be sued into your next lifetime."

"Got it," I said, reaching for her Montblanc. I might not trust a lot of people, my parents included, but I trusted Madeline.

She reached into her drawer, pulled out another set of papers. "Your flight details."

I scanned the paper. First-class ticket. Car service on both ends. Everything arranged. "I leave tomorrow. That's…soon."

"Is that a problem? You have other work I'm not aware of?"

"Nope. I'm good. Except I'd like to go to the airport with Elsa."

"Very well." She nodded. "I will make that adjustment."

I tucked the flight information into my bag and stood. "I better get packing."

She'd already turned back to her tablet.

I left, smiling at Madeline's assistant Gwyneth on my way out. "See you later. Good luck with all the nannies."

She got to her feet. "Don't suppose you could get me an autograph from Rose?"

"I might find myself in a shallow grave in Madeline's basement if I do."

"She has a basement?" Gwyneth asked.

"Wouldn't surprise me in the least." I raised my hands as though painting a picture. "I'm sure it contains multiple gravestones. *Here Lie The Nannies that Disappointed Me.*"

"Shouldn't you be on your way?" Madeline asked.

I jumped. Madeline stood in her doorway.

"I'm already gone," I said.

"Good."

I grimaced at Gwyneth and headed for the elevator.

"Oh, and Zoe?" Madeline said.

I paused, turning around. "Yes?"

"The gravestones in my basement say *They seemed so promising.*" Then she was gone.

"Did you know she had a sense of humor?" I asked.

Gwyneth shook her head.

"Better not let anyone know or you might wind up in the basement along with—"

"Now, Zoe." Madeline's voice drifted out of her office and down the hallway.

"I'm gone!"

And I was.

I'D NEVER BEEN to Los Angeles. Although at least I'd been on a plane before, thanks to the Stockports. I made my way down to the lobby, out onto the street, and onto the subway.

I sat and pulled out my phone. Googled Rose Marlowe. Pages and pages of results. One of the highest-paid actresses in Hollywood. Five Academy Award nominations. One win. Married to the equally famous actor Caleb Penrose for fifteen years. Only one mention of their kid.

Rose had been accused of assault by a paparazzi for stalking the boy.

Talon. Why the hell did parents feel the need to be "original" with kid names? I'd bet anything when Kiersztyn hit 18, she'd be changing that spelling.

I scrolled more.

Divorce rumors.

They'd apparently been circulating for months, given the article dates. Apparently Rose and Caleb hadn't been seen together at any public events for six months now. "Sources" (probably some bored intern in the office) close to the couple claimed they were living separate lives despite still sharing a home.

I switched to searching Maxwell Marlowe, legendary producer. Founder of Eureka Films. The man behind some of cinema's most iconic franchises. And according to several articles, stepping down as CEO due to health concerns.

I dug deeper. Found an old newspaper article from thirty years ago:

LOS ANGELES—Isabella Marlowe, 40, wife of renowned film producer and studio head Maxwell "Smokey" Marlowe, died Monday night in what authorities are calling an accidental drowning off the Southern California coast.

The Marlowe family was reportedly aboard their private yacht, anchored near Catalina Island for a midsummer holiday when Isabella was discovered missing early in the morning. Her body was recovered early Tuesday morning by the U.S. Coast Guard.

Officials have not released further details, though preliminary statements suggest no foul play is suspected. An autopsy is pending.

Known for her work with children's literacy charities and her appearances at Hollywood's most exclusive events, Isabella was a beloved figure in Los Angeles social circles. She and Maxwell Marlowe shared four children and nearly two decades of marriage.

The news has sent shockwaves through both the entertainment industry.

A spokesperson for the Marlowe family declined to comment.

A private memorial service is expected in the coming days.

And then I found another one:

ISABELLA CALLAHAN DEAD: BUT WAS IT AN ACCIDENT?

She was beautiful, beloved, and married to one of the most powerful men in Hollywood. Now she's dead.

Isabella Marlowe, 40, wife of producer Maxwell "Smokey"

Marlowe, was found drowned off Catalina Island. Officials are calling it an accident.

But insiders say the marriage had been "on the rocks for months." One source claims Isabella was "miserable" and "wanted out." Another says Smokey was seen on deck just before she disappeared into the water.

Was it a tragic misstep…or is Tinseltown hiding something much darker?

We'll be watching, Smokey.

I got off at my stop and headed home to pack. My phone rang.

I flopped down beside my suitcase, staring up at the ceiling as I answered.

"Well?" Elsa asked.

I hit speaker and kicked off my shoes. "You'll never guess who I'm nannying for. Never in a million years."

"Then I'm not going to try. Who?"

"Rose Marlowe."

Silence. Then: "*The* Rose Marlowe? The actress?"

"The one and only.

"Holy shit. I didn't know she had kids."

"Thirteen-year-old boy named Talon."

"Jeez. LA. Hollywood. Movie stars. Secret scandals."

"Yeah. But not this job. This job is going to be uneventful."

Elsa laughed.

I really hoped those weren't going to be famous last words.

Chapter Three

Los Angeles was a furnace. Hot and full of exhaust. I stood at the curb of the arrivals area, scanning the vehicles idling at the curb pumping out ribbons of even hotter air.

A car was supposed to meet me. But which one?

I dragged my suitcase back into the terminal and pulled off to the side. A young man in black uniform held a sign: *Zoe Smith*.

Early twenties. Hair slicked back. Dark sunglasses.

The polished look of money.

He caught me looking at him. I waved, then walked over, dragging my suitcase behind me. "Hi. I'm Zoe. Do you want my ID?"

"No." He smiled, shaking his head. "I've already seen your picture."

"You have?"

He nodded, extending his hand. "Welcome to Los Angeles. I'm Bertie. How was your flight?"

I shook his hand, and he seemed surprised. I realized he was reaching for my suitcase.

"Sorry," I said, dropping my hand.

He laughed. "That's quite alright. You're the first person I've ever picked up that did that."

"Nice to meet you," I said, surrendering my suitcase.

He gestured to the doors. "This way."

I followed him back out into the heat.

He walked over to a black SUV and put my suitcase in the back, then circled to the passenger door.

"You okay if I ride up front?" I asked. "I always feel weird in the back."

He shot me a grin. "Works for me."

I got settled, then Bertie pulled away from LAX. Or at least tried to. Traffic crawled along at the slowest pace imaginable. Horns blared. Airport security whistled and yelled at cars that lingered too long.

"Is your traffic always this bad?" New York got congested, but somehow it always seemed to be moving. This seemed like a parking lot.

He laughed. "This must be your first time in LA."

"Is it that obvious?" I wiped the sweat from my brow.

"Don't worry," he said, adjusting the air conditioning. "You'll get used to it. Took me three years to figure out that any time I get on the 405, I needed to pack like I was going away for the weekend. Water. Snacks. Sleeping bag."

I laughed. "Where are you from originally?"

"Detroit." He kept his eyes on the road. "Came out here after college. Why would anyone want to live with snow and ice when you can have sunshine year-round?"

"I dunno. I kind of like the seasons."

"Me too." He turned to me with a playful smile. "And it's called summer."

I laughed.

We merged onto the freeway. Palm trees lined twelve lanes of crawling traffic.

"So, what brought you to nannying?" he asked, switching lanes.

I wrinkled my nose. "Necessity at first. My college fund dried up overnight."

"Tough break."

"Yeah." The memory of Tania's betrayal still felt raw. "I had been hoping to study journalism before… well, before everything fell apart."

"Journalist to nanny is quite the career shift."

I shrugged. "I got lucky working for Madeline. She doesn't put up with any bullshit from her clients. And the pay is surprisingly good. Plus I can still write on the side."

"Well, you're in the right city for that." Bertie's eyes darted to the rearview. "Everyone here is working on a screenplay or a novel."

Industrial blocks and faded billboards blurred by.

"So what's Los Angeles really like? I have a feeling it's nothing like New York."

Bertie checked the mirror again, then leaned back in his seat. "Better weather and worse traffic. Everything you've seen and nothing you expect at the same time. Beautiful and ugly. Glamorous and desperate. Fame and obscurity. All living side by side."

"You're very poetic."

"You're not the only writer. I've got ten scripts in my bedside drawer."

He checked the rearview again, tightening his fingers on the steering wheel.

"Is everything okay? You keep looking behind us."

Bertie hesitated. "Don't be obvious about it, but take a look at the gray sedan three cars back. Has it been with us since the airport?"

I adjusted the side mirror, angling it until I could see

the car in question. A nondescript gray sedan, windows tinted nearly black, following at a distance.

"I don't remember seeing it. But there was so much traffic. Why? Who is it?"

"Probably just the paparazzi." His tone was casual, but his eyes were fixed on the mirror. "They're always swarming about, trying to get shots of Rose or Caleb. They must have thought I was going to pick one of them up."

"Are they a big problem for the family?"

"The Marlowes are used to them." Bertie shrugged. "But you're not. Just know they're like fleas. They'll attach themselves anyone connected to celebrities. Nannies included."

"Why?"

"Celebrity blogs like *PopFix* or *GlamTrap* will pay top dollar for a blurry shot of a baby toe if the kid's got the right last name."

He accelerated.

"Jeez."

"Don't worry. I'll lose this one." Bertie jerked the wheel, slicing through three lanes of freeway. Horns blared. Someone flipped us off.

He veered onto the shoulder and sped up, passing several vehicles.

The SUV fishtailed slightly as he took an off-ramp under an overpass.

We shot down the road into a rundown industrial area, all chain-link and graffiti. He turned, then again, pulling into the back lot of a building that looked abandoned. Just a few delivery trucks rusting in place and a broken vending machine baking in the sun.

We waited for ten minutes after he stopped, both of us

watching out the window, my hands shaking. But the gray car never reappeared.

"I think we're clear," Bertie said.

"Yeah."

"You know not to talk to anyone about the Marlowes, right? Not even a doctor. A therapist. Or your mother."

"No worries there. I signed my NDA."

"That doesn't stop everyone. Paparazzi pays big money for insider info."

"Well, Marlowes aside, I'd never do anything to put Madeline's company in jeopardy."

He pulled back onto the highway.

"You're very protective of them," I added.

He flushed. "Thanks. They've been good to me."

We climbed into the Hollywood Hills.

"It's greener than I expected," I said, watching the landscapes flash past my window. Palm trees towered over winding streets. Bougainvillea cascaded down fences in violent purples and pinks. White stucco houses hid behind manicured hedges, their glass walls catching sunlight like mirrors.

"Everyone thinks LA is just desert and concrete, but the wealthy keep their microclimates well-watered thanks to the fires.

He turned onto a private drive that curved upward. Wrought-iron gates loomed ahead, black and ornate. A white wall bore the name *Starshine* in flowing script.

I glimpsed a dense curtain of hedges beyond the bars, manicured to within an inch of their lives. The house itself stayed hidden, like it was choosing not to reveal itself to those that didn't have access.

Bertie pressed a button on a remote attached to the rearview. The gate swung open and a second later we were through.

"This place once belonged to Cary Grant. And before him, a couple of silent film stars whose names I can't remember."

The driveway curved around a stand of ancient oaks.

The house materialized through the trees. Three levels of glass and concrete, all sharp angles and clean lines. White walls. Marble columns. A cobalt blue door at the center like a jewel.

My stomach knotted. Another grand house. Another wealthy family. I'd been through this before—twice now—and both times it had ended in what could only be called chaos. Hopefully this time it would be different.

Bertie parked near a side entrance, away from the imposing front door. "Here we are. Home sweet home."

I got out. Cooler air. Dead quiet.

Bertie got out and retrieved my suitcase from the back.

A woman paced on the flagstone path near the front door, phone pressed to her ear, her face a mask of irritation. Late forties, impeccably dressed in a tailored pantsuit. Sleek dark hair pulled back in a severe ponytail, not a strand out of place.

She paused mid-sentence when she spotted me, her eyes narrowing.

"Where the hell have you been?" She strode over, not bothering to move the phone from her mouth. "No. I'm not talking to you. I'm talking to Bertie. Rose is furious."

Bertie shrugged. "LA traffic."

Her gaze swept over me, assessing and dismissive. "How much is the old man paying you?"

I blinked. "Who?"

"Maxwell."

"He's not paying me. I get my check from Madeline."

Her smile was cold. "And if I double it, will you go back to New York City?"

I opened my mouth without even knowing how to respond, but then the person on the other end of her call started speaking again. She waved her hand at me, then spun around and walked away. "Alright, alright. I'm listening."

"Ignore her," Bertie said.

"Who is she?"

"Rose's sister Nova. The whole family is crazy."

I eyed him. "I wish you'd told me that in the car."

He grinned. "Uh uh. You might have made a run for it."

I laughed. "You might be right about that."

Bertie led me inside. "Pro tip: if anyone asks why you're late for anything, just claim you got stuck in traffic. Want to stop for a latte but you're running late? Traffic. Overslept and need an extra twenty minutes? Traffic. Got distracted shopping and lost track of time? Traffic. It's everybody's excuse for everything in this town."

"Got it."

Nova might have been unwelcoming, but Bertie was making up for it.

We walked along a hallway lined with framed movie posters, most featuring Rose. Her entire career laid out chronologically, from child star to ingénue to leading lady.

Bertie stopped and pointed outside to a wrought-iron gate set into the high wall surrounding the property. "There's access to the road out there if you want to go for a walk or run. Code is 4259."

High walls. Security cameras. Another fortress.

Just like the Stockport estate and Lyon Island.

Different coast, different family, same golden cage.

Chapter Four

THE HALLWAYS OPENED INTO A BRIGHT, airy living room as we walked deeper into the house. Glass walls flooded the space with sunlight. White couches arranged in a welcoming circle around a massive stone fireplace. I couldn't imagine when it was used.

Did LA ever get cold?

"Wait here," Bertie said. "I'll put your suitcase and carryall in your room. Ms. Marlowe should be with you shortly."

I nodded.

Ms. Marlowe.

Rose.

He disappeared down a hallway. I stood in the center of the room, conscious of how I smelled after the flight.

Behind me, a glass display case housed a collection of gleaming of awards. Emmys, Golden Globes, and two Oscars. All bearing the name *Eureka Productions.*

I wandered toward the wall of windows dominating one side of the room. Los Angeles sprawled far, far below, a mosaic of rooftops, palm trees, and concrete softened by afternoon haze. It almost looked almost peaceful. An appropriate view for a Hollywood star.

Up high, looking down on everyone else.

A long, gleaming pool stretched out like a jewel to my right. A dog darted between lounge chairs. A fully dressed man floated on a pink flamingo in the water. A woman was seated on the edge. I only let myself glance. Didn't want anyone to think I was spying.

I walked over to one of the couches and sat.

Then stood.

I sat again, perching on the edge of the couch. A white box sat on the coffee table, wrapped with silver ribbon.

"I hope your travel went well." The voice came from behind me. "Madeline speaks very highly of you."

I jumped up from the couch and spun around. Rose Marlowe stood behind me, one hand on her hip like she was posing for a camera. White silk pants. Leather bralette. Loose blazer. A silver whistle hung around her neck. Her blonde hair fell in perfect waves, skin flawless as airbrushed photos.

I'd seen her on screens of every size, on billboards and in magazines. She was shorter, tinier, than I expected, but still occupying space like someone twice her size.

"I—yes, the fine was flight. I mean the flight was fine." I hated how starstruck I sounded. "Thank you."

She smiled and walked over to me. "Please, don't be awed. I'm a normal person, same as you."

I laughed a little. "I doubt that."

"You might be surprised." She waved at the couch. I sat again, then she joined me. "Believe it or not, I have all the same human problems as anyone else, just with a layer of fame on top that exacerbates everything. Would you like something to eat or drink? Maybe some water? You must be thirsty after your flight."

I nodded. "Water would be great."

Rose grabbed the silver whistle round her neck and blew one long blast that echoed through the cavernous room.

What on earth?

Within seconds, a maid appeared in the doorway. "Yes, Miss?"

"Sparkling water for Zoe and myself. The Italian one, not the French. And make sure the glasses are properly chilled."

The maid bowed, then disappeared. Oh boy. Was I going to be summoned with a whistle as well?

"You have a beautiful home," I said.

"Thank you. It's a bit chaotic at the moment, I'm afraid."

Looked perfect to me. But perfect houses usually hid the worst secrets.

She smoothed an invisible wrinkle from her linen pants. "How is Madeline? It's been ages since we've had a proper catch-up."

Her question surprised me. "You know Madeline?"

Rose laugh sounded almost like music. "We went to boarding school together. Same graduating class. We still keep in touch, though it's become more sporadic over the years."

The maid returned with two crystal glasses filled with water on a silver tray. She set out coasters on the wood table, then placed our drinks before retreating.

Rose picked up her glass and took a delicate sip.

I did the same. Even though I was parched and wanted to gulp it all in one go.

"My father is retiring and will be turning the business over to the family soon. So we're all here under his roof while he decides which one of us is most deserving."

"That sounds…" I searched for a diplomatic word.

"Absurd? Medieval? Psychologically damaging?" Rose said.

I laughed. Maybe she wasn't so different after all.

"Of course it will be me that wins in the end, but in the meantime, we all have to go through this ridiculous charade."

A door slammed somewhere. Shouting voices. A dog barked. Water splashed. Then silence, like someone had hit a mute button.

"Would you like to meet everyone?" She stood. "They're all out by the main pool. It might be easier to introduce you to them all at once rather than having them ambush you individually."

Main pool?

I really was in Hollywood.

"Sure." I downed the last of my water and got to my feet. Though the prospect of multiple introductions at once made me anxious.

I followed Rose across the living room to the French doors and we stepped out onto a narrow landing. We walked down smooth concrete stairs flanked by more glass, arriving on a balcony over the deck.

The infinity pool stretched toward the cliff. Rose paused at a railing. "Welcome to the madhouse. Now let me give you the crash course on the Marlowes."

The pool deck swarmed with people pretending the others didn't exist.

Rose pointed to a young woman—early twenties at most—perched on the pool's edge with her feet in the water, clutching a cocktail in both hands, hair pulled back in a sleek blonde ponytail, highlighting cheekbones that could cut cucumbers. "Olivia. Maxwell's latest wife. She spends most of her time drunk, which is the only way to handle this family, so I don't blame her."

Olivia's eyes darted around the pool area, landing on me before skittering away. She looked like a rabbit surrounded by wolves.

"Nova's over there." Rose nodded toward a woman in her forties sprawled on a chaise lounge, somehow managing to talk on her phone and type on a laptop while glaring at everyone.

"I met her at the front door. She offered to pay me double if I turned around and went back to New York."

"That sounds like Nova. And yet, you're still here."

"I didn't believe her."

"You should have. I'm sure she meant every word."

"Well, I wouldn't want to let Madeline down. She's done a lot for me."

Rose smiled. "I'd like to say Nova's bark is worse than her bite, but that's probably untrue. She's a high-powered entertainment lawyer. And if you ever see her without that phone glued to her hand, she'll be dead. Or in prison."

Rose gestured to the fully clothed floater. "That's Gordon, Nova's husband. Stay-at-home dad."

"How many kids do they have?"

"They don't. Versailles and Monaco are the dogs."

Either Versailles or Monaco jumped into the pool, then scrambled out, then shook itself, spraying water everywhere.

"Watch it!" Olivia shouted.

She tried to back away but knocked over the bottle of red wine sitting next to her. Crimson liquid spilled across the concrete and into the pool, blooming like blood in the water.

"For fuck's sake, chill out," Nova said, without looking up from her phone. "It's just fucking water."

Olivia's lower lip trembled, and for a moment I thought she might cry.

A man sprawled nearby, laptop balanced on his knees, phone pressed to his ear. "Dailies," he was saying. "Reshoot schedules." He glanced up. Met my eyes. Looked away.

"That's Jaxon, my brother," Rose said. "He's been working with our father as interim CEO for the past few months while Maxwell's been…indisposed. He and Nova are twins. Fraternal."

A young woman in her thirties lounged nearby, staring at her phone, occasionally laughing at something on-screen, each outburst drawing an irritated glance from Jaxon.

"Willa, Jaxon's wife. Former script editor. Now she mostly spends her time texting God-knows-who and annoying my brother. And that's Liam, the youngest." Rose pointed to a man in his early thirties with a shaved head, filming himself with his phone. "YouTube influencer, whatever that means."

Liam flipped his phone around, grinned into the lens, and walked backward toward the pool. "Day seven of Marlowe Madness!"

He jumped.

The splash was seismic. Water exploded across the deck.

Nova shrieked. Her laptop crashed to the ground. Olivia burst into tears. Gordon's float tipped and dumped him underwater.

He emerged seconds later, clutching the dog to his chest. "Versailles can't swim!"

I glanced at Rose. She smiled, seemingly entertained and glanced at me before shrugging. "Liam is such a scamp."

A woman sat in the shade, watching Liam. She held up her arm and tapped her watch.

Liam spat out a mouthful of water, then swam to the edge, climbed out, and trotted over to her.

"Who's that?" I asked.

"No idea. Liam's latest girl, I guess. They change too frequently to keep track of their names."

Liam grabbed a towel from one of the lounges and wandered off. At the far end, Caleb paced alone. Shorter than I'd expected.

"I'm sure you recognize him," Rose said.

I nodded.

"He's having an affair. So if you see him behaving weird, just chalk it up to that. Although I'd appreciate it if you didn't let on. I prefer Talon not know. At least for now."

I blinked. "Okay."

She studied my face, then touched my shoulder. "It's Hollywood. Infidelity is practically written into our marriage contracts. Now, two more people you need to be aware of. My father, Maxwell. He rarely leaves his room. But if you see an ornery old goat wandering around yelling at people, that'll be him."

"And Talon?" He didn't seem to be around the pool.

"Probably hiding in his room with a book, the little introvert. Come on, I've got something to give you first."

I followed her back up the stairs and into the living room. She gestured to the small white box sitting on the coffee table. "That's for you."

I lifted the lid. A silver whistle on a delicate chain.

"Everyone in the family has one. Test it out. Three short blasts."

I blew three sharp notes. The sound echoed off the ceiling.

Rose nodded. "Perfect."

"Everyone has one of these?"

She nodded. "Family tradition. Not everyone uses theirs. Drives me crazy."

I put the chain around my neck.

I couldn't think of why I'd need it, but ready or not, I was officially a Marlowe now.

Chapter Five

"YOU CALLED?"

I turned around. Talon stood in the doorway. Thirteen and as tall as me, all elbows and knees. Thick glasses magnified his eyes. Messy hair that hadn't seen a brush. He studied me like I was a puzzle to solve.

I glanced down at my whistle. Three short blasts. That's how Rose called her kid?

"That's Talon's call sign if you need to find him. Sometimes it's hard to be heard above the rabble."

"Okay," I said.

"Talon, why don't you show Zoe her room?"

Talon let out a long sigh. "Can't the maid do it?"

Rose gave him a pointed look. "No. And it'll help the two of you get to know each other. So don't be a little shit and do it."

He kicked at the floor once, then nodded. "Fine. Come on." He made it sound like I was a stray dog he'd been ordered to walk.

Rose glanced at her slim gold watch. "I need to run. I have an audition."

Talon frowned. "Now?"

Rose crossed to her son, planting a kiss on his forehead. "I'll see you for dinner."

And just like that, she was gone.

Talon looked over at me. "She's probably having an affair. She's been acting weird lately."

I blinked.

Jesus, were there no secrets in this family?

"This way." I half expected Talon to pat his leg and bring me to heel.

I followed him down a hallway. "If you don't mind, I'd prefer to call you by name instead of using the whistle."

He shrugged. "Whatever."

We entered a room at the far end.

Floor-to-ceiling windows. City view. Modern bed with dark pillows. Stone fireplace.

"This your room?" I asked.

He shook his head. "No, it's yours."

My suitcase sat at the foot of the bed.

"You have your own small private pool as well." He gestured toward a set of glass doors on the left leading to a courtyard. "I don't like to swim, so it didn't make sense for me to have this room."

I walked to the doors and looked outside. An oval shaped pool glimmered in the California sunlight, surrounded by palms and their dappled shade. The size of a regular pool to me. Utterly private, enclosed by tall walls, with a pair of chaise lounges and a table with an umbrella at the far end on the deck.

I turned to look at him. "Is this some kind of trick? This is way too nice for staff quarters."

He shrugged. "You're one of the family now. Much as you might not want to be. My room is to the left of yours.

Granddad is upstairs, along with my parents and the others."

Right.

Nova. Willa. Jaxon. Gordon. Liam. The nameless girl-friend. I was going to need a flowchart to keep track of this family.

"I'll let you get settled," Talon said. "Dinner is at six."

He left. I locked the door behind him.

The room was minimalist like the rest of the house. Walk-in closet big enough to live in. Marble bathroom with a conference-room-sized shower. Expensive toiletries, the kind I usually just smelled at Sephora, lined the shelves.

I hung up my paltry wardrobe in the closet, tucked my suitcase away, then pulled out my phone and called Elsa.

"I made it," I said.

"And?"

"Want to see my digs?"

"You know it."

I gave her a tour via FaceTime, watching her eyes widen as I panned across the room.

"Holy shit. You hit the jackpot."

"It's insane," I said, walking to the windows. "Check out this view."

I showed her the city sprawling below, all glass and concrete catching the light like scattered diamonds. "I keep waiting for someone to tell me there's been a mistake."

"After what you went through with the Stockports and those creepy twins, you deserve to be pampered," Elsa said.

"They weren't creepy."

"Uh huh."

I laughed.

"How many secrets have you stumbled across?" she asked.

"A few. But everyone seems to know about them. At least everyone in the family."

We chatted for another few minutes before disconnecting. Elsa seemed to be a lot more relaxed than during our ride to the airport. Maybe things had settled down with the Carlsons.

I went into the bathroom and took a shower, lathering my hair with shampoo that probably cost more per ounce than a decent bottle of wine. After drying off, I dressed in the nicest outfit I'd brought: dark jeans and a white lace and cotton top that Elsa always said brought out my eyes. I blow-dried my hair and even applied a touch of makeup.

Then I opened the glass sliding door and walked out to the pool.

The water caught the sunlight. I'd need to buy a bathing suit.

The courtyard connected to a balcony that ran past both our rooms.

I glanced at the time on my phone. It was almost dinner time. I followed the scent of frying garlic to the kitchen. A chef in whites plated food at a massive island.

I thought back to Frenchie cooking for me and swallowed my disappointment that he was still so far away.

"Hello, I'm Zoe. The new nanny," I said to him, feeling self-conscious. "I wasn't sure where I eat. I was just told to be here for six."

The chef nodded toward a door on the far side of the kitchen. "You'll find your seat through there."

"Thanks you." I said, heading in the direction he'd indicated.

I pushed through the door and stopped dead in my tracks.

The dining room looked like a magazine spread. Long wood table. Succulent centerpiece. One entire wall was tiered desert plants: cacti, agave, spiky palms rising in perfect rows. Every person from the pool sat around the table. All conversation stopped when I entered.

"I'm sorry." I cleared my throat. "I was just looking for where I eat."

Rose smiled and gestured to an empty chair at the far end of the table. Next to Talon. "There."

They wanted me to eat with them? All of them? I walked toward the empty chair next to Talon, feeling their eyes track every step.

Crystal glasses. Fine china. More silverware than I knew what to do with.

"We don't bite," Jaxon said as I sat. "At least, not until dessert."

Willa elbowed him. "Don't tease the nanny."

She made me sound like the family pet.

There was an empty seat across from me. But a second later, Liam strolled through the door and sat in it. "Molly has work. She won't be joining us tonight."

Nova looked up from her wine glass. "Who the hell is Molly?"

Liam blinked. "My girlfriend? She's been staying here for the past week?"

"Oh right," Nova said. "The wallpaper."

He glared at her. "Bitch."

"Freeloader."

Liam snorted. "That's rich, coming from someone who's still living off the family trust."

Nova crossed her arms. "We're all living off the family trust."

"Not me. I've got YouTube cash. And Molly's just living off *me.*"

"Yeah, well, soon enough she'll turn into an infestation

like the last one. Then we'll need a tent and fumigation crew to get her out of here."

"Shut up."

Rose set down her wine glass with a decisive *clink*. "Alright, that's enough, children."

I shrunk down in my chair, hoping no one would notice me.

The chef entered with the maid, both carrying trays loaded with food. They walked around the table, setting dishes on the table. It all looked like edible art. Colors that shouldn't exist in nature, textures that belonged in art galleries.

Conversations exploded around me, overlapping and chaotic. I gave up trying to follow any single thread.

Liam nudged Talon. "Subscriber count hit over two million this morning. Which means I'm buying myself a falcon. A real one."

"You are not," Rose said.

"I promised my subs."

Gordon looked at him. "You know that word used to mean something completely different."

"I forbid you to be in charge of a bird of prey," Rose said.

Nova pressed the phone to her ear even harder. "The clause clearly states residuals revert after the third quarter, so if they're trying to backdate the contract, they're bluffing."

"How you doing, baby?" Gordon slipped a piece of chicken under the table. Versailles (or Monaco?) snapped it up like a vacuum cleaner.

"I need more wine," Olivia said. "Where's that maid with the Cabernet?"

I glanced over at Talon. His nose was buried in a thick astronomy book. "Betelgeuse isn't actually the brightest,

Liam. It's just closer. The apparent magnitude versus absolute magnitude—"

"Did you say, 'beetle juice'?" Liam asked.

Talon rolled his eyes. "Betelgeuse. It's a star."

"Stop antagonizing my son," Rose said, reaching for the salt.

Liam grinned.

Caleb flipped a page in his script. Then he underlined something with a pencil and started mouthing words.

"Can you please not whisper during dinner?" Nova said. "It's distracting me."

"I'm not whispering," Caleb said without looking up.

Talon glanced down at his plate and made a face. "I'm not hungry. I'll get a sandwich later."

Rose pointed to his food. "Eat."

"Speaking of infestations. I think the dog has fleas again," Gordon said, scratching Versailles behind the ears. "Little bastards."

Rose exhaled loudly. "For God's sake. Not while we're eating, Gordon."

Olivia glanced around. "I still need that wine."

"The contract language is ironclad," Nova said into her phone. "If their lawyer tries to claim otherwise—"

"How was the audition?" Willa asked, talking over Nova.

Rose shrugged, spearing a piece of asparagus. "Fine."

Jaxon glanced at her. "Which director?"

"Howard."

Jaxon took a bite of steak. "I don't remember him announcing a new property. What's the project?"

"I'm not going over it again," Rose replied with a sigh.

Caleb frowned. "I don't think my character would say, 'You're not talking like a human.' It feels forced."

I glanced from face to face, trying to follow at least one conversation thread but finding it almost impossible.

Nova tossed her phone on the table and turned to me. "So how much is father paying you to spy on us all?"

The table went silent.

Everyone turned to look at me.

I froze. "What?"

Nova's eyes never left mine.

"You heard me, spy."

I looked over at Talon.

He shrugged.

Liam leaned forward, elbows on the table. "Yeah, come on, Zoe Smith, nanny. Tell us. We're dying to know."

Chapter Six

I LICKED MY LIPS. "I'm not a spy. I'm a nanny."

Nova scoffed, tapping her phone. "Talon is 13. Why the fuck does he need a nanny?"

"Why does any child need a nanny?" I replied.

Rose set her wine glass down. "Stop interrogating Zoe, Nova. Maxwell wanted Talon to take a year off school. That's why we have a nanny. And Talon agreed to it."

"I didn't, actually," Talon said.

Rose eyed him. "Hush."

Nova shook her head. "Bullshit. That was all you."

"Because I know what it's like to work your childhood away. And I'm not about to do that to my son regardless of what he wants."

Talon had gone back to his book. He didn't seem interested in acting. Not that I'd really gotten a chance to know him yet.

"And what do you think, Caleb?" Nova asked.

"I'm not leaving our son alone all day. Especially when we're gone on shoots."

Rose nodded.

Nova tightened her lips. "We're trying to close ranks as a family, not open ourselves up to more prying eyes."

"She's not prying," Rose said. "She's nannying. And she signed your ridiculous seventy-page NDA, didn't she?"

"It wasn't seventy pages."

Liam had his phone out, pointing it at me.

I turned away, hiding my face.

"What are you doing?" Nova asked.

"Live streaming." Liam turned the camera on her. "Say hi to HotBunny69."

Nova lunged across the table, snatching the phone from his hands, then hurling it to the floor. It hit the marble with a *crack* and shattered.

"Jesus, Nova." Liam turned around, snapping his fingers, attracting the attention of the maid who stood near the door. "Be a love and bring me another phone from the office."

"Don't you dare," Nova said. "Set one foot outside that door and you're fired."

The maid froze, trapped between them.

Rose pulled the silver whistle from beneath her blouse. Blew it hard. "Everyone shut up."

A phone rang. Jaxon pulled it out of his pocket.

Rose turned to stare at him.

"Jaxon Marlowe. Uh huh. Uh huh. I've told you this several times. Just because you invest in a movie doesn't mean you get the money back immediately." He got to his feet and walked out of the room.

Willa threw her fork down on the table.

Nova looked back at me. "I'm still waiting for an answer."

I met her eyes. "I'm not a spy. I'm a nanny."

"Of course you are." Her voice dripped with disbelief.

Olivia downed her fourth glass of wine.

Liam nudged me with his foot. "So, you got a boyfriend?"

Rose rolled her eyes. "Zoe isn't interested in any of your influencer friends. Or you. And even asking that question is all kinds of inappropriate."

Liam looked affronted. "I'm taken. Molly, remember?"

"Who?" Rose asked.

"Jesus Christ. My girlfriend!"

Rose leaned across the table and grabbed Talon's book. "No reading at the table. It's family time."

"Mom, please. Dad's reading."

She hesitated, glancing over at Caleb before handing it back. "You're right."

Olivia knocked on the table twice, then raised her glass. The maid walked over with the bottle of wine. Jeez. Didn't any of these people use names?

"No more," Nova said, eying her. "You drink too much. And that will make you fat. I'm not sure which is worse."

Olivia flushed. "I don't need my stepdaughter policing my actions."

Nova snorted. "I'm old enough to be *your* mother. Besides, you won't be here much longer."

Olivia paled. "What does that mean?"

"Maxwell won't stop at wife number five. His wandering eye never retires."

Olivia stood, almost falling over. "How dare you!"

"Oh, I dare," Nova said.

Olivia shoved her chair back, wobbling on her heels. Stumbled against the wall. Weaved toward the door, using the table for balance.

"Do you need help?" I asked, already standing.

"Ignore her," Rose said. "We all do."

"I don't mind."

Olivia grabbed my arm, using it for balance. I led her through the door and toward the living room. She pulled away when we got there.

"Leave me alone," she snapped. "I know exactly why you're here and what's going on, and I won't stand for it."

She almost tripped but caught herself before walking off.

She knew exactly why I was here?

Didn't everybody know?

I was supposed to be the nanny.

I returned to the chaos. Everyone yelling over everyone else.

"Is that what we're calling box office bombs now?" Rose said. "Unconventional choices?"

"If anyone bothered to read the reviews," Willa replied, "they'd see that critics appreciated the artistic vision—"

Liam laughed. "Three percent on Rotten Tomatoes isn't appreciation."

One of the dogs leapt from Gordon's lap and onto the table and grabbed a piece of steak, knocking over Willa's water glass as it bolted away.

"Goddammit, Gordon!" She jumped to her feet. "For once in your life, control your fucking dog!"

Nova's face reddened. "Don't you dare yell at my husband!"

"It's not her fault," Gordon said. "Monaco is still learning manners."

"She's ten years old!" Willa screamed. "She's not learning anything. She's poorly trained!"

I stared. How did they function like this? A reality show where everyone fought for camera time?

Liam leaned toward me. "You've made it five hours.

And Nova's just pissed 'cause she hadn't bet on you lasting longer than the last nanny."

I blinked. "She didn't make it five hours?"

"Hell no. She walked out during dinner. Didn't even bother to collect her things. We had to FedEx them. The one before her made it a week. Nanny number two lasted the longest. Three months. I've got a grand riding on you sticking out a month." He patted my hand. "So try and hang in there, yeah?"

Chapter Seven

Talon disappeared first when dinner wound down. I waited five minutes, then excused myself. No one noticed. Nova was screaming about pyrotechnics; Caleb was running lines with Rose; Willa and Jaxon were fighting over schedules.

I escaped down the hallway, trying to remember the route.

Left at the Oscar case? Right at the abstract painting?

This minimalist maze would take time to figure out.

I found myself back near the kitchen.

Time to ask for directions.

Bertie sat at the counter, eating dinner. He waved me over.

"You eat here?" I asked, crossing the room.

He speared a potato. "Of course."

I jerked my head toward the dining room. "Not allowed?"

"Opted out," he replied with a smirk.

"How do I do that?"

"You don't." He laughed. "The nanny always sits with the family."

"Damn it."

He gestured to the empty chair across from him. "How'd dinner go?"

I dropped into the seat with a sigh, resting my elbows on the table. "Nova broke Liam's phone."

He shrugged. "Sounds mild."

I raised my eyebrows. "Mild?"

"Last week, Nova broke three plates and chucked a wine glass at Liam. She has excellent aim."

I laughed. "Does it ever get any less chaotic?"

"Only when they're not speaking to each other."

"And how often does that happen?"

He swallowed a bite of lamb. "About once a month. They're due for a falling out fairly soon."

I leaned back in the chair. "I got accused of spying. Nova seems convinced I'm here to report back to Maxwell."

"Aren't you? Who've you got your eye on to take down first?"

"You too? I'm not a spy!"

Bertie studied my face. "Come on. Talon is more mature than any of the adults. Why does he need a nanny?"

"I don't know. Ask Rose."

Bertie picked up a linen napkin and wiped his fingers. "Everyone thinks Maxwell hired someone for intel on the family. To see who's fit to run the company. You show up right when he's deciding? Perfect timing. Plus Madeline and Rose go way back. Being a nanny is the perfect cover."

"But it's not true."

Willa appeared in the doorway. She hesitated when she saw me. "Is there any sparkling water?"

Bertie pushed his chair back and got to his feet. "I can grab you one."

"It's alright. Just show me where to get them."

Bertie turned back to me. "You want one?"

I shook my head. "I was just looking for my room and got lost."

He gestured to the door I had come through. "Turn right at the Oscar case. You'll find your way back."

I stood. "Thanks."

Then I left the kitchen, following his instruction. It didn't take long to find my way back to the residential wing. But before going to my own room, I stopped at Talon's door and knocked.

Silence.

I knocked again. Could almost hear the sigh. And then, "Come in."

I pushed open the door. Same size as mine, but the walls were painted galaxies. Solar systems mapped like star charts. Paper planets hung from invisible wires, swaying in the AC.

Astronomy books lined the shelves. A telescope dominated the window.

He lay on his bed, not even looking up when I entered.

"What are you reading?" I asked, stepping inside.

He tilted the book so I could see the cover. *Rudin's Principles of Mathematical Analysis*.

"Are you enjoying it?"

"It's okay. I disagree with some of the theorems."

I raised my eyebrows. "Mind if I ask you some questions? Since we're going to be spending a lot of time together."

Talon dog-eared his page and closed the book. "Sure. Is this about the spy thing?"

"No. And just for the record, I'm not a spy."

"I know that."

I blinked. "You do."

He nodded. "Uh huh. There is no spy. Everyone is just paranoid that my grandfather will find out all their secrets and use it as a reason to not hand over the business. It's stupid. Maxwell doesn't have time for stuff like that. He's ill."

I sat at his desk. Bertie was right. Talon was more mature than the adults downstairs.

"What's ailing Maxwell?" I asked.

"Don't know. Not sure anything is. Could just be a manipulation tactic to get the family under control."

"Does he do that often?"

Talon shrugged. "About every three months. Manipulation is the cornerstone of Hollywood."

I laughed, glancing around his room. There were framed certificates on the wall next to his desk. A diploma with his name on it. From Berkeley. For a BSc.

I stared at it. "Is that yours?"

"Yes."

"But…it's a college diploma."

He pointed to a framed article hanging beside it. "I graduated last year."

I got up and looked at the article: *Hollywood Heir, 13, Becomes Youngest Ever Berkeley Grad.*

"So you're a genius."

He grimaced. "I hate that word. It's reductive. I just process information differently than most people."

"That's it?"

He grinned. "Sure."

I sat again. "Alright, tell me the truth. Why do you need a nanny? Because it doesn't really look like you do."

Talon sighed. "I begin my PhD next year, but Rose and Maxwell want me to take a year between studies."

"Why?"

"Because Rose resents Maxwell for making her work as a kid. She never had much of a childhood, and he's probably trying to make sure that I don't resent her in the same way."

"And he doesn't want you to be alone while you're on break?"

He nodded. "Most times there is no one here. Rose and Caleb are usually away on set. Jaxon and Nova are at their offices. And even though Gordon is here, he's busy with his dogs. And Willa—" He shrugged. "But I like being alone."

"I get that. I'll try and give you space if that's what you want."

He adjusted his glasses. "You mean it?"

"Sure. You're old enough to know what you like."

"Thanks."

I nodded.

"So you're not going to beat me if I don't do you what you say?"

I stared at him, horrified. "What? No! Of course not!"

A small smile tugged at his lips. "Just checking."

"I like your sense of humor, Talon."

"Thanks."

I stood to leave. "Have a good night."

He gestured to my whistle. "You don't have to wear that if you don't want to."

I touched it. "No?"

He shook his head.

"Rose just wants everyone to have one because of Grandma. She drowned. And I guess Rose figured if she had a whistle, she could have alerted someone. Now we all have to wear them."

"Makes sense."

He shrugged, clearly itching for his book.

I left his room, closed the door behind me, and headed to my own. Maybe I could figure out how to introduce some fun into Talon's life, especially if he was going back to school next year.

God, I couldn't imagine being in college at that age.

I took off the whistle and laid it on my bedside table. Then I walked to the sliding glass doors. Liam was on the patio filming himself. He grinned and waved when he saw me, pointing the camera at me. I lowered the blinds, shutting him out.

I changed into my pajamas and climbed into bed, checking my phone and seeing a voicemail from the unknown number. I thought about playing it, but then changed my mind and deleted it.

I wasn't interested in anything my father had to say.

Chapter Eight

I WOKE up and blinked hard.

It was so quiet. Where was I?

Right. The Marlowes. Los Angeles. Not New York. The other side of America. I stretched, reaching for my phone.

No new calls.

Thank God. Maybe my father had given up.

I rolled out of bed and hit the shower. Last night's dinner played in my head like a bad reality show. Despite what Bertie said, surely all their meals weren't like that?

I toweled off, got dressed, then walked to the window and opened the blinds. Bright sunshine poured into the room, nearly blinding me.

I squinted against the light, letting my eyes adjust. The sky was a perfect cloudless blue, the kind of cerulean day that made people move to California in the first place.

Talon sat on the deck, reading. I slid open the glass door. An elaborate breakfast waited on the small table. Fresh fruit, buttery pastries, yogurt, granola.

"Morning," I said.

"Morning." He glanced up at me. "I hope it's alright, but I prefer breakfast and lunch out here instead of with the family. But if you want to eat in the dining room…"

"Nope. I'm good out here if you don't mind the company."

He shook his head, already buried in *Gray's Anatomy*.

"Did you get bored of your last book?" I asked, sitting across from him.

"No. I already finished it."

I raised my brows. "You finished *Rodin's Book of Math*?"

"*Rudin's Principles of Mathematical Analysis*."

"Yeah, that one?"

He nodded.

"You really are a genius."

He stuck out his tongue.

I laughed. Then filled my plate with fruit and a croissant before pouring myself a cup of coffee from the silver carafe. The breeze ruffled his hair, and for a moment, Talon looked younger than thirteen.

I tore off a piece of the croissant and it flaked apart in my hands, buttery and still warm. He dug into a bowl of strawberries.

"Did you train to be a nanny?" he asked after several bites.

"Other than being a kid myself? Not really."

"You didn't want to be one when you were little?"

I shook my head.

"So what's your philosophy about children?"

I thought for a moment, chewing on a chunk of croissant. "Never lie to the kids I look after. Always tell the truth."

"And do you do that?"

"I try."

"And is that it?"

I shrugged. "Don't really need anything else."

"I guess not. So if you didn't want to become a nanny, why are you one?" He popped another strawberry in his mouth.

"Kind of a long story."

"I got time."

I laughed, setting my croissant down and wiping my fingers on the cloth napkin. "I wanted to be a journalist. I was registered at Columbia. But…" I broke off.

"What?"

"My mother stole my tuition money."

His eyes widened. "Seriously?"

I nodded. "Had to waive my registration. Delay studies."

"Why did she do that?"

"Because she's a thief."

"Really?"

I shrugged.

"Do you still talk to her?"

I shook my head. "Nope."

He studied me. I sipped my coffee

"Do you still want to be a journalist?"

"Actually, I've been thinking about writing a novel. I just need to get a laptop. And start."

Talon pushed a strawberry around his plate with his fork. "You should do it. Human experience is infinitely varied yet universally relatable."

I laughed. "That it is."

"Everyone in this town writes, but sometimes I don't think they say anything."

I eyed him. "You are far too wise for your years."

We ate in comfortable silence as I surveyed the pool. "You ever swim?"

"Nope." He shook his head. "None of the Marlowes do."

I blinked. "None?"

"Only Isabella. After she died, they were all too scared of the water, so they stay out."

"And yet the house has two pools."

He shrugged. "It's California. Gordon likes to paddle. And Liam likes to splash."

I sipped my coffee. "Do you know what to do if you fall in?"

Talon stared like I'd asked if he knew how to breathe. "You get out."

Not if you can't swim. Panic kicks in. Your body fights you. "It's not that easy."

"No?"

I shook my head. "I need a bathing suit. Know any affordable stores?"

"My mom shops on Rodeo Drive."

I wrinkled my nose. "Those stores are a bit pricey for me."

He tilted his head, considering. "Right, you're saving for a computer so you can become a writer. Melrose. Regular stores, regular prices."

I nodded. "Why don't we do that this afternoon?"

He groaned, dropping his forehead to his book. Finally —kid behavior. "That sounds boring."

"Well, I'm not leaving you at home."

He groaned louder.

"Sounds like bribery is in order."

He stiffened and sat. "Bribery?"

"Come shopping with me and I'll take you to wherever you want to go."

"A bookstore?"

I nodded. "Sure."

"I'll be ready in ten minutes." He was already on his feet.

I finished eating, looking out over the perfect pool. Even the plants looked styled. How long before I found the cracks?

I went to my room, slipped on a pair of sandals, grabbed my purse, and walked down to the living room.

Rose was texting on her phone. She put it away when I entered.

"Talon and I thought we'd go shopping."

"He wants to go shopping?" She sounded baffled.

I nodded. "I want to get a bathing suit for the pool."

"Then you are a miracle worker. Bertie is at your disposal. You can find him in the west wing. Turn left at the kitchen."

"Thank you."

Caleb entered, dressed in dark jeans and a button-down shirt. "I'm heading out, love. I've got that audition."

"Which one?" Rose asked.

"*Cold Sun*."

Rose frowned as much as her Botox permitted. "I haven't heard of it."

"Futuristic noir." Caleb gave her a kiss and headed for the door.

"Good luck," Rose said.

I followed her directions to another wing entirely. Listened at doors until I heard sports commentary and knocked

The door opened a second later. Bertie appeared dressed in jeans and a Lakers tee. "You made it through to the morning!"

"I did. Would you be able to take me and Talon shopping?"

He raised an eyebrow. "You got the kid to agree to leave the house?"

"Bribery," I replied.

"Ah." He hit the remote, turned off the TV, and grabbed his jacket. "Let me show you a shortcut."

He led me down a hallway and out a side door, into the garage—though the word didn't do the space justice. It was massive, with polished concrete floors, gleaming beneath long strips of recessed lighting. The ceiling could swallow a second floor without trying. A glass wall gave the garage a panoramic view of the manicured grounds. The cars were displayed more than parked.

Six parking bays stretched across the space. Three cars in front: white BMW, black Rolls Royce, the SUV from yesterday. Three more behind, each showroom perfect. In the back corner, something hidden under black tarp. Chrome wheel tips peeked out underneath.

Talon appeared with his book, fist-bumped Bertie, and climbed into the SUV.

We pulled out into the LA morning.

Chapter Nine

I bought two bathing suits.

One black, one navy. Both one-piece. Nothing flashy. I paid cash, cringing when I handed over the money. Why was everything in LA so expensive? Nix that. Why was everything everywhere so damn expensive right now?

I made good money with Madeline, but I was still nowhere near restoring my tuition fund.

I returned to the car and found Bertie scrolling on his phone and Talon reading in the back seat. Both looked content. I'd rushed, but they obviously could have waited for hours without caring.

I climbed in, setting the shopping bag at my feet. "Bookstore next?"

Talon looked up with a smile. "Yep."

I glanced at Bertie. "You know where we're going?"

"Sure do. Fact And Fiction?"

Talon nodded.

Three blocks later, I noticed Bertie checking the rear view again.

I twisted in my seat, looking out the back window. "You see that gray car again?"

"Not sure," he said.

Talon leaned forward. "What gray car?"

Neither of us answered. Me, because I had just spotted the car two vehicles back. And Bertie, because he was concentrating on the road.

The gray car hung back, then sped up as we hit a red light. Pulled even with us. Drive with sunglasses and a baseball cap. Then the car surged ahead and disappeared.

Bertie glanced over at me. "Must be imagining things."

"Maybe."

"It's probably just paparazzi," Talon said.

"Yeah." But why no camera? Why not look over? Maybe I was being paranoid.

I looked back through the rear window. Nothing but a line of random cars behind us now. Talon was watching me.

I smiled at him.

He returned to his book. I leaned back against the headrest, looking out the window. It felt surreal to be in Los Angeles. Palm trees lining the road, bright blue sky. New York already felt a thousand years away.

Traffic was a mess. We crawled the last mile. And when we finally reached the bookstore, there wasn't a single parking spot in sight.

Bertie double parked. "Go ahead. I'll circle around and find a spot. Text me when you're done. I'll come meet you."

The bookstore squeezed between a tattoo parlor and designer dog boutique. *Fact and Fiction* in faded letters. Inside, dying air conditioning. Shelves crammed with astrophysics, engineering manuals, pulp novels.

Talon headed straight for the back, zeroing in on a tiny section labeled *THEORETICAL SCIENCES*.

I browsed the novels. Nothing caught my eye. Found him later with a stack at his feet, reading about black holes.

"Take your time," I said. "I'll meet you outside when you're ready."

He didn't even look up. "Okay."

I pushed open the door and stepped back into the heat.

The street was alive. Music spilled from the tattoo shop, someone was hawking sunglasses and star maps on the corner, a woman walked a dog with bright pink fur. I wandered down the block, peeking into windows. A surf shop. A vintage record store. A café that looked like it hadn't been cleaned since the seventies.

Restaurant and vintage stores across the street. Self-driving cars rolled past, no one behind the wheel.

I retraced my steps to the bookstore. I saw Caleb, walking along the sidewalk toward me, heading for the pedestrian crossing.

I stopped.

He did a double take. Recognized me. The color drained from his face. Then he flushed deep red, glancing across the street.

I followed his gaze to the restaurant.

Caleb looked back at me, then walked up. "Hi, Sophie."

I blinked. "Zoe."

"Right, right, that was the other nanny. What are you doing here?"

I gestured to the bookstore. "Shopping with Talon."

"Ah. That didn't take him long to convince you to bring him here."

"Quid pro quo."

He nodded, his gaze straying back toward the restaurant. "Kids always know how to work the system, don't they?"

"Did you want to speak to him?"

"No. No. Just scouting locations for my film. Trying to find a street with some atmosphere."

"Well, this is a good one. It seems very LA."

"It does at that." He shoved both hands into his pockets and met my eyes. "How's the job going?"

How *was* it going?

"Well, I've only been at it less than twenty-four hours."

"Right, right." His eyes darted past me, again toward the restaurant. "Well, I should get moving. More locations to scout."

"Of course."

He nodded, then turned on his heel and walked off down the block. A moment later he rounded the corner and disappeared from sight.

What the hell was that about?

I found Talon still in the back of the bookstore.

"You find anything?" I asked.

He nodded and pointed to three: particle physics, cosmology, and a battered paperback about chaos theory. I accompanied him to the register and he paid with a credit card. Black.

"I bumped into your dad outside," I said, holding the door open for him.

Talon looked surprised. "Here?"

I nodded.

"Weird. He never comes to this side of town." He stopped and gestured to the restaurant. "Probably meeting his lover there. I told him about it awhile back."

I stared at him. "His lover?"

"Yeah, he's having an affair too."

"He said he was scouting locations."

Talon scoffed. "Actors don't do that. At least not any of my father's caliber."

I pulled out my phone. "I'll let Bertie know we're ready to go."

"Wait," Talon said, eying the restaurant. "We should go check her out."

"Who?"

"My dad's lover."

I winced. "I don't think that's a good idea."

Too late. Talon bolted across the street. Shit.

I sprinted after him, catching up just after he entered the restaurant.

Eight tables. Dim lighting. Tiny glass vases with single roses. Romance central.

A man in a tuxedo materialized in front of us, all stiff posture and disapproving eyebrows. He looked me up and down, then gave Talon the same treatment. I couldn't figure out if he thought we weren't suitable clients or the age gap was too much.

"We're fully booked." His sniff that suggested he could smell our lack of a reservation from ten feet away.

Talon didn't blink. "Reservation for Burt Reynolds."

"Talon," I said.

"One moment." The maître d' consulted a list, then looked back up at us with a brand-new face. "Of course, sir. Follow me, please."

Talon grinned like he'd robbed a bank. My sneakers squeaked on the polished floor.

The maître d' led us to a corner table behind a massive fern. It was private but with a view of the entrance.

I sat. "Burt Reynolds?"

"It's the fake name my dad uses when he books hotels, rentals, whatever and wants to be anonymous."

"It's not fake. There used to be an actor by that name."

"Oh."

I leaned forward. "We should go home."

"Not until I see who Dad's meeting."

Talon consulted the menu, then flagged down the waiter. "We'll do the calamari, the tuna tartare, the truffle fries, crab cakes, the mini sliders, and the flatbread. Oh, and the burrata too."

"Yes, sir. And to drink?"

"Two lemonades." He looked over at me. "Unless you want vodka."

"No, I don't want vodka."

The waiter disappeared.

I leaned forward. "I can't pay for all that."

"Don't worry. My treat."

"I'm worried. I don't want to get fired."

He looked confused. "Why would you get fired?"

"Because I'm supposed to be responsible for you. I'm trying to prove that I'm not spying on your family. And spying on them is hardly the way to do it."

"Relax. You'll be fine."

I slumped back in my chair, staring at the door.

"I bet it's someone from his last film. Or maybe that actress he keeps pretending he doesn't know. Or his old vocal coach. Mom hated her."

"Well, I don't want to know."

He looked surprised. "You're not even a little curious?"

"No. Not even a little. I hate secrets."

The door opened and he reached out and grabbed my wrist. A woman had just walked in. She wore big sunglasses that swallowed half her face and a wide-brimmed hat pulled low over her forehead. Her clothes were simple but expensive—white linen pants and a silk blouse. She hesitated just inside the doorway, scanning the room like she was looking for someone.

Talon stiffened. "It's her."

"She could be here for anyone."

But even I didn't believe it.

Chapter Ten

THE WOMAN GLANCED OVER. She froze.

"Is that your mother?" I asked.

Talon's eyes widened.

Rose spotted us, and her perfect forehead creased into a frown.

"Good thing Dad left when he did," Talon whispered.

"Yeah."

Rose dug her phone out of her handbag. Tapped the screen and typed a little, then tucked it away before walking over to our table.

"She's probably tracking his location on his phone," Talon said.

I was too busy wishing the floor would open up and swallow me whole to answer.

"What are you two doing here?" Rose asked.

My cheeks burned. I had no idea what to say.

"We were at the bookstore across the street." Talon pointed to the bag at his feet. "Decided to stop by for lunch."

"Very good," Rose replied, sounding distracted.

The maître d' hustled over, bowing slightly. "Ms. Marlowe, what an unexpected pleasure. May I get you a chair?"

"No." She shook her head. "Just make sure my son has a good meal. Put it on my tab. I need to get to an appointment."

"Of course."

"Are you sure you don't want to join us?" I asked.

"Paparazzi will show up soon. I can't deal with them today."

She bent down and kissed Talon on the forehead, leaving a smudge of lipstick. Then she straightened and gave me a smile. Seconds later, she was gone.

"See?" Talon said. "You weren't fired."

"It's still early."

He laughed.

The waiter appeared with our lunch, laying out plate after plate.

I scooped some calamari onto my plate as he left our table. "I've never worked for a family that's this open about their secrets. I can't decide if it's refreshing or unsettling."

Talon snorted. "My family has *plenty* of secrets they don't discuss. Even me. That's why they're all so terrified about Maxwell hiring someone to spy on them."

I studied him. "I can't imagine what secrets a thirteen-year-old has."

He raised an eyebrow. "And you never will."

"If you say so. Why would your grandfather need feedback on who to leave a company to anyway?" I tossed a piece of squid into my mouth. "Can't he just decide for himself?"

Talon shrugged. "I think he just likes collaboration. He's used to taking feedback on films, scripts, all that stuff. Maybe this isn't any different to him."

"You have a point."

"But it's not you?"

"I swear," I said, raising a hand. "Now, tell me about your schooling. What subjects do you like best?"

"Astronomy and physics are my favorites. I want to be the youngest person in space."

The door opened. Talon took a breath and gripped my wrist. "Lana Ferris. I bet it's her."

I turned to glance over my shoulder. A blonde woman was scanning the room.

"She had a minor role in Dad's last film."

The maître d' approached the woman. They exchanged a few words, and he gestured toward our table. Lana stared at us, her confusion evident. Then she shook her head and retreated out the door.

My heart sank.

Talon was right.

"She was expecting someone else."

"Yeah." He nodded. "*Dad*."

"How do you feel about it?"

"Most people in this city are sleeping with someone else."

"Yeah, but this is your dad."

He shrugged. Maybe he was trying not to let it bother him. We ate in silence, then boxed up the leftovers. I texted Bertie.

He pulled up in the SUV minutes later.

"Have a good lunch?"

Talon handed him the leftovers. "We were trying to catch Dad's affair partner."

Bertie glanced at me then back at Talon. "And did you?"

Talon shrugged. "Maybe? But we saw Mom. I think she's onto him. It was fun, right, Zoe?"

"Let's not make a habit of it," I replied with a wince.

Talon got in the vehicle, dug out one of his books, and started reading. I climbed in beside Bertie and leaned back in the seat as he pulled into traffic.

"How did you start working for the Marlowes?" I asked.

"I was a driver for the production company, then switched to chauffeuring the family. I definitely prefer this, although my client is a little shit."

"Hey!" Talon said.

Bertie grinned, then he put an arm back and the two bumped fists.

The light turned green, and I spied the blonde actress again, standing at the corner talking on her phone. She caught my eye and looked away quickly.

We headed home through palm trees and billboards. One featured Rose advertising face cream. Fantasy colliding with reality.

We turned onto Mulholland and climbed, the city sprawling below with endless streets disappearing into haze.

"This is my favorite part of the drive." Bertie nodded toward the view. "Reminds you how small everything really is."

It felt vast and unknowable, not small at all. A city of secrets and lies.

Talon said he had secrets too. How many could a thirteen-year-old have?

I had secrets too. Madeline thought my father was dead. I'd lied, worried she wouldn't hire me otherwise. Technically, he was dead to me. But lies had a way of surfacing.

Besides, even still living, he was dead to me. I just hoped she'd never find out about him.

The gates swung open and we drove through. The house loomed ahead, all glass and angles catching the afternoon light.

The gates closed behind us, but they weren't sealing us in so much as sealing the world out.

Chapter Eleven

I washed my new swimsuits and hung them to dry. My own pool in LA? It still felt a little surreal. Just a few days ago, I was living in a cheap hotel. Life changed fast.

I washed up and headed out of my room for dinner. Caleb was pacing in the living room. He saw me and darted over, seeming somewhat agitated, glancing around as if afraid of being overheard.

"Soph—Zoe." His smile seemed like acting. "I'd appreciate it if you wouldn't mention to Rose that we bumped into each other on the street today. She wouldn't like that I was visiting my old manager."

"I thought you were location scouting."

"Right. Right. And then I went to see my old manager."

First day on the job, and I was already being asked to keep secrets. "I won't say a word. But I told Talon I saw you."

Caleb nodded. "That's okay. I already talked to my son." He patted me on the shoulder like I was a good little doggy. "Thank you.

I stood there wondering if I should mention that we also saw Rose, but he was already gone.

I found Rose in the hallway. The woman moved like there was always a red carpet beneath her feet.

"Zoe." Her million-dollar smile looked performative too. "I've been looking for you."

"Is everything okay?"

"Yes, yes, of course." She waved an elegant hand. "But I'd appreciate it if you wouldn't mention to Caleb that we bumped into each other today. He wouldn't like that I was visiting my old manager."

I blinked, trying to keep my expression neutral. "Sure. But Talon saw you."

"Oh, I already spoke to him."

"I promise not to say anything."

"Thank you." Another pat on the shoulder, the opposite of Caleb's.

Then she was gone.

I heard them before opening the door. Deep breath. Was all of LA like this? I'd fallen down a Hollywood rabbit hole. Just no talking cat.

I took the empty chair next to Talon.

Molly sat beside Liam tonight. He looked terrible—pale, flushed. She tried checking his forehead. He brushed her away.

"I'm good, Molls."

Her lips tightened.

Nova glared at him from across the table. "You know how important this dinner is. Couldn't you at least come sober?"

Liam rolled his eyes. "It's not like the old bastard is going to leave me the business, so I can come as I like."

"You could at least try to make it seem like you care."

Liam slouched farther in his chair. "Why?"

"So you can advocate for one of us."

He laughed. "Even if I did, it wouldn't be you."

Nova glared at him. "Asshole."

"Petty tyrant."

"Jesus Christ," Willa said, rubbing her brow. "Jaxon."

He glanced up. "What?"

"I've got a headache. Tell them to shut up."

"You got a mouth," Jaxon said. "You do it."

"She uses her mouth for other things," Liam said.

Willa turned white. "Shut up!"

Liam opened his mouth. Molly touched his arm. His shoulders relaxed. For a second, he just looked tired.

The doors opened and Rose entered.

She walked over and greeted Caleb with a kiss on the cheek. "How did your audition go today, darling?"

Caleb kissed her back. "Excellent, darling. And yours?"

"Phenomenal."

"No, no, no," Nova said. "We are not doing this."

Rose straightened. "Doing what?"

Nova folded her arms. "Kiss, kiss, yell, yell. You two only start playing lovey-dovey when you're about ten minutes away from nuclear warfare."

"I don't know what you're talking about. Do you, Caleb?"

He shook his head. "Not at all. We never shout."

Nova snorted. "Please. I've seen smoother acting in shampoo commercials. So whatever you've got planned, save it. At least until Maxwell has signed on the dotted line."

Rose took her seat beside Caleb.

Gordon picked up his water glass and held it out to his lap dog. It started lapping water.

Willa looked over at him. "That's disgusting."

Gordon scowled. "It's no different than you or I drinking out of it."

"Do you know where Monaco's mouth has been? I've never seen a dog more invested in its lack of balls."

Liam cleared his throat.

Willa glared at him. "Shut up."

Liam raised his hands. "I didn't say anything."

No wonder Talon graduated early. He kept his nose in his book for every meal. Not that I blamed him. It apparently helped him stay out of the chaos.

I slunk a little lower in my seat, trying to stay out of everyone's sight lines. I didn't want to catch any strays.

Then the dining room door opened.

Olivia entered, guiding a thin, reedy man wrapped in a red velvet bathrobe that looked like it hadn't seen a washing machine in weeks. His shock of white hair needed brushing, and his chin had enough silver stubble to sand furniture. He smelled like he had soaked in a nicotine bath.

Olivia hovered beside him, helping him to the table.

He slapped her hand away, his voice a raspy rumble. "I don't need help. I've been getting around on my own volition for seventy-some goddamn years. I'm not a goddamned invalid."

Rose wrinkled her nose. "You told the doctor you'd stop smoking."

Maxwell barked a laugh. "If I stop now, I truly will die. Nicotine is the only thing keeping my organs alive."

"That can't possibly be true," Willa said.

Nova sighed. "Dumb and useless and annoying. You are certainly a trifecta of talent."

Willa elbowed Jaxon. "Are you going to let her speak to me like that?"

Jaxon looked up from his phone. "Huh?"

Willa glared at him, folding her arms and sinking back in her chair.

Maxwell sat at the head of the table. Olivia took the seat beside him, reaching for her wine glass and taking a large gulp. Fair enough.

The chef and maid brought out our food, including two small plates for Monaco and Versailles which were set on the floor.

Jaxon turned to Maxwell and cleared his throat once they left. "I need to chat with you about something later."

"If it's work-related, the answer is no," Maxwell replied without looking up from his plate. "I meant what I said about taking a year sabbatical. I gave you a brain, didn't I? Although given you married this one"—he gestured to Willa—"maybe I'm being a little generous."

Willa slammed her palm down on the table, glaring at her husband. He sunk down farther in his chair.

Maxwell took a sip of wine and turned to Talon. "What did you get up to today, kid?"

"Went to the bookstore," Talon said.

"Atta boy. The brains must have skipped a generation, all of them emptying into you. Well, maybe not my Rosie." He glanced over at her with a smile, something almost warm in his eyes. "She's got real thoughts in that pretty head of hers."

Rose preened.

Then Maxwell pointed a fork at me. "Who the fuck is that?"

"That's the nanny," Rose said.

Maxwell squinted, then aimed his fork at Molly. "Isn't that the nanny?"

"No," Nova said. "That's Liam's girlfriend."

"Hmm." Maxwell studied me. "Wasn't expecting anyone so young."

Olivia looked annoyed and gulped down the rest of her wine.

Maxwell waved his fork in my direction. "I thought your friend said she had a lot of experience?"

I stiffened. "I've done alright so far."

A hint of amusement flickered in his eyes. "What do you think of the family? How do we stack up against the rest of your charges?"

The table fell silent. All eyes turned to me, waiting. I had never felt more like a bug under a microscope.

"Well, so far, no one's been murdered. So I'd say it's going well."

"That's not very funny," Willa said.

"I like her." Maxwell laughed. "Got a sense of humor. Unlike most of the humorless clods floating around this table."

Willa stiffened.

"Where you from?" Maxwell asked.

"Connecticut, originally. New York, lately."

"I hate that goddamn city. Too wet. But now that you've been to California, you probably won't go back. No one ever does. What about your family? Where are they?"

I tensed. This wasn't territory I was going to explore with a table full of strangers. "Still in Connecticut." At least I thought they were.

"You got siblings?"

I shook my head. "Only child."

"Nice." He nodded. "I wanted to stop at the twins, but Isabella wanted more. And thank God, otherwise I wouldn't have gotten my Rosie."

She smiled again.

"Jesus Christ, Dad," Nova said. "Mother warned you not to have favorites."

"Well, she's not here, is she?"

Silence dropped like a curtain. Sudden. Suffocating. I preferred the squabbling to the trauma.

Chapter Twelve

I knocked on Talon's door after dinner.

"Come in."

I opened the door. As usual, the kid was on his bed with a book. "Want to go for a walk?"

He hesitated, looking down at his page.

"It's okay if you want to stay and read."

He nodded. "I prefer that. Thanks, Zoe."

"Want me to look in on you later?"

He stared at me like I'd suggested counting his toes. "Why?"

I shrugged. The kid was already more self-sufficient than most adults I knew. "I used to tuck my other kids in."

"Oh." He thought for a moment. "Maybe we could do that."

I smiled. "Sounds good. I'll see you in an hour or so?"

He nodded.

I closed his door, grabbed a sweater and tied it around my waist, and slipped outside using Bertie's gate code. The night air carried the medicinally sweet scent of eucalyptus.

Security cameras blinked red eyes as I passed

fortresses of walls and gates. Spanish, Art Deco, Contemporary—different styles, same purpose. Keep the world out.

I stopped again to look at the view. Talon didn't need a nanny. Thirteen going on thirty, credit card in his wallet. What *was* I doing here? Taking money to babysit a kid who could parent himself?

Maybe I should talk to Madeline? Or Rose? See if there was something more I could be doing? But why? Maybe I should just enjoy this time of less responsibility.

It only felt strange because I wasn't used to it.

I wondered what Frenchie was doing right now. He was probably somewhere in the Mediterranean on that sailboat, trying to keep the twins from literally murdering each other. Or fixing something that had broken. Or he was cooking.

I missed him. I had never felt so alive than when we were together.

Maybe it was the circumstances? Everything on Lyon Island had been so life and death. I could text him again, but I didn't want to harass him. Maybe he wasn't interested in staying connected.

"Stop torturing yourself," I told myself out loud. "Just enjoy the damn view."

A scraping sound came from behind me.

I whirled around, squinting into the darkness but seeing only shadows.

"Hello?"

No answer.

I pulled out my phone and turned on the flashlight, sweeping the beam across the road. I stood still, watching for a bit, but after not hearing or seeing anything, I switched it off and kept walking.

Probably just my imagination. After the Stockports and

Lyon Island, I was understandably paranoid about finding danger in every shadow.

A woman jogged past me, wireless earbuds in, neon stripes on her leggings glowing in the dark. She didn't even glance my way.

But her presence reassured me.

If she wasn't scared, than neither was I.

Streetlights grew sparse. Houses spread farther apart. The night thickened. Time to head back.

A shadow fell over me. A man loomed in the dark.

I screamed and swung my fist, connecting with his shoulder.

"Jesus Christ!" Liam stumbled back. "It's me."

I dropped my hands to my side, my heart pounding. "You scared me!"

"Sorry, sorry." He rubbed his shoulder. "I thought you saw me."

He was dressed in black from head to toe. I gestured to him. "Seriously?"

He grinned.

"Why are you following me?"

"Maybe you're following me."

I planted my hands on my hips and glared at him.

"Just teasing." He tucked his arm into mine like we were old friends on an evening stroll. I shook him loose.

"Thought you might like some company," he said. "Plus I know all the good spots along Mulholland. Want to see something cool?"

I hesitated.

"Best view in LA. I won't let you say no."

Oh for Pete's sake. "Okay."

I followed him against my better judgement. We walked a few minutes in silence before he veered off toward a dark corner where the guard rail had a gap. He slipped through, then turned back, waiting for me to follow.

I picked my way through and onto what turned out to be a small clearing at the edge of the hillside.

Los Angeles sprawled below, a galaxy of lights shimmering in the dark, all the way to the ocean. It made me feel small, and strangely full of possibility. No wonder people called it Tinseltown.

"Told you." Liam sat on a large rock at the edge of a clearing and pulled a joint from his pocket. The lighter flared in the darkness, illuminating his face for a moment. In that flash of light, he looked younger, almost vulnerable.

I walked over and sat next to him.

"So," he said, exhaling a plume of sweet-smelling smoke. "Now that it's just the two of us, you can come clean."

"About what?"

"Spying for Maxwell." He took another drag. Then held it out to me.

I shook my head.

He waved his hand. "Rose won't mind."

"Yeah, but Madeline might."

"She's not here."

"Doesn't matter."

He raised his brows. "So you're not only pretty. You're ethical."

"And I'm not a spy."

"But just in case you are, hear me out—"

"Alright." I sighed, willing to play along. "What's your pitch? You're the youngest, therefore you're the best choice?"

"Nah." He laughed. "I don't want the old man's empire. I want to put in a good word for Rose."

That surprised me. "Rose?"

He nodded. "Nova's too uptight for creative work. Jaxon panics under pressure. But Rose solves puzzles, looks out for people. That matters in business."

Liam pulled out his whistle. "Like this thing. Isabella died because she couldn't get help. So what does Rose do? Make sure each of us can reach out as long as we have breath in our lungs."

He leaned over, checking my collar. "Where's yours?"

I smacked his hand away. "I left it at home."

"If you're out wandering in the dark, maybe you should wear it."

"Why's that?"

"Paparazzi can seem overwhelming when you're not used to them."

"You're definitely right about that."

We sat in silence for a moment. A bat swooped low over our heads.

"My turn for a question," I said.

"Hit me."

"Why were you following me, really?"

Liam's grin returned. "Thought maybe you were meeting someone."

"Meeting someone? I don't know anyone here."

"Your boss."

"My boss is in New York."

"Not that boss." He raised his eyebrows. "The mysterious boss you send your spy reports to."

I stood with a sigh. "I'm going back to the house."

He scrambled to his feet. "Don't be mad."

"I'm not. Just tired. Still on New York time."

I made my way back to the road, with Liam at my heels. He scrubbed out his joint on the asphalt, then tucked his hand inside my arm again.

This time I let him.

We walked back in silence to the side gate. After he opened it, I turned to face him. "Thanks for showing me your favorite spot. It really was beautiful."

"That's how California gets its hooks in you. Soon you'll never want to go home."

I laughed. We closed the gate behind us to find Nova pacing on her phone while smoking.

"He's a fucking idiot," she said into her phone.

"Maxwell know you've taken up the family habit?" Liam asked.

She started, then dropped her cigarette and stubbed it out. "I'll call you back later." She disconnected the call. "What are you two doing out?"

"Walking," I said.

"Me too." Liam nodded. "Fresh air. Stars. All that jazz."

Nova narrowed her eyes. "You never go for walks."

"Turning over a new leaf. Might start a health kick." Then he pulled out another joint and lit it.

"Goodnight, Liam," I said, heading for the door.

He waved.

Nova followed after me. When we reached the door, she blocked me from opening it with her foot. "Hold on."

I sighed. *Now what?*

"Are you alright?" she asked. "Liam can get…handsy."

"I'm fine."

"He didn't try anything?"

I shook my head. "Nope."

Nova nodded. "I know I can come off as…brusque."

Is that what she calls it?

"But I'd appreciate it if you put in a good word for me."

I stared at her, bewildered. "With who?"

"*Maxwell.*" Her tone suggested I was being deliberately

obtuse. "I've swept real shit under the carpet for this family. I deserve to be rewarded, don't you think?"

"It's not up to me. I'm just the nanny."

God, how many times did I have to say it?

"Uh-huh." Her smile was cold. "We'll talk again later."

She sauntered off, leaving me at the door.

I went to Talon's room. Knocked softly. No answer, but the light beneath his door went suddenly dim.

I cracked it open and peered inside.

Sure enough, it was dark.

I walked across his room and found him curled up in bed. On his side, blankets bunched around his chest, book lying closed beside him. He hadn't closed his blinds, so the moonlight flooded into his room, brightening his face. His eyes were closed.

I picked up the book and set it on his bedside table. The light switch was swaying like it had just been switched off.

I tucked the blankets up around his neck, then smoothed back his hair. "Good night, Talon. Sweet dreams."

A tiny smile flickered on his face.

No one had tucked me in at his age. Or younger. But I could do this for Talon. Make him feel safe.

I rubbed his back, then slipped out, softly closing the door behind me.

Chapter Thirteen

EXHAUSTED BUT WIRED. Late in LA, later in New York.

I texted Elsa: *You awake?*

A second later she FaceTimed me.

I hit *accept*.

"How's it going?" She tucked a red curl behind her ear.

I hesitated. What the hell could I say? "Crazy."

She laughed.

"But in a good way. I think I kind of like them. And California too. It's so pretty here."

Elsa moaned. "Oh my God, Zoe, you're going to fall in love with the place and never come back to New York, aren't you?"

"Maybe," I replied with a smile. "After all, I do have my own private pool."

She glared at me. "If you decide to stay, I will come out there personally and drag you back."

I snorted, raising my fist. "I'd like to see you try. Just so you know, I took out one of the younger Marlowes tonight."

Her eyes widened. "What happened?"

"Nothing. He spooked me in the dark."

"Oh my God. Are you okay?"

"I'm fine. But his shoulder *might* have a little bruise."

She laughed.

"How are you doing?" I asked. "The Marlowes might not be behaving themselves, but I hope the Carlsons are."

"No." Elsa sighed. "They're still fighting."

The Marlowes squabbled constantly, but the squabbling seemed to have the staying power of lighting a match in the wind—it flared up, then it was out.

"They're pretty much estranged," Elsa said. "Just staying together for the sake of the baby. I wish parents wouldn't do that. I don't think it's good for Kiersztyn to be subjected to all that hostility."

"Are you thinking of leaving?"

She chewed on her bottom lip. "I don't want to. Kiersztyn needs stability, and…"

"That's not your responsibility, Elsa."

"I know. And I'm starting to think that it might be a good idea. I'm just not ready to pull the plug."

"Talk to Madeline. She'll either help you or find you something better."

"Yeah, I know." Elsa tried to smile, but it didn't really take. "But forget about me. Tell me what Rose is like."

I shrugged. "She treated me like family the second I walked in the door. It's a bit odd, to be honest."

"I'll say."

"All the Marlowes are like that. Sometimes I feel like they talk to me like I've been here for years. They either think all nannies share the same brain, or—"

Or maybe it was that they were trying to win over the spy.

"Or?" she asked.

I shook my head. "I don't know."

"Well, I'm glad they're treating you well. You deserve a *much* better position after the last two."

"Thanks."

"And speaking of two. It's late. Go to bed."

I laughed. "I will. Love you."

She smiled. "Talk to you later."

We disconnected and I plugged my phone back in, then snuggled down into the bed. Only to hear loud voices outside in the hallway.

I got up and walked to the door with a frown, cracked it open and peered out into the dark hallway. Nova and Gordon stood at the far end, lost in shadows.

"I told you to leave the investigating to me," Nova said.

Gordon threw his hands wide. "You haven't gotten anywhere."

"I'm doing my best."

"And I'm tired of waiting."

"Jesus, Gordon. It's not an easy thing. It's still an open—"

"I don't care. Do it. Or I will." Then he spun on his heel and walked off.

Nova dropped her shoulders, then stiffened, turning to look down the hall. Even though it was too dark for her to see me, I pulled back.

A second later, I looked out again. She was gone. A door slammed somewhere in the house. I wondered what they were talking about.

No.

No, I didn't.

The last thing I wanted was to be involved in another family's secrets.

I went back to bed and climbed in. At least this time, sleep came quick.

I woke again. It was dark—pitch black—and cold. That was odd.

The mattress felt strange under me. I reached out for the bedside lamp. Nothing. I bolted upright, scrambling out of my bed, feeling along the wall for the switch. Finally I found it and flipped it on.

I wasn't in the Marlowe home. I was back in the room in the basement in the Stockport house.

How the hell did I get here?

I shoved open the door and stepped into a long hallway. Then ran along it, trying to find a way out. I tested every door I passed. Locked. Locked. Locked.

But at the end of the hall, one door gave way.

I stumbled through—and found myself outside. The cold wind hit me first. Then the rain. And the smell of salt. I was standing on Lyon Island, at the cliff's edge, looking down at the churning ocean.

Rose stood on the shore below, pouring a bottle of red wine into the water. She glanced up when she saw me, smiling like she'd been waiting. She lifted a hand and beckoned me to join her.

I looked for the stairs, but they were gone. I had no way down. So I shook my head.

I heard the scrape of a shoe on the ground behind me. I turned around and saw Carlotta.

She held a dog in her arms. Monaco, I think.

She scowled. "Go away."

Then she shoved me hard.

I screamed.

Falling.

And woke with a jolt, my heart racing.

The sheets were wrapped around my legs. I kicked them off and dropped back against the pillow, forcing myself to inhale and exhale.

It was just a stupid dream.

But then I heard a noise.

I froze, holding my breath, listening hard. *What was that?*

Silence.

It was only my second night. I wasn't used to the noises yet. It was probably just the house settling and I was paranoid after everything that had happened with my last two jobs. I reached down and pulled the blanket up to my chin.

Another sound. This one a thud.

Then what sounded like a splash outside my room.

Talon? Or Liam?

I scrambled out of bed and grabbed my robe, throwing it on as I went to the blinds, pulling them back and peering outside at the pitch-black pool area.

I couldn't see anyone.

I walked to the sliding glass door and unlocked it. Stepped out onto the patio and searched for a light switch but failed to find one in the dark.

"Hello?"

No response.

I waited for my eyes to adjust, but the moon was hidden behind clouds, making it nearly impossible to see anything in the darkness. I shuffled along the patio, inching toward the pool.

Finally, I reached the edge. There was something dark in the water. I crouched down, squinting at the shape.

What was it? Fabric of some sort?

I reached out, scooping the water toward me, trying to get a better look. My fingertips brushed against something rough and organic.

A palm frond.

I blew out a breath of air, then plucked it out of the water and tossed it onto the deck. Glanced up at the tree that stood over the pool as a breeze stirred the leaves above, turning the shadows into dancers around me. I wiped my wet hand on my housecoat, then took one last look around the darkened pool area. Everything was still now.

The water lapped against the sides. I headed back to my room. I was just jumpy. I pulled the sliding door closed behind me, making sure it was locked.

Then I shuffled back to bed and climbed under the covers, settling against the pillows.

I closed my eyes. Willed sleep to come. Scared myself over nothing. But sleep wouldn't come.

I stared at the ceiling, replaying the noise in my head. The splash seemed a little loud for a palm frond. Maybe it was a raccoon. Did they even have raccoons in LA? I had no idea.

Sleep.

Right.

I closed my eyes again.

And then another noise jolted me upright: a sharp clatter out by the pool deck.

I grabbed my phone from the nightstand, thumbed the flashlight app on, and marched straight to the door. Threw it open—

And froze.

A soaking wet man stood at the door, dripping all over the tile, his bright orange hair plastered to his skull.

Staring at me like *I* was the surprise.

I screamed.

"Oh shit."

He raised something black and pointed it at me. I dropped to the floor, heart pounding, every instinct screaming *gun!*—

Only a bright flash exploded in my face. Then another.

And another. Flashing in rapid succession. For half a second, I thought I'd been shot—but there was no crack of a gun going off—no sound at all aside from…a *click*.

It wasn't a gun.

It was a camera.

It took me longer than it should have to stitch that together.

But I couldn't see. The light was blinding, then it wasn't, then it was again. White spots danced across my vision.

I stumbled backward, disoriented. My heel caught on the door jamb. I fell, arms windmilling.

I landed hard on my butt, the impact knocking the wind out of me.

I tried to catch my breath. Then I scrambled to my feet, lunged for the door, and slammed it shut, flicking the lock.

My bedroom door burst open. Talon stood there in pajamas, his hair sticking up in all directions.

"What's wrong?" His eyes were wide. "I heard you scream."

"Camera," I said.

He grabbed my whistle from the nightstand. Three sharp blasts pierced the air, echoing through the house like a screaming alarm.

Chapter Fourteen

"PAPARAZZI," said Rose. "We've caught them on the property before but couldn't figure out how they got in. Seems they climb the neighbor's tree and jump into the pool."

She sat next to me, her arm draped around my shoulders. The weight felt both comforting and strange. Talon was crouched on the floor with his back to the wall. He appeared to be reading, but I hadn't seen him turn a page since he sat.

Footsteps sounded in the hallway.

Nova appeared in the doorway, her expression unreadable. "Bertie, Jaxon, and Liam are searching the property. No sign of him yet."

Rose's arm stiffened. "He couldn't have gotten out."

Nova crossed her arms. "Maybe he climbed another palm tree."

Rose stood. "Well, I want him found. I've got a kid to protect."

Talon didn't look up from his book. "I'm fine."

Rose ignored him, brushing past Nova and heading out of the room.

Nova leaned against the doorframe. "You'll start getting used to them eventually. It will become normalized. At least when Rose, Caleb, or Maxwell are with you, the rest of us aren't targeted. Maybe Talon a bit. Wunderkind."

Talon extended his middle finger without looking up from his book.

"I've arranged for an arborist to take down the neighbor's tree tomorrow," she said.

I blinked. "You can do that?"

She smiled, her teeth gleaming. "He's a lotto winner. We're old Hollywood. Yeah, I can do that."

She walked out. I sagged on the bed. Then she popped her head back in. "I hope you'll tell Maxwell how well I handled this situation."

I almost threw a pillow at her, but she was gone, the door clicking shut behind her. I looked over at Talon. He closed his book and met my eyes.

"*Are* you used to it?" I asked.

He nodded. "They've always been there. In a weird way, they're like family. Only they're the ones no one wants around."

I almost laughed.

"You want me to stay with you?" he asked. "I don't mind."

"No, I'm good." I stood. "I think I'll get a cup of tea from the kitchen."

Talon stood, tucking his book against his chest. "Don't let the paparazzi scare you, Zoe. They just want pictures. As soon as they figure out you're not famous, they'll never bother you again."

"Solid advice. Thanks."

"Good night." He gave me a smile, and then he was gone.

I pulled my robe tight and headed to the kitchen. Voices outside. Flashlight beams sliced through darkness, catching tree branches. The search party continued.

Gordon sat at the kitchen island, laptop open. He closed it when he saw me. "Zoe."

"I didn't mean to disturb you," I said, hovering in the doorway. "I just thought I'd get a cup of tea."

He pushed the laptop aside.

"Not at all. I'm just taking a break from searching."

Either Versailles or Monaco trotted over and sniffed at my ankles. I reached down and patted a dog head, earning a tail wag.

I filled the kettle and set it to boil.

"Mugs are in that cupboard." Gordon pointed to one of about fifty.

"Thanks."

I could hear Jaxon outside, yelling that he'd already searched there.

Gordon ran a hand through his thinning hair. "I think the bastard must be gone. There's only so many palm trees you can hide behind."

I laughed. "Does this happen a lot? The paparazzi showing up?"

"It used to before they put the new security system in. Or at least that's what Nova told me. It was before my time."

We watched out the window. The kettle clicked off. I made tea. "Want one?"

"Sure. Why not?"

I got another mug from the cupboard, dunked in a tea

bag and added hot water, then carried it over and set the mug in front of him. "How long have you been married to Nova?"

"Six years." He wrapped his hands around the mug, looking down into the steam. "Best thing that ever happened to me. She pulled me out of a dark time in my life."

Monaco (I think?) settled at his feet with a contented sigh.

I gestured to the dog. "What is she?"

"Yorkie. Though sometimes I think there's a bit of gremlin thrown in there for good measure."

I laughed.

"She belonged to my first wife."

That surprised me. "That's not Nova?"

"No." He shook his head. "Beth. She died. Hit and run. Nine years ago now."

"Oh—I'm sorry. I didn't know. I wouldn't have—"

He waved a hand. "Don't apologize. I like talking about her. She was the love of my life. And yes, Nova knows I call her that. Always has."

I took a sip of my tea.

"We ran a vintage store on La Brea. I was sick that day, stayed home. She walked home alone. Broad daylight. Car drifted onto the sidewalk, hit her. Wasn't even hard, but she hit her head on the curb." He snapped his fingers. "*Gone.*"

"That's awful."

"I had a hard time after she was killed. I started drinking. Then I met Nova at AA and well…if it hadn't been for her, I don't know where I'd be today."

"Did they catch the driver?"

Gordon shook his head, his face darkening. "Not that the police tried very hard."

"I'm sorry."

"If I'd been married to Nova at the time, I'm sure no stone would have been left unturned. This town runs on celebrity clout, and I was a nobody. If you're famous, they'll work hard. If you're not, good luck." He rubbed his head. "Sorry, I shouldn't be burdening you with my miseries. It's the tenth-year anniversary coming up, and I think it's hitting me hard."

"I can imagine," I said.

His fingers drifted toward his laptop.

"I should get some sleep," I added.

"Of course." He nodded. "It's been quite a night."

I paused at the door. "While you have me alone, aren't you going to ask if I'm the spy?"

Gordon laughed. "No."

"Why not?"

"Because I know who the real spy is."

Then he opened his laptop and started reading again.

I stared. He knew? Why hadn't he told Nova?

Was this what they'd argued about?

Now he looked impatient. "Is there anything else?"

"No." I flushed. "Goodnight."

I headed back to my room and sat on my bed, sipping my tea, trying to calm my nerves. But my eyes kept drifting to the blinds covering the glass doors to the pool. Had I locked them? I got up to check: yes, locked.

But I checked them twice more after that.

I climbed into bed, blankets to my chin. The orange-haired man kept flashing through my mind. For a moment, I'd thought I was being shot.

I couldn't tell them how scared I'd been. They were used to paparazzi. I'd seem foolish. I wanted to call Elsa, but it was too late. Frenchie was too far away.

Madeline?

No. She was paying me to handle things.

I listened for sounds outside. Nothing. I set my mug down and turned off the light.

Sleep felt impossible.

Chapter Fifteen

A CHAINSAW RIPPED me awake from my dream.

I bolted upright, heart pounding, and stumbled out of bed and to the window, yanking the blinds up.

California sunshine blazed through the glass. Men in hard hats swarmed the pool area, dismembering the palm tree chunk by chunk. Nova stood on the deck, phone pressed to her ear, supervising the execution.

I stepped away from the window and glanced at the clock. Just past eight. After the previous night's excitement, I'd hoped to sleep longer, but that wasn't happening now.

I lowered the blinds again for some privacy.

Then I showered, listening to the massacre outside. When I finished dressing, I walked down the hall and knocked on Talon's door. No response.

I knocked again, a little harder. "Talon? You awake?"

"Yeah."

I opened the door to find him hunched over a textbook, still in pajamas. Hair sticking up, glasses askew. He'd been up for hours.

"Did you sleep?" I asked.

"Uh huh."

It sounded like a lie.

"What do you want to do today?"

"Stay in and read?"

The chainsaw roared to life again. I winced at the sound. "Why don't we go out and explore? There must be something you'd like to do."

"Anything?"

"Well, within reason," I said.

"What's outside of reason?"

"Murder, gambling, starting a cult."

He laughed. "How about the Griffith Observatory? Nobody ever wants to take me there."

An observatory? Somewhere dark, quiet? "Sounds perfect to me."

He perked up immediately. "You mean it?"

"Yeah. But we need some breakfast first."

Talon looked the happiest I'd seen him since my arrival. He closed his book and rolled off the bed. "I'll get dressed."

"Meet you downstairs."

The dining room was empty. The chef had laid out a Hollywood breakfast buffet: fruit, pastries, bacon, waffles, eggs, avocado toast. I filled my plate and found my seat. Talon joined me five minutes later.

I'd just taken my first bite of yogurt and granola when the door banged open.

Liam wandered in, wearing pajamas and a robe, a joint dangling from his fingers. He made a beeline for the bacon, grabbed a handful, then plopped down at the table. He didn't bother with utensils, tearing into the bacon with his fingers.

"What are you two up to today?" he asked with his mouth full.

"The observatory," Talon said.

"Cool. I'll come."

Talon brightened. "Swell!"

I wanted to protest, but I couldn't bring myself to dim his enthusiasm.

Liam turned to me. "Did you recover from your midnight photo shoot?"

"I'm fine. Did you find the guy?"

"Nope. Slippery little weasel, whoever he was. At least he didn't get any photos, we think. Well, except of you. I'd pay to see those. The expression on your face must have been something."

I glared at him, then turned to Talon, who was arranging fruit in a perfect circle around his plate. "How did you graduate so early anyway?"

Talon shrugged.

Liam said, "The bastard would finish doing lessons ahead of everyone else and ask for more. His teacher got irritated. Started giving him harder and harder equations and shit. He solved them all anyway. So they sent him for testing, and it turned out he was really smart." He reached over and ruffled Talon's hair. "Smarter than me. Smarter than the whole goddamn family."

Talon beamed.

"Was it hard? Going to college when you're so young?" I asked.

Talon shook his head. "No. I like learning."

"But everyone would have been older than you."

"Most kids my age are boring. Adults too." His eyes widened. "Sorry."

I laughed. "That's okay."

Relief washed over his face.

"It's why Nanny 2 eventually left," Liam said. "She

kept trying to pretend she was smarter than him. Eventually, she found other work."

"Must be lonely," I said. "Being that smart."

"I need to brush my teeth. I'll meet you at the car." Talon stood abruptly and walked out, leaving his plate half-full.

"Did I say something wrong?" I asked.

Liam shrugged. "Dunno."

I narrowed my eyes. "Why are you really coming with us?"

"What?" He feigned outrage. "I've always wanted to see the observatory."

"Bullshit. You could go anytime. Why today, with us?"

Liam leaned toward me. "You know why. I'm spying on the spy."

I almost rolled my eyes. Not this again. "How many times do I have to tell you? I'm not spying on your family. I'm the nanny."

Liam snorted. "He's a thirteen-year-old kid who's about to get his PhD in astrology—"

"Astronomy."

Liam waved his hand. "Point is, does the dude really need a nanny?"

It did seem ridiculous when he put it like that. Liam seemed more in need of a nanny than Talon did. Maybe I was missing something. I should talk to Rose about my reasons for being here. Clear it up once and for all.

"Half an hour." I stood. "If you're not ready, we're leaving without you."

"Yeah, yeah." Liam picked up another slice of bacon and bit into it.

I returned to my room to grab my purse.

The chainsaws had finally stopped. I looked out the window to see a member of the crew sweeping up sawdust.

One less way in. Somehow, that didn't feel safer.

Chapter Sixteen

As we explored the Griffith Observatory. Liam and I hung back while Talon darted between exhibits, knowing more than the information signs.

"See this?" Talon pointed to a diagram of planetary orbits. "They've left out the Kuiper Belt objects that affect Neptune's trajectory."

"And that's a bad thing?" I asked.

He stared at me like I was an imbecile. "Yes, because you can't understand orbital mechanics without accounting for gravitational perturbations."

"You can't?" Liam asked.

Talon sighed. "It's like trying to explain why a car swerves without mentioning the pothole."

I nodded, pretending I understood what he meant.

Liam ruffled Talon's hair. "Regular professor, this one."

Talon pulled away and ran to another display, this one about deep space exploration missions with an interactive Voyager model.

"I'm going to be an astronaut one day," he said, studying the space probe. "The youngest one in space."

"Well," Liam said. "If anybody can do it, it's you. I just hope I'm around to see it."

Talon glared at him. "It's not going to take me that long."

Liam threw up his hands. "Got it!"

"Come on," Talon said. "Let's watch the show."

He led us to the Samuel Oschin Planetarium. A sign read: *Journey to the Edge of the Universe — A Deep Space Exploration.*

Front row. I sat between them, immediately regretting it. Liam fidgeted—bouncing knee, shifting, picking at his laces.

The lights dimmed, the stars blossomed across the dome above us. A minute later, the narrator's voice—I recognized him from a popular science fiction TV show in the sixties—filled the room and began talking about distant galaxies and cosmic phenomena.

Liam leaned over, his breath hot on my cheek.

"Bathroom," he said in a low voice. "Be right back."

I nodded, relieved when he slipped away. I could finally enjoy the show without his constant movement.

I sank deeper into my seat, letting the vastness of the cosmos above wash over me. There were billions of stars. Countless worlds. My problems (having had my tuition stolen by my mother, being thousands of miles away from my best friend) seemed microscopic by comparison.

A few minutes later, a tap on my shoulder jolted me back to reality.

I turned to glare at Liam.

But it was an usher.

"Are you with Liam Marlowe's party?" the man asked in a hushed voice.

"Yes." I nodded. "Is he okay?"

"Could you please come with me?" His face gave nothing away.

I turned to Talon, touched his arm. "I'll be right back."

He nodded, too engrossed in the cosmos spinning above to be concerned about me.

I followed the usher out of the dark theater and into the hallway, blinking in the light. "What's going on?"

"Mr. Marlowe asked that I find you." He led me toward the washrooms. "We were going to call an ambulance, but he said he insisted that he talk to you instead."

My pulse quickened. "An ambulance. What happened?"

"I'll let him explain." The usher gestured to the washroom door.

I pointed to it, then myself.

He nodded and I entered, allowing the door to swing closed behind me.

The room was empty except for Liam, sitting propped against the wall by the sinks. His usual cockiness was gone. Instead, he looked small, pale, and vulnerable. A thin film of sweat coated his forehead, but he managed a weak grin when he saw me. "Hey, Nanny 911."

I turned around and locked the door, then walked over and crouched next to him. "What happened?"

"Had a seizure." His voice was hoarse. "No big deal."

"No big deal?" I couldn't keep the shock from my voice. "You need to go to the hospital."

Liam shook his head, then winced. "Just feeling nauseous. Blurred vision. It'll pass. Need some help getting up is all. In a minute."

I eyed him. "Is it drugs."

He scowled at me. "No, it's not drugs."

I got up and grabbed a wad of paper towels from the dispenser, then turned on the tap and soaked them. I wrung them out and wiped his face, then the back of his neck.

He closed his eyes. "Thanks."

"Hospital."

"No." His voice had an edge now. "I'm epileptic. I know what to do."

That caught me off guard. "You're epileptic?"

"Yes. No one in the family knows. And I'd like to keep it that way."

"Why? It's nothing to be ashamed of."

"Please," he said.

I raised my hands, then tossed the paper towel in the garbage can. "I promise I won't say anything."

"Good." His color was gradually returning. "Can you help me up now?"

I slipped my arm around his shoulders and helped him to his feet. He swayed, gripping the sink for balance. We waited a moment, then he spread his arms wide. "See? Good as new."

He swayed again, catching himself on the porcelain.

I caught him before he could fall. "Let's get you out to the car."

"The kid—"

"I'll come back for Talon."

He nodded, laying a hand across my shoulders.

Together we made our way to the door. I unlocked and opened it.

As soon as we stepped into the hallway, he pulled away from me. "I'm feeling better. I'll head to the car. Meet you there."

"I don't think that's a good idea. You shouldn't go alone."

"I'm fine. Really."

"Liam."

He forced a smile. "Don't make me fire you, Nanny Zoe. And don't tell the kid. He'll just worry."

I hesitated, but he was already making his down the hallway. What was I supposed to do? Run after him? He was a grown adult. And I really didn't like the idea of leaving Talon alone.

Not with paparazzi crawling about.

I returned to the theater just as the show was ending, with the narrator wishing everyone a long life. I slipped back into my seat as the house lights came up.

Talon blinked, returning to Earth.

"Sorry I took so long," I said.

He looked around. "Where's Liam?"

"He wasn't feeling well. He's meeting us at the car."

Talon frowned. "He left the show?"

"Yeah, he—"

"Whatever." Talon stood, looking deflated. "Can we go now?"

I nodded. "Yeah, we can go."

We left the observatory into bright afternoon sun. Tourists snapped photos of the Hollywood sign. Talon stalked ahead, hurt by his uncle's abandonment. Why couldn't Liam just tell him about the epilepsy?

We found Liam sprawled across the back seat, smoking a joint. Talon yanked open the passenger door, slammed it shut. I smacked Liam's feet, slid into the back.

The car reeked of cannabis. I plucked the joint from his hand and ground it under my foot.

"Hey, I wasn't done with that."

I pointed to Talon. "Yes, you were."

Liam raised his brows.

I glared, slamming the door behind me.

Liam leaned forward. "You okay, T?"

Talon didn't answer.

Liam cleared his throat. "Didn't mean to bail on you like that."

Talon kept his gaze fixed straight ahead. "Whatever."

"Come on." Liam plucked at his sleeve. "The Mars show will still be here next week. I'll bring you back. Just the two of us. Promise."

"It's deep space. And you always say that. Remember the La Brea Tar Pits? And the Natural History Museum?" Talon finally turned around, his expression hardening. "You promised to take me to those too."

"We went to those, didn't we?"

"No."

"Right." Liam ran a hand over his face. "Shit, I'm sorry."

"You also always say that."

"I mean it this time, T. Scout's honor." He held up three fingers in what I assumed was meant to be a pledge. "Next Friday. I'll clear my whole schedule."

"You don't have a schedule."

"Not any more I don't."

"And you were never a Scout."

Liam looked offended. "How do you know that?"

"Because Mom told me you spent your summers smoking pot behind the tennis courts at Maxwell's country club."

I stifled a laugh. Liam glared at me.

"Fine. Whatever honor is better than scout's. Marlowe honor."

"That's not saying much," Talon said.

"You wound me, nephew." Liam clutched his chest dramatically. "Straight through the heart."

"Good thing you don't have one."

"Ouch!"

Talon grinned.

Liam ruffled his hair. Then he leaned back against the seat, caught my eye and mouthed, *Did you tell him?*

I shook my head.

Relief washed over his face. He patted my shoulder, then seemed to relax. "How about Grill-N-Go Burger? I'm famished."

"You know I'm not allowed to eat that," Talon said. "Rose says it's bad for digestion."

"Yeah, well Rose ain't here, is she?"

Talon and Liam both turned to look at me.

I blinked. "What?"

"You won't tell Mom, will you?" Talon asked.

I hesitated.

"Come on," Liam said. "Don't start spying now, spy."

I glared at him, then turned to Talon. "Rose hasn't mentioned anything about your diet to me."

"Then that's a yes." Liam tapped Bertie on the shoulder. "Grill-N-Go, my good man."

Bertie nodded, pulling away from the curb. "Yes, sir."

And we were off.

Chapter Seventeen

LIAM AND TALON were dueling with french fries in the back seat. I'd moved up front, grateful to escape the food fight while Bertie navigated afternoon traffic.

I glanced back. Talon's face was bright with excitement and Liam's playful smirk had returned. Hard to believe this was the same man who'd been collapsed on a bathroom floor an hour ago.

"En garde!" Liam lunged with a particularly long fry.

Talon parried with his own, then jabbed back. "Touché!"

Bertie accelerated, then braked hard. I was thrown back against my seat. "What's going on?"

His eyes flicked to the mirror. "That gray car again."

I turned around, glancing out the rear window. Sure enough, there was a gray sedan three cars back. "Are you sure it's the same one from the airport?"

"Not positive." Bertie changed lanes abruptly. The gray car followed. "Could be a coincidence."

We turned onto Sunset Boulevard, the car still behind

us. A minute later, it signaled and turned off onto a side street.

"Nah," Liam said, glancing back. "The two of you are just paranoid."

I glanced at Bertie.

He shrugged.

I settled back in my seat. Maybe Liam was right. The traffic light ahead turned yellow. But Bertie accelerated through just as it changed to red.

We were the last ones through.

But then a black van pulled out from a side street, sliding in directly behind us. No front license plate.

"That van's riding our bumper," I said.

Bertie checked the mirror again. "Asshole."

The van edged closer, almost touching our rear bumper. Then it nudged us—not hard enough to cause damage but definitely deliberate.

The SUV shuddered.

"Son of a bitch." Bertie tightened his fingers on the steering wheel.

Liam twisted around in his seat. "What's happening?"

"Some idiot tailgating," Bertie said, voice tight.

Liam turned to look out the back window. "Damn paparazzi."

"Are you sure?" I asked.

He stiffened, watching. "Maybe not."

The traffic light ahead turned red. Bertie started to slow, but Liam leaned forward. "Don't stop."

Bertie swung into the turn lane, ran the red light. We swerved between oncoming cars, horns screaming as we shot through the intersection.

I gripped the dashboard.

The black van followed, accelerating.

Bertie sped along Laurel Canyon where the road

wound uphill. The van stayed with us, gaining ground on the straightaways.

"What do they want?" I asked. "Because if it's not paparazzi, it's not pictures."

"Don't know." Bertie took a curve too fast. "And I don't want to find out."

We reached Mulholland and turned east, the van still behind us. The road narrowed, snaking along the ridge of the Hollywood Hills.

Liam grabbed Talon and pushed him below the window line. "Get down!"

I twisted around. "What—"

The van accelerated, pulling alongside us. The passenger window lowered and a man wearing a black balaclava leaned out, metal glinting in his hand.

"Reverse!" Liam yelled. "Reverse!"

Bertie slammed on the brakes and threw the car into reverse, tires screaming against the pavement. The van shot past, then skidded to a stop, blocking the road ahead.

"Go back!"

Bertie spun the wheel, executed a perfect turn, and accelerated in the opposite direction. My stomach lurched.

The gray sedan appeared at the intersection in front of us.

"Those aren't paparazzi," I said.

"No shit." Liam had his phone out, punching in numbers. "Drive, drive! Stay down, Talon. Don't look."

Bertie swung left onto another street.

The sedan followed, the van now behind it.

"We're on Woodrow Wilson," Liam said into the phone, his voice surprisingly calm given the situation. "Two vehicles. Armed men. Yes, with fucking guns. At least I think it was a gun."

We hit a straightaway. Bertie floored it.

"Take Cahuenga," Liam said. "Then right on Pilgrimage Bridge."

Bertie nodded, executed a sharp turn. Tires squealed against the asphalt.

My heart slammed against my ribs.

I reached back for Talon's hand and he grabbed it. I turned to look at him. He was hunched over, his eyes wide. "It's okay," I told him. "We're going to be fine."

"You said you don't lie to your kids."

"Then I must be telling the truth."

The car bounced over uneven pavement, engine straining as Bertie pushed it to its limits. The Hollywood Bowl flashed past, then he took another right.

"They're still back there." Bertie checked the mirror. "About four car lengths."

Liam remained on the phone, rattling off street names as Bertie drove. "Coming down Highland now. I think they're going to try and box us in at Franklin." He paused, listening. "Understood."

Bertie swerved around a slow-moving Prius, narrowly missing a parked delivery truck. Then just as Liam predicated, the van appeared in front of us.

Bertie yanked the wheel left, burning through a yellow light onto Franklin Avenue. Horns blared. Someone shouted obscenities.

"Go north on Beachwood," Liam said. "There's an empty lot near the Beachwood Canyon Market."

Bertie nodded, took the turn. The streets narrowed as we climbed into the hills again, houses pressing close on either side.

"There," Liam pointed.

Bertie swung into what looked like a weed-choked driveway, then continued up a dirt path obscured by overgrown shrubs. We bumped along for twenty yards before he cut the engine and killed the lights, backing up against a dilapidated wooden fence.

Everyone froze. The only sound was our collective breathing and the tick-tick-tick of the cooling engine.

Talon's hand was squeezing mine so tight it hurt. I squeezed back.

Seconds stretched into minutes. A car engine growled in the distance, growing louder, then faded again.

"Did they see us?" Talon asked.

Bertie shook his head. "Don't think so. They'd be here by now."

Liam was still on the phone, voice low. "Yeah, they seem to be gone. Yeah. Yeah. We'll stay put a few more minutes to be sure."

He disconnected and let out a slow breath.

"Are the police on their way?"

"I don't think so. Why?"

I stared at him. "You didn't call the police?"

"Of course not."

"Then who was on the phone?"

"Jaxon. He's checking the roads. Making sure it's safe."

I released Talon's hand and dug my phone from my purse. "Well, I'm calling the cops."

Liam undid his seat belt, darted forward, and plucked the phone from my hands. "No."

I unbuckled as well and stuck out my hand. "Give it back."

"Nope."

"Liam."

"No police. Let the family deal with it."

"Talon's a child. Those men had guns!"

"Jaxon's people have it handled."

"Jaxon's people?" I repeated. "What's that supposed to mean?"

Liam shrugged. "It means sit tight. He's got security. Connections. Whatever. They'll take care of the problem. Tell us when it's safe to come home."

I glanced over at Talon. He was still curled over.

Liam's expression softened. He reached over and rubbed his nephew's back. "You okay, T?"

Talon nodded, though he seemed awfully pale, breathing in shallow bursts. French fries were scattered all over the back seat.

"See?" Liam smiled. "He's fine."

"He's not fine," I said. "He's terrified. And so am I."

Talon straightened. "Who were those men?"

Liam shook his head. "Nobody important."

"They had guns."

"Probably just movie props. This is Hollywood, after all."

I stared at Liam. "Stop lying to him."

Bertie's phone rang. We all jumped. He answered, listened briefly, then hung up. "Jaxon says Mulholland is clear. We can head home now."

He started the engine. It sounded too loud.

"Don't forget to buckle up, Zoe," Liam said.

I glared at him. Then I did up my belt, crossing my arms. Bertie eased back onto Beachwood Drive, heading north and away from where we'd last seen our pursuers. He drove slowly, following all the road rules.

Nobody spoke.

We arrived and Liam got out of the car. "Come on, T. I'll get the chef to make you more fries."

Talon shook his head.

"Go," I said to Liam. "I'll get him inside."

Liam hesitated, then gave me my phone. "Remember what I said. This stays in the family."

Then he walked off.

I got out of the SUV and opened the back door. Talon didn't move. "Are you okay? Did you get hurt?"

He sniffed. "I peed myself."

The confession came out small and humiliated.

I untied the hoodie around my waist, then fastened it around his. "There you go. Straight to your room and shower. This will stay between us."

Relief flooded his face. "Thanks, Zoe."

"Of course," I said with a smile. "And just for the record, I'll need to do the same myself."

He gave a little laugh, then ran off to the house.

Bertie appeared at my elbow. "I'll get the car detailed."

I ignored him and followed Talon.

I was annoyed at them both.

From inside, I heard Rose screaming at someone. Indistinct words fueled by obvious rage. I saw her stalking down the hallway toward Talon's room. She flung the door open and disappeared inside, slamming it behind her with enough force to rattle the artwork on the walls.

Liam glanced over at me, shrugging.

I ignored him, making my way down the hall to my room. I closed the door behind me and my knees buckled. I slid down the wall until I was sitting on the floor.

Masked men. Guns. A car chase through the streets of LA.

This was no movie.

This was real life.

I dropped my head into my hands. What had I gotten myself into?

Chapter Eighteen

I REALLY SHOULD HAVE CALLED the cops. Maybe I should have fought Liam for my phone. Or taken Talon and made a run for it when we stopped at that empty lot.

But where? I didn't know Los Angeles. Not like Liam and Bertie.

And those men had guns.

There was a knock on my bedroom door.

I got to my feet and answered it.

Rose stood in the hallway. She was pale. I could almost see the bone beneath her flesh. "Talon told me how you were there for him. Thank you."

I nodded. "Of course."

My voice shook. I cleared my throat.

"It must have been terrifying."

"Yes."

She reached out and took my hand, giving it a squeeze. "I'm sorry my dumb asshole of a brother called Jaxon instead of the cops."

The fury in her voice made me step back. She was

always so composed, so perfectly put together. Seeing her this raw was unsettling. "How is Talon doing?"

"Better." She released my hand. "Could you watch him until I return? I need to track down Caleb. He's not home. And Talon doesn't want to be alone."

"Of course."

Rose nodded, squeezed my hand again, then strode off down the hall.

I blew out a breath, then made my way to Talon's door and knocked.

No response, so I pushed it open. "It's Zoe."

He was curled up in bed in his pajamas with an open book in his lap, but he wasn't reading.

I walked over and sat on the edge of the bed beside him. "Hey."

"Hey."

We sat in silence for a long moment.

Then his eyes filled with tears. "I was really scared."

"Me too."

He wiped his eyes. "Really?"

I nodded. "That's why I needed to hold your hand."

He laughed. It was small, but it was something. "Thanks for not telling Rose about the accident."

"Of course not. That stays between us."

"You want a bedtime story?" I asked after another lingering silence.

"I'm kind of old for that, Zoe."

"Yeah, I guess you are. Dumb idea."

He pursed his lips. "But if I did want one, what would it be about?"

"I don't know. Maybe something about the moon?"

"Okay." He snuggled down into his bed. I turned, tucking the covers up around him. Then I curled up beside him, resting my head on my arm.

"Once upon a time, there was a little boy whose mom was always sad because she never had any cheese for her crackers. So one night, when the moon was full and bright, he decided to climb up and get her some."

"The moon isn't made of cheese, Zoe."

"This one is."

He almost smiled.

"He built a ladder out of old telescope parts and climbed all the way up to the moon."

I paused.

"Go on," he finally said.

"The boy had to be very careful walking so as not to bounce too high, because the gravity was so much weaker than on Earth. One wrong step and he might float away into the darkness between the stars."

"But oxygen," Talon said.

"This is a special moon. It has plenty of that."

He laughed.

"Anyway, the boy found craters filled with different kinds of cheese. Some sharp like cheddar, others soft and creamy like brie. All that cheese glowed with a gentle silver light that sparkled like the stars. He filled his pockets, making sure not to take too much. After all, the moon needed to stay whole and bright."

Talon's breath was slowing.

"Then he heard a sound. A gentle humming coming from the dark side of the moon. He walked around to investigate and found hundreds of other children there. Kids from all over the universe who had come to gather moon cheese for their families. They traded between them, making sure they had their favorite flavors."

Talon smiled.

"The boy spent the night learning about the moon from his new friends. They taught him which craters had the best cheese, and how to listen for the moon's heartbeat deep underground. And when morning came on Earth, it was time to go home, even though it was still dark on the moon. The boy climbed back down his telescope ladder, his pockets heavy with the most wonderful cheese. When he gave it to his mother, she smiled for the first time in months, and her smile was as bright as the moon itself. 'You went all the way to the moon, just for me?' she asked. The boy nodded. 'Of course,' he told here. 'Some things are worth the journey.'"

I stopped talking, looking over at Talon.

He seemed to be asleep.

I got up from the bed, smoothed his hair and headed to the door. Rose was standing just inside the door, watching. "You're a good storyteller."

I flushed. "Thank you."

"Good night, Zoe."

"Night."

I slipped out and closed the door behind me, leaving the two of them alone. Caleb appeared in the hallway, walking toward me. "How's Talon?"

"Sleeping. Rose is with him now."

"I think I'll join them," he said with a nod.

Caleb knocked softly, then entered the room and closed the door.

I headed to my own bedroom.

I searched the wall, looking for a light switch. I found one and turned on the outside light. Then I went out onto the deck, looking at the place where the tree used to be.

In a strange way, I missed it.

I sat in one of the chaises and lay back, looking up at the stars. But it reminded me of the planetarium. Maybe I should go for a swim instead. Try and wear off some of the adrenaline.

There was a knock behind me. I started, turning around. Jaxon held a cup of tea in each hand. "Don't get up. I just wanted to chat."

He walked over and took a seat in the chair beside me, setting the tea on the table between us. "Olivia made you some black tea. Figured you could use something stiff after that ordeal."

"That was nice of her."

He laughed, the light flashing on his Patek Philippe watch. "Don't get used to it."

I took a sip. It was hot and bitter. Perfect.

"Liam said you were angry he didn't call the cops. But you need to know the family is used to solving their own problems."

"Those men had guns."

He nodded. "I know. And I thought you'd be pleased to know that I filed a report with the police."

"Do you need me to speak to them?"

He shook his head. "Liam and Bertie provided descriptions. They said they'd be in touch if they needed anything more."

"What do you think they wanted?"

Jaxon shrugged. "Attempted carjacking, maybe. Or maybe they were paparazzi. They can be ruthless in getting the shot. Maybe they thought Rose was in the car."

"You think paparazzi would do something that extreme? Put masks over their faces and chase a car with a child in it?"

Jaxon took a sip of tea. "Once when Rose was on the red carpet for *The Orange Tree*, a photographer shouted out that Talon had been killed on his way home from school. The look on her face went viral."

My stomach flip-flopped. "That's sick."

"Welcome to Hollywood. If the cameras can catch

more than the usual commercial shot, it can net those bastards a lot of money. Look, I know this family can seem chaotic. But we protect our own. And what happened today won't happen again. I guarantee it."

"How can you be sure?"

"Because now we know someone's targeting us. And we'll be more careful." He stood, collecting his mug. "Again, I apologize. If you need anything, Zoe, you just let me know, okay?"

I nodded.

"Goodnight," he said.

"Goodnight."

I watched him walk around the balcony. There must be another entrance to the house along there. I opened my phone and googled Rose and *The Orange Tree* and red carpet. I found the photo a few seconds later.

Rose's face was twisted in pain. Her mouth open, eyes wide. A devastating photo. It almost felt obscene to look at.

The accompanying headlines were brutal: *Rose Marlowe's Red Carpet Meltdown* and *Orange Tree Star Loses it at Premiere*. One article speculated that there must be some kind of disagreement between her and the director for her to look that angry. Another went into excruciating detail about the "obvious tension" between Rose and her co-stars. Another suggested she was having a nervous breakdown.

I put my phone away and closed my eyes. I couldn't imagine being so famous that people made up stories about you. Let alone having someone shout fake news about my child's death just to capture my reaction. It was beyond cruel. Sadistic really. So maybe it wasn't that big a stretch to imagine the paparazzi dressing up in masks and guns, chasing us through the hills?

It would be a hell of a shot. Only Rose wasn't in the car.

And that gun had looked real. Not that I knew a lot about guns. But the way the man had held it…there was nothing theatrical about that.

Regardless, I was grateful to be here. Now that the palm tree was down, I felt safe enclosed behind the Marlowe walls. The warm air wrapped me in a hug. And despite everything, exhaustion began to pull at me. And soon I was drifting away beneath a blanket of stars.

Chapter Nineteen

I YAWNED.

Blinked.

Why was it so bright?

I opened my eyes. The sun was shining directly into them. I was outside. Still on the chaise next to the pool. Of course I was tired from the events of yesterday, but I had no idea I was *that* exhausted.

I groaned, stretching my neck. It was stiff from sleeping at an awkward angle. I rolled off the chaise and collected my phone from where it had fallen onto the deck.

My phone screen was black. Dead. The charge had run out.

I made my way around the corner and along the balcony, spotting a set of stairs at the far end. I walked down, passing Talon's room. His curtains were still closed.

The stairs led down to the main pool area.

So I had been right about another access point.

I returned to my room and entered, heading for my charger on the nightstand. It was gone.

But I knew I had left it there.

Now it was just the lamp, a glass of water, and the silver whistle.

Maybe it had fallen?

I crouched, reached under the bed. Found the cord. Plugged in my phone.

Then I got up.

And stilled again.

The pillow had been moved as well. I was positive I'd covered my pajamas with it when I'd gotten dressed that morning. Now they were poking out from underneath.

Alright.

I needed to take a breath.

A lot had happened in the past few days. An intruder. An attempted carjacking—or whatever it was. Maybe I was just imagining that my things had been moved. And I was feeling groggy. I'd obviously not had the best night's sleep out there on the patio.

I opened the closet. My suitcase was lying on its side, but I'd left it standing up. A chill ran over me. Even my hanging clothes were slightly left of where I had hung them.

I stepped out and made my way into the bathroom. My toothbrush was in a different slot in the holder, now next to the mouthwash instead of by the toothpaste.

The towel from my shower was folded over the bar. Far too neatly. Because I had jammed it in there after my shower, thinking I should straighten it. Then not bothering to.

So now there was zero doubt. *Someone* had been in my room. But who? Was it one of the family? Or an outsider?

I collapsed onto my bed, staring at the floor.

I couldn't accuse a family member. I didn't want to jeopardize my job, let alone Madeline's business. But what if it was paparazzi? Or one of those men with the guns? Then staying silent could be risky.

But why would anyone want to search my room? Was someone in the family looking for proof that I was the spy? And if so, then why mess with my toothbrush? Unless they'd thought I'd hidden something inside the holder?

I went to Talon's room and knocked softly on the door.

Rose answered. She was still in last night's clothes but looked like she'd just stepped out of hair and makeup. She entered the hallway, closing the door behind her. "Zoe?"

I hesitated.

"What is it?"

I took a breath. Might as well get it over with. "I think someone has been in my room. My things have been disturbed. I think it might be the paparazzi again. Figured I should tell someone."

Rose's face went cold. Different from her movie anger. A mask slipping.

She marched past me and entered my bedroom.

I followed, feeling anxious. Maybe I shouldn't have told her after all?

Rose stood in the center of my room.

She checked the full-length mirror, running her fingers along edges. Moved to the abstract painting, pulled it out to peer behind the frame.

Finally, she inspected the blinds. "Gotcha."

She pulled the silver chair over from the desk, climbed up, then yanked something small and black from up top.

She jumped down, held up a mini camera. Matchbox-sized. I recoiled.

Someone had been watching me?

"I'm so sorry, Zoe." Rose whirled around and strode toward the door. "But don't worry. I'll take care of that lecherous pig."

A second later, she was gone.

Lecherous pig?

Who was she talking about?

I had no idea whether I was supposed to follow her or not, but then I heard Rose's voice: "Come!"

So I trotted along behind her like a dutiful dog. All the way up to the third floor.

She tried to open the first door on her right, but it was locked. She kicked it hard. "Open the blasted door!"

A second later, Molly answered. "Yes?"

Rose pushed past and barged inside. Molly glanced at me. I shrugged, standing awkwardly in the doorway.

The room had a collection of vintage silver rockets and robots. A couple of posters of early sci-fi movies hung on another wall: *Forbidden Planet* and *The Day the Earth Stood Still.*

Liam sat in a chair next to the window, smoking pot. He held out his joint. "You come to join me?"

Rose chucked the camera at him. "What did I tell you about this bullshit?"

The camera hit him in the chest and bounced onto the floor.

Liam looked down at it, then back up at Rose. "I have no idea what you're talking about."

"You put a camera in Zoe's room," Rose said, pointing at me. "You did the same thing to Nanny 1."

"Yeah, but that was a prank. It wasn't even hooked up to anything at the time." He pointed to the camera. "Somebody else did that, and I'm being framed."

Rose crossed her arms. "Bullshit."

He glanced over at me. "I swear to God, Zoe. It wasn't me."

I saw no duplicitousness in his eyes. For some strange reason, I believed him.

"When did it happen?" he asked.

"Yesterday, I think."

"There you have it. I was with Zoe all day at the observatory. I came to bed when I got home, which Molly can attest to. When would I have had the time?"

"Then who?" Rose asked.

Liam shrugged, stubbing out his joint in a flying saucer-shaped ashtray. "Could be anyone. Half the family thinks she's Maxwell's spy. Maybe they're trying to get dirt on her."

"Or maybe you're lying," Rose said.

"Come on, Rose. You know I'm a shit liar." He shook another joint out of a little metal box and lit it.

I cleared my throat. "I slept out by the pool last night, so I suppose anyone could have gone into my room."

Liam sank back in his chair, coughing. "There we go."

Molly stepped forward. "You need to leave. The stress isn't good for Liam."

Rose stared at her. "Who the fuck are you?"

She paled. "Molly."

"My girlfriend?" Liam said.

Rose waved her hand. "I can't be expected to remember these things."

"She's been here three weeks," Liam said.

Rose stepped forward and plucked the joint out of his hand. "You're not supposed to smoke in the house. Maxwell's orders."

Liam opened his mouth to protest, but Rose had already raised the joint to her lips. "I need to calm my fucking nerves."

She took several long puffs, then handed it back to him. Then she turned on her heel and walked out of the room.

I glanced over at Liam. "Sorry for disturbing you."

"Nah. I hope you find your Peeping Tom."

"Thanks."

I left the room and made my way back to the stairs. Rose had stopped at the top, gripping the banister, looking down and blocking my escape route. So I stayed put until she finally turned to look at me. "Are you going to quit?"

"No." I hadn't expected her to ask me that. "But I thought maybe you were going to fire me for accusing your family of spying."

"Absolutely not." She laughed with what sounded like surprise. "You're a blessing on this household."

Heat crept up my neck. "Thanks."

Rose pressed her hand to her forehead. I'd seen the gesture in *The Orange Tree*. Acting or real? "I feel a bit undermined by the family sometimes. They acted dreadful toward Nanny 1."

"And Nanny 2?"

"Well, she deserved whatever backlash came her way."

I had no idea how I was supposed to respond.

Rose leaned against the banister and met my eyes. "I didn't want to take one of Madeline's nannies. My family's unhinged. Add Hollywood, and it's a pure insanity cocktail. I don't have many friends and didn't want to risk our friendship."

I nodded. That seemed to be a pervasive fear among the wealthy: constant underlying suspicion that everyone around them had an agenda. That true friends were had to come by.

"But Madeline assured me that you could handle a hell of a lot."

"I can," I said, raising my chin.

"So you are really not going to quit?"

"Nope. I like Talon."

This smile was genuine. All the others had been performance.

"Also, I'm not a spy."

Rose laughed. "That I know. They're all just paranoid."

We went back downstairs. Rose returned to Talon's room and I went to mine.

I was about to enter when I felt like I was being watched.

I looked down the hallway.

Olivia stood there, a bottle of wine tucked under her arm. She scuttled away like a startled crab when I saw her and disappeared around the corner.

Odd.

I went back inside and closed the door behind me. I still didn't feel comfortable, so I looked around for anything else that looked out of place, starting with the bathroom.

No camera in sight.

I searched every inch of the bedroom. When I got to the desk, I found another small camera, this one tucked behind the lamp.

I grabbed it, studied the angle. Focused on the chair, not the bed. Rose's camera had watched the door. Just comings and goings. What was the point?

Maybe they hadn't had time to adjust the angles properly.

I walked to the pool, tossed it in.

One less eye watching.

Chapter Twenty

I WAS STILL FEELING GROGGY, so I washed my face and brushed my teeth, but I had a feeling this was something only coffee could solve.

I made my way to the dining room and found Olivia hunched over at the far end of the table, staring down at her eggs. She didn't bother to say good morning. Neither did I.

Gordon was busy with Monaco and Versailles. They sat beside his chair, their tongues lolling out. "Who's a good girl? Who wants bacon?"

I poured myself a cup of coffee from the silver carafe on the sideboard and slipped out. The idea that someone had planted cameras in my room had stolen my appetite. At least for now.

I only hoped that they were installed yesterday and not before I arrived.

On my way back to my room, I bumped into Rose in the hallway.

"Perfect timing," she said. "Caleb and I are taking Talon for the day, so you're free to do as you like.

Bertie is at your disposal if you need to go anywhere."

"I'll probably just stick around the house. I'm still tired after yesterday."

Rose nodded, continuing down the hallway. "I put a taser on your bedside table in case you need to keep the family in line."

I laughed as I entered my room and walked over to set the coffee on my bedside table. Sure enough, sitting next to the charger, was a small black and yellow taser.

Shit. She wasn't kidding.

I opened my purse and chucked the taser inside.

I got out one of my new swimsuits but felt nervous about changing. I glanced around the room. Were there more cameras I hadn't found?

Paranoia was exhausting, but I couldn't shake the sense that I was still being watched.

I went into the bathroom, hung a bath towel over the glass shower wall, then changed inside.

I got a pool towel, grabbed my phone and coffee, and went out to the pool. I set my items on the table next to the chaise. I sat for a moment, drinking my coffee.

I dipped a toe in the water. It was nice and warm, so I dove in.

Sunshine sparkled on the droplets clinging to my arms as I swam.

I did several laps across the pool. Front crawl, then backstroke, letting my body find its natural rhythm. The physical exertion felt good. My muscles loosened with each stroke, washing away yesterday's chaos.

After a while, I dove down and collected the camera. Then I surfaced and set it on the side of the deck.

I swam for about an hour.

Finally, I hoisted myself out of the pool, then walked

over to the chaise lounge and toweled myself off. Then I lay down on my stomach. The California sun immediately began drying my skin.

It was very quiet.

All I heard was the gentle lapping of water against the sides of the pool, the distant sound of crickets, palm fronds rustling overhead.

Warmth seeped into my bones. I closed my eyes. The world began to fade away as the sun worked its magic…

A shadow fell over me.

I heard footsteps. Jerked awake, wiping drool from my lips. Blinking, I saw Liam laying in the chaise beside me, holding a large drink with pineapple and red cherries. I could smell the alcohol. And of course he was smoking a joint.

He held up his glass. "Want one?"

I checked my phone. 9:30 a.m. "It's a little early for me."

"You only live once," he replied with a grin.

"Where's Molly?"

"She has to work."

"What does she do?"

"Nurse."

I don't know why that surprised me. "How did you two meet?"

He shrugged, taking another drag from his joint. "At a party. Can't quite remember. You got a boyfriend? Girlfriend?"

I hesitated.

He took a sip of his drink. "Ah, you do."

I flushed. "It's not quite that easy."

"Why not? You afraid of commitment? Or is it them?"

I sat up, wrapping the towel around my shoulders. "His job takes him around the world."

"So does yours."

"Not in the same way."

"So what does he do?"

"Works for a family. Like I do. Only in security."

"And the problem?"

I hesitated.

Liam nudged me. "Come on. I'm good at relationships."

"I thought the one before Molly lasted only three weeks."

Another grin. "They were three amazing weeks."

I laughed. I liked Liam. And I really hoped he was telling the truth and wasn't who put cameras in my room. "We went through some intense stuff together. Life and death kind of stuff."

Liam's eyes sharpened. "And?"

"I don't know. I guess I keep wondering if what happened between us was real, or just…adrenaline."

He sipped his drink. "Where is he now?"

"Europe somewhere. On a sailboat with no cell service."

Liam snorted. "Rich people problems. Let me guess— he's gorgeous, mysterious, and emotionally unavailable?"

"It's not like that."

"It's always like that." He stubbed out his joint on the table. "Trust me, I've been the gorgeous, mysterious, emotionally unavailable guy. We're never worth the wait."

I glared at him. "You don't know him."

"I know the type. Question is, are you going to waste your time pining for him?"

I turned back to the water.

Was I?

I didn't know.

I was too busy trying to figure out why I felt so insecure. Maybe because I felt so far away. That had to be it. Maybe if I had stayed in New York, I might have felt more confident.

I sighed, rubbing my head. "Are you feeling better after your seizure?"

"Yeah." He took a drag. "Still a bit shaky, but the pot helps."

I studied his face. He looked pale beneath his tan, with dark circles under his eyes. "Why don't you simply tell your family you're epileptic?"

"I don't want their pity. They'd start treating me like I'm made of glass. I just want to keep having fun and be myself, you know?"

"Yeah."

"The second they find out, everything changes. They'll be watching me like a hawk all the time, waiting for me to have another episode."

"But what if you need help?"

He shrugged. "That's what Molly's for. She knows what to do if things get bad. And of course, we have the damn whistles."

I laughed. "Is that why you're with her? Because she's a nurse?"

Liam raised his brows. "You think I'm that shallow?"

I flushed. "I didn't mean—"

"Maybe a little." He gave me a slight smile. "But she's also the only person who doesn't treat me like a walking disaster. She just lets me be me."

I settled back against my chaise, watching the reflection of the clouds in the water, while Liam puffed beside me.

"Is it true that none of the family knows how to swim?" I asked.

He raised an eyebrow. "Where'd you hear that?"

"Talon."

"Yeah." Liam took another sip of his drink. "After Isabella drowned, Maxwell didn't want any of the kids near the water."

"I'd think it would be the opposite."

"Yeah, well, that's Hollywood for you. Drama trumps logic. Don't tell anyone, but about ten years ago I took private lessons."

"So you can swim?"

"Figure somebody should know how, considering we have two pools."

I studied him for a moment. Had a feeling he was more responsible than he let on. He met my eyes. "I really didn't put the camera in your room," he added.

"Cameras," I said, pointing to the second one on the pool deck.

Liam stubbed out his joint, then held out his hand and gestured with his fingers. "Gimme."

I sighed, got up and walked over to collect it. Then I returned to my chaise and dropped the camera in his hand.

He set down his drink to examine it. "Shitty quality. The kind of crap you buy off Amazon for relative pennies. Given how easy you found it, I'd bet on Olivia. She'd want something easy to set up. Not a whole lot going on upstairs."

I stared at him. "Why would Olivia want to watch me?"

"Afraid you'll take her job."

I was confused. "What job?"

Liam stared at me. "Didn't anyone tell you? Olivia was Nanny #2 before she became Wife #5."

I stared at him. "Olivia was Nanny #2?"

He set the camera down on the table. "Yeah."

"I didn't know that."

"Maxwell was never the same after Isabella drowned. She was his great love. So he'd marry, discard, marry, discard. Wouldn't surprise me to learn Maxwell had wives the family didn't even know about."

"I read about your mom online."

"Yeah." He picked up his drink, took a long swallow. "The whole family was on the boat that night. All six of us. She was unhappy, threatening divorce. They were arguing. Anything we did irritated her. So all of us kids huddled together downstairs, trying to stay out of her way." His voice grew more distant. "Last thing I said to her was that I hated her."

I shivered despite the sunshine. "I'm sorry."

He shrugged. "I was five years old. Being a brat. Then morning rolls around and she's nowhere to be seen. Nova thought she swam for shore, which was bullshit because she didn't know how to swim. Jaxon thought she'd gotten off on another boat. Rose tried to convince everyone that she was somehow back home. But I knew she was gone for good. Took two weeks for her body to wash ashore. For a while, everyone thought Dad that killed her. But there was no evidence."

"What did happen?

He lit another joint. "Rose thinks it was an accident. Lost her footing and fell overboard."

"And you?"

"Suicide. She was always miserable. Wanted to leave California and go to Europe where her friends lived, but Maxwell wouldn't let her. So she got out the only way she knew how."

He was quiet for a moment, then sighed. Picked up his joint, took a long drag, then dropped it in his drink while standing. "Can I have the camera?"

"Help yourself."

Liam picked it up and headed toward the back of the house.

"I'm really not the spy, Liam," I said.

He turned back toward me and grinned. "Sure."

"Gordon knows who it really is. Ask him."

"Gordon?" Liam repeated with obvious surprise.

I nodded. "He told me he knew who it was."

"Son of a gun. I'll ask him. Thanks, Nanny Zoe."

And then he disappeared. Leaving me alone in the hot California sun.

Chapter Twenty-One

I spent the remainder of the day swimming in the pool and relaxing on the deck. It was just the medicine. Yesterday's scare seemed a million miles away. Even the camera situation didn't seem as messy. Sunshine and swimming in your own pool really was a cure-all.

But when I headed down the hallway to the dining room for dinner, Nova was waiting for me by the living room. "Talk to you in private?"

I stiffened. "Sure."

She led me into Maxwell's office. Sleek, modern space. Floor-to-ceiling windows overlooked the Hollywood Hills. Wood paneling covered one wall. A massive mid-century desk dominated the room—nearly empty except for a laptop and a small, succulent, sculptural white lamp. Awards covered the back wall—Oscars, Emmys, framed certificates.

Nova closed the door behind us. "What are you going to tell Maxwell about the past few days?"

I sighed. "Nothing."

Nova took a step toward me. "It's time to drop the pretense. It's just the two of us talking now."

"There's no pretense to drop." I crossed my arms. "I'm not a spy."

"Did he hire you to monitor how I'm handling business affairs? Because I can show you the books."

"I don't know anything about business affairs. Nor do I want to know. Please stop asking."

Nova studied me for a moment. "You're good. But not that good."

"I don't know what I can say to convince you."

"The truth."

I wanted to stamp my foot like a kid throwing a tantrum. But somehow, I refrained. "I am telling the truth."

"Then why are you here?"

I threw my arms wide. "Because Rose needed a nanny. And I needed work. I swear I don't have some secret agenda. I don't care about the business or who's going to inherit what. I am simply here to look after Talon."

"Rose doesn't hire staff without Maxwell's approval. Nothing happens in this house without his say-so. And right now, when he's deciding who gets the company, he suddenly approves her to hire a nanny?" She shook her head. "I'm not that naive."

"Then I don't know what to say, because it's the truth." I stepped up to the door, but Nova was still standing in front of it. "Move. Please."

She didn't, and for a moment I wondered if I would have to scream. Then she stepped aside, and I bolted for the door.

"It's not over," she called out. "We'll talk again."

I ignored her, heading to the dining room. It was empty, although the food was all set out buffet style. Crystal serving dishes held an array of gourmet options: grilled salmon with an herb crust, roasted vegetables, and some kind of quinoa salad.

I got my plate and realized my hands were still shaking. Nova was intimidating. Had she been the one who put cameras in my room? No. I had a feeling she'd just browbeat me if she wanted information. Either that or water torture.

I filled my plate with salmon and vegetables. And didn't bother waiting for anyone to join me. I hadn't heard Caleb, Rose, or Talon return yet. And, aside from Nova, I had no idea where anyone else was.

Family photos lined the wall. Premieres, award ceremonies, fake smiles. One caught my attention: the family on a yacht. I got up for a closer look.

The boat was named *The Reel Escape.*

It looked to be some kind of family portrait, but no one seemed particularly happy. It must have been taken shortly before Isabella's death, because Liam was very young. He also looked cranky, glaring directly at his mother with undisguised hostility. Nova and Rose were sticking their tongues out at each other. Maxwell stood smoking, staring out at the camera with an expression of bored indifference, as if he couldn't wait for the photo session to end. Jaxon had struck an identical pose to his father, an unlit cigarette dangling from his lips.

Isabella stood slightly apart from the group, holding a toy robot under her arm, looking over at Maxwell with an enigmatic expression—not quite smiling, not quite frowning. Something knowing and sad. Like the Mona Lisa.

Willa entered, glancing over at me.

Heat crept up my neck. I returned to my seat.

"That photo was taken the morning Isabella died,"

Willa said. "Before they set sail. That's the last picture anyone took of her."

Why put a photo that would remind the family of that day? That felt uncomfortably odd.

"Her death royally fucked up the kids," she said.

I swallowed a chunk of salmon. "What do you mean by that?"

Willa began filling her plate. "Well, Liam became a useless turd. Doesn't do anything productive except occasionally stream on YouTube. Rose is paranoid about everyone's safety—hence the whistles. And she can't even come to terms with the fact that her husband isn't having an affair, but she thinks he is."

I nearly choked on a carrot. "Caleb's *not* having an affair?"

"Nope." Willa shook her head and joined me at the table. "He's too much of a coward. Besides, he's still in love with her." She pointed to the picture with her fork. "Nova couldn't rescue her mom, so she had to rescue Gordon instead. A classic case of guilt transference. And Jaxon wouldn't know love if it bit him in the ass. Instead, he spends his whole life trying to win Maxwell's approval, but the old man gives it all to Rose instead."

She speared a piece of roasted vegetable with her fork, examining it. "It's textbook trauma response, really. Everyone developed their own coping mechanism for losing Isabella. Problem is, none of them ever dealt with the actual grief. They just found ways to avoid it."

I looked back at the photograph. "Did you know her? Isabella?"

"Before my time. But her ghost lives in every room of this house." Willa chewed her asparagus. "Did you know Jaxon was in a movie as a kid? *The Last Witness*."

I shook my head. "I don't think I've heard of it."

"That's because it was universally panned." She cleared her throat and recited in a theatrical voice: "'Jaxon Marlowe, the young lead in *The Last Witness*, delivers a performance so stiff and lifeless it's hard to tell if he was acting or just reading off cue cards. In a movie where the stakes are life and death, young Marlowe's performance makes the audience feel like they're watching the clock. While *The Last Witness* had the potential to be a solid thriller, its lead actor's painfully terrible performance turned it into an unintentional comedy.'"

I winced. "That's harsh."

Willa laughed. "Jaxon never acted again after that. It was left to Rose to carry on their mother's legacy."

"Why would you memorize the review?"

"Are you kidding? It's family lore. Nova brings it up every time Jaxon gets too big for his britches." She took a bite of her quinoa salad. "The poor kid was only twelve when they cast him. Maxwell thought it would be good for the family brand to have another Marlowe on the big screen. Only he chose the wrong one."

"Does Jaxon miss acting?"

She shook her head. "God, no. He hated it. But whenever Rose gets praised for a performance, you can see the pain in his eyes. It's like he's still that twelve-year-old kid getting obliterated by critics."

"That's sad."

"That's Hollywood." She pushed her chair back from the table. "I'm going to get some sparkling water. Do you want any?"

I shook my head. "No, thanks."

She left the dining room and I continued eating.

By the time I finished, Willa still wasn't back, so I took my plate into the kitchen, then headed down to my bedroom. I shoved the taser down the back of my jeans, then made my way outside and around to the side gate.

I spotted Bertie and Willa near a copse of palm trees, having what looked like an intense conversation. They stepped apart when they saw me watching.

Willa headed back into the house without a word.

Bertie walked over to me. "Hey, Zoe."

"Bertie."

"Can I help you?"

I gestured to the gate. "I'm just going for a walk."

"Want some company?"

I shook my head. "No, thanks. I'd like to be alone."

He waved, then headed toward the garage.

I punched in the gate code. The mechanism clicked, and the gate swung open. I stepped out onto Mulholland Drive, then stopped. Maybe I should have said yes to Bertie's offer? After everything that had happened, from the car chase to the paparazzi, maybe it wasn't such a great idea to be wandering around alone.

I peered out at the street and touched the taser at my back. If anyone came at me, at least I'd be prepared.

But I didn't see any gray cars or black vans. In fact, Mulholland was perfectly quiet. The wealthy residents of the Hills were probably all safely tucked away behind their own gates and security systems.

I was probably the only one stupid enough to be out here alone.

Chapter Twenty-Two

I WALKED MULHOLLAND, watching out for suspicious vehicles. None appeared. At Liam's spot, the city sparkled below like fallen stars. Beautiful, but I knew LA was different without money, influence, fame. For nobodies like me.

I had to remember that the life I was living right now was temporary, bought and paid for by my service to the Marlowes. As much as they might make me feel like family, I wasn't, and I never would be.

Up here in the Hills, life was manicured. From the plants to the people. But down there in the city, people sat in traffic for hours just to get to jobs that barely covered their expenses.

I sighed, retracing my steps back toward the house.

Near the Marlowe estate, headlights swept around the curve. I ducked into bushes by the gates, reaching for the taser. My foot hit something flat.

But then the car slowed, pulling into the driveway. The gates began to open. I peered out from behind the bushes to see Rose, Caleb, and Talon returning from their day out.

Talon was seated in the back. I waved when he saw me. He tipped his head, looking confused as he opened his mouth—

I put my finger up to my lips: *hush.*

He nodded, settling back in the car, but keeping his face turned toward me. Once the car had entered and the gates closed behind them, I finally stood.

I don't know why I didn't want Talon to say anything to his parents. Maybe I didn't want them to know that I was still spooked from the other day. Which was silly because I was fairly sure Rose would understand. She'd given me a taser after all.

I turned on my phone's flashlight. A black leather wallet lay in the dirt. Well-worn. I flipped it open. Driver's license in a clear slot. That orange hair. The paparazzi from the other night. *Denton Hatch.*

Age fifty-four, address in Venice Beach.

He must have dropped the wallet when he fled the other night. Or maybe he left it here in case he got caught, intending to come back? Only he got scared off.

I closed the wallet, then walked around to the side gate, punched in the code and entered. Talon met me at the kitchen door.

"What were you doing in the bushes?" he asked.

"I got spooked when I heard the car coming."

His eyes widened. "Did you think it was the black van?"

"Maybe? How was your day out?"

He shrugged. "Okay. Jaxon sent a bunch of security with us, so I felt safe enough."

I squeezed his shoulder. "I'm glad."

He spotted the wallet in my hand. "What's that?"

"A wallet. I found it by the bushes. It belongs to the paparazzi who fell in the pool."

"Seriously?"

I nodded.

From somewhere deep in the house, we heard Rose. "Talon! Time for bed!"

We made our way out of the kitchen and down the hallway to the living room to where Rose was waiting. Talon bounced over to her. "Mom! Zoe found the paparazzi's wallet."

Rose looked over at me.

I nodded, holding up the evidence to show her. "I found it outside by the front gates. It belongs to that man from the other night—the one with the orange hair."

Rose extended her hand as she walked over to me.

I gave her the wallet and she opened it, studying the man's license photo. "They're like a pack of wolves that follow us everywhere. But him, I don't recognize."

"You know them by sight?" I asked.

She nodded. "I send half of them Christmas cards. Keeps them on our side for when I want to be left alone."

"And the other half?"

She bared her teeth. "Leeches."

"What should I do with it?" I asked. "Turn it over to the police?"

Rose sighed, looking tired despite her flawless makeup. "No. I'll get it back to him. I don't care about the trespassing anymore. We've got bigger problems than some freelance photographer trying to make a buck at my expense."

"I can deal with it if you like," I said. "I don't mind."

Rose smiled, handing the wallet back. "Thanks, Zoe. I'd appreciate that."

"Can I come with you to return it?" Talon asked.

"No," Rose said.

He scowled.

She kissed his head, then put her arm around Talon's shoulders. "Come on. You've had a long day."

"Goodnight, Zoe."

"Night, Talon."

I watched them leave, then headed to the kitchen for tea. Jaxon was on the phone. He gestured me in.

I walked over to the stove and grabbed the kettle.

"I have explained this several times," he said.

I took the kettle to the sink, trying my best to ignore him pacing behind me.

"No, I was quite clear about that from the beginning." Another pause. "Look, if I understood what kind of movies the fucking proletariat liked, I wouldn't be in this situation, would I?"

I felt awkward. Should I turn on the tap? Wait until he was done his call? I decided to pour the water. Jaxon could leave if I was being too loud.

"And if I'd known Jake Pierce was going to get in trouble for fucking the babysitter, I wouldn't have hired him, would I? The whole project went to hell because of his personal—"

I plugged the kettle in.

"No. No, I'm not taking responsibility for his poor life choices. We did our due diligence on the script, the budget, everything. We couldn't have predicted he'd throw his career away for a twenty-year old."

He disconnected, leaning against the counter, breathing heavy.

I thought back to what Willa had said about him. That he wouldn't know love if it bit him in the ass. She'd sounded so matter of fact about it, like she'd accepted that her husband was incapable of genuine affection.

Depressing.

I wondered why she stayed married to him. The

money? This house? The lifestyle that came with being a Marlowe by marriage? Or maybe like a lot of us through life, she was simply caught in a web of dysfunction that made leaving seem impossible.

The kitchen was soon filled with the gentle hiss of water heating up.

"Goddamn nanny," he said.

I glanced over at him.

"Not you," he said. "Jake's."

"Sounds like Brad was the problem, not her."

He grunted. "Worst part of my job, working with fucking investors. They think throwing money at a project guarantees a return."

"Then why do it?"

"It's the family business."

I thought back to my family business. Fraud. Con-artistry. If everyone followed in their parents' footsteps, the world would be more of a mess than it was.

"Have you seen Nova?" he asked.

I shook my head.

He started to leave, then hesitated at the doorway, turning back to study me.

"Not. A. Spy," I said as he opened his mouth.

He glared, spun around, left. Maybe I should get that printed on a T-shirt.

I pulled out my phone and typed *Denton Hatch Los Angeles* into Google. Then hit search and waited for the results to load. I figured I'd find his management company or something.

Instead I found his office.

DENTON INVESTIGATIONS - PRIVATE INQUIRY SERVICES.

Huh? That didn't sound like paparazzi to me.

I clicked the webpage.

Below the above title was a head shot of the orange-haired man I'd encountered by the pool. He almost passed for respectable when dressed in a suit and tie. A far cry from the soaking wet man I'd found on the pool deck.

His services were listed as: *Infidelity Investigations, Background Checks, Missing Persons, Corporate Security, Surveillance Services, and Process Serving.* At the bottom of the page: *Licensed and Bonded - Serving Greater Los Angeles Area since 2013 - 24/7 Availability.*

It gave a phone number and an address in Venice Beach. The tagline read: *Discretion Guaranteed. Results Delivered.*

I sat back, pursing my lips.

He really wasn't a paparazzi at all. He was a private detective. What was a PI doing climbing over the Marlowe's fence with a camera? Who hired him?

Maybe Willa was wrong. Maybe Caleb was having an affair. And someone had hired Denton to get the evidence. Or maybe it was Rose he'd been after.

Or perhaps Denton Hatch was both paparazzi and detective? I could see how that could be a thing in LA. The line between surveillance and stalking probably blurred pretty easily in a city full of celebrities.

I scrolled down to the contact information and called the number. It went straight to voicemail. I left a message. "Hi, my name is Zoe Smith. I have your wallet. You dropped it at the Marlowe house the other night. Give me a call and I'll give it back to you. Or I can drop it off at the police station."

I left my number, hung up as the kettle clicked off. Maybe I shouldn't have mentioned the police. But after he'd scared me, fair was fair.

Chapter Twenty-Three

I SPENT the weekend exploring Los Angeles, seeing more of Melrose and all of Rodeo Drive. Now I was at Venice Beach, watching an eclectic mix of street performers, tourists, and locals. A man painted silver stood motionless as a statue while kids dropped coins at his feet. Roller skaters weaved between vendors hawking everything from tarot readings to handmade jewelry.

In some ways, LA reminded me of New York. Both cities were full of people chasing dreams. Wall Street fortunes and Broadway stages in New York, movie deals and record contracts here. Same ambitions, different costumes.

Manhattan felt vertical and urgent. LA sprawled horizontally under an endless blue sky. Time moved slower here, promising perpetual summer and incessant reinvention. Less real somehow, like a movie set where everyone played roles.

I sipped my latte, scrolling through photos on my phone. There was me squinting in the sun on the beach, trying to look casual while street performers juggled fire behind me. A selfie outside the Beverly Hills Hotel. And my personal favorite: the Melrose Trading Post with its vintage band tees and overpriced sunglasses.

Rollerbladers and muscle-bound guys filled the beach. Despite the crowd, I felt lonely. This would be more fun with Elsa.

So I called her.

She answered on the second ring.

I blinked back tears. "I miss you."

"Me too." I could almost hear her smile. "Tell me everything. Any more adventures?"

I hesitated.

"There are! You get all the exciting gigs."

"I don't know that I would call this exciting," I said.

"Spill."

I laughed and told her about the paparazzi incident. But I kept quiet about the attempted carjacking, not wanting to worry her.

I felt better after we both laughed about it.

"What's Rose like?" Elsa asked.

"Well, she really loves her son, which is a nice switch from some of the families I've worked for."

"No kidding."

"You sound happier," I told her.

"That's because I have a surprise."

I straightened. "Now it's your time to spill."

She laughed. "I talked to Madeline about my situation, and she suggested I take a little break to think about whether I want to stay with the Carlsons or find something new. So I have two weeks off at the end of this month."

"And?"

"I'm coming to LA. If you want me to."

"Yes!"

"Madeline's going to cover my hotel costs. And we can hang out whenever you're free."

Joy bubbled up in my chest. "I know it hasn't been long, but I still can't wait to see you, Elsa."

"Me too."

"Let me know when you get your flights."

"I will."

We chatted longer, then disconnected. I finished my latte, grinning. Elsa was coming! New York suddenly felt closer.

I went for a walk. The afternoon sun was warm, and the eclectic mix of shops made for interesting window shopping along Abbot Kinney Boulevard. Then I turned down Horizon Avenue. The name nagged at me. I'd seen it somewhere recently.

Then it hit me: Denton Hatch's office was on this street.

I pulled out my phone and googled him again, then mapped his address. His office was only four blocks away. I still hadn't heard back from him about his wallet. Maybe I should just walk down and tell him in person?

His ad had said 24/7 availability, so maybe someone would be in the office.

But did I really want to run into him again? He had scared the crap out of me that night. Then again, maybe I had startled him too. He'd looked surprised to see me.

I stepped aside for tourists. I could check out his office without going in. I walked toward his building, passing vintage shops, a coffee roastery, and crystal stores.

His narrow two-story building sat between a tarot reader and a bulk soap refill shop. *DENTON INVESTIGATIONS* painted in gold letters on glass. A red neon sign: *OPEN.*

I hesitated. Was this weird, showing up unannounced?

I peered inside but didn't see anyone. Maybe the sign was lying? Only one way to find out.

My heart thudded in my throat as I walked up to the door, pushed it open, and stepped inside.

A glass partition separated the reception area from the main office with professional space beyond: wooden desk, papers, files, computer.

A small plant sat on the windowsill. On the wall were a collection of framed certificates: Denton Hatch's California Private Investigator License, a City of Los Angeles Business License, a Qualified Manager Certificate, his membership from the California Association of Licensed Investigators, and a Certified Professional Investigator (CPI) credential.

This was no film noir seedy detective agency. Denton Hatch appeared to be legitimate.

A minute later, a woman bustled out from the back office. She was in her fifties, with blonde hair pulled into a practical ponytail and wearing jeans and a blazer. She seemed shocked to see me. "I'm sorry. I didn't hear you come in. May I help you?"

"I was hoping to see Denton Hatch."

She paled. "He's not here. I'm not sure where he is. Are you looking to hire him?"

I shook my head. "No. I found his wallet. I left a message but didn't hear back from him. So I thought I would drop and let him know again by since I was in the area."

She stared at me. "You found his wallet?"

I nodded. "Yes. Out by the Marlowe house on Mulholland."

"The Marlowe's house?"

Another nod. "Do you want my number?"

"Sure." She got out a pen and paper, and I scribbled it

down along with my name. "I'll let him know where to pick it up as soon as I see him."

I started to leave but paused in the doorway. "Does Mr. Hatch also work as a paparazzi?"

The woman laughed. "Heavens, no. Why?"

"No reason. Just wondering."

The phone rang and she leapt for it.

I left, walking back toward Abbot Kinney Boulevard. If Denton wasn't a photographer, what had he been doing with a camera at the Marlowe house? He was clearly there to take pictures of someone.

His assistant had seemed worried. Why?

I pulled out my phone and requested an Uber. Maybe Denton wasn't there to spy on the family at all. Maybe he had been paid to spy on me. See if he could figure out what I was supposedly reporting to Maxwell.

I sighed.

The Venice crowd swirled around me—tourists snapping photos, locals with designer dogs, street artists arranging easels for the evening rush.

A man in a yellow jogging suit watched me. Too hot for the weather. Aviator sunglasses. I looked away.

When I glanced back, he was walking toward me.

"Excuse me," he said with a heavy Russian accent.

I glanced behind me. But there was no one there. I pointed to myself. He nodded.

He spoke again, this time in Russian.

I shook my head. "I'm sorry, I don't understand."

He tried again, speaking more slowly but still in the same foreign tongue.

"I really don't understand. English?"

He looked frustrated.

My Uber pulled up to the curb in front of me, tapping

the horn. I stepped toward the vehicle and the man backed away.

Then the Russian waved at me.

I got into the Uber and it pulled away from the curb. I turned around watching the man out of the rear window. A car pulled up to the exact spot where I'd gotten in the Uber.

My stomach dropped.

A gray sedan.

The man jogged over and got in.

I held my breath. The car sat idle, then did a quick U-turn, peeling off in the opposite direction.

I kept watching. Each time a car made our same turn, my pulse spiked.

When a blue sedan followed us onto the freeway on-ramp, despite the color, I had to convince myself it wasn't the one I'd seen.

"Everything okay back there?" the driver asked.

I flushed, forcing myself to turn around and face forward. "Yeah, sorry. Just thought I saw someone I knew."

Maybe it was just a coincidence. A lost tourist asking for directions before getting picked up by a friend. Los Angeles was full of gray cars. Hell, half the vehicles on the road seemed to be gray or silver.

But I couldn't shake it. That same gray vehicle had been tailing us for days.

Chapter Twenty-Four

I PUSHED off from the wall, arms cutting through the water. I fell into a rhythm: stroke, stroke, breathe, stroke, stroke, breathe. Back and forth and back and forth, flip-turning at each end, muscles stretching, finding my groove.

The pool area was silent except for the sound of splashing water as I glided beneath the surface.

I glanced up as a shadow passed over me. Talon. Heading to the breakfast table. I kept swimming.

Until hunger got the better of me.

I surfaced, hoisting myself out of the pool and reaching for my towel. I dried myself off, pulled on my coverup, and walked to where breakfast had been laid out.

Talon was seated on one of the chairs, his nose buried in another thick textbook.

"Morning," I said, sitting. Our food had already been plated. Scrambled eggs, sausage, salsa, and three slices of watermelon.

"Morning." He closed his book, looking up at me. "How do you do that thing where you breathe to the side?"

I toweled off my hair. "Bilateral breathing?"

He nodded. "Looks hard."

"Just takes practice. I could show you if you'd like."

His eyes widened behind his glasses. "You'd show me how to swim?"

"Sure. If you're interested."

He frowned. "I don't have swim trunks."

"Shorts work fine until we can get you proper ones. If you'd like, we could start today."

"What if I can't do it?"

"We won't know until you try."

He pursed his lips. "Okay."

"Great." I stabbed my fork into one of the sausages, then cut off a chunk and chewed. "What did you do this weekend?"

His face brightened. "We went to the UCLA library. It's my favorite place. They have an amazing astrophysics section."

"Is that where you're doing your doctorate?"

He shook his head. "Harvard."

I blinked. "That's so far away."

"I know." He shrugged. "But I'll be okay."

He seemed confident enough. But I couldn't imagine sending my fourteen-year-old off to university alone at that age.

"Bertie's coming with me."

I blew out a breath. "Good."

A second later, Rose appeared around the corner of the house, impeccable as always. She walked over to us, then bent over and kissed her son on his forehead. "I've got an audition to get to. Be good for Zoe."

He scowled. "I'm always good."

She kissed him again, then disappeared around the corner with a wave.

Caleb appeared about ten minutes later. "Got that call-back. Wish me luck." He also kissed Talon on the forehead.

"Good luck, Dad."

He left and we looked at each other, bursting into simultaneous laughter.

"You really don't mind that they're having affairs?" I asked.

"I just want them to be happy."

"You're a good kid, Talon."

He beamed. "Thanks. You—"

Nova walked over, her arms crossed and a scowl on her face. "There's a police officer here to see you, Zoe."

I set down my coffee cup. "A police officer?"

"Yes."

Talon glanced over at me.

I shrugged. "Did they say what they wanted?"

She shook her head. "She wouldn't tell me."

"Maybe it's about the carjacking."

"They don't know about that."

"Jaxon said he reported it."

"He probably just wanted to make you feel better. We prefer to handle these things in the family. And I'd prefer you not mention it now."

I gaped. They hadn't reported the carjacking?

"Hurry up and get dressed." She made a shooing gesture with her hands. "I'd prefer the paparazzi not see a cop car on the property. Tongues will start wagging. And I'd prefer not to have my day ruined by a call from TMZ."

I glanced at Talon. He'd been watching, fascinated. I sighed. "Rain check on the swimming lesson?"

He nodded.

I went straight to the shower. If this wasn't about the carjacking, what was it about?

Maybe my father had committed another fraud and

they were trying to track him down. Maybe they had traced my number when he'd called me.

Shit.

I really didn't want to talk about him. Not with the cops. Not here.

I got out of the shower, dried myself off, then squeezed the water out of my hair. After that I got dressed and made my way to the living room.

A woman in a navy pantsuit stood with her back to me, studying one of the abstract paintings on the wall. She was in her fifties, with brown hair cut into a sharp bob that framed her angular face.

She turned around, gesturing to the painting. "Is this a Roethke?"

"I have no idea," I replied with a shrug.

Nova swept into the room. "Yes, it is. Number 63." She extended a hand to the officer. "Nova Marlowe, family attorney. I'll be sitting in on this interview."

The officer smiled. "There's no need for that."

"Oh, there's always a need."

Nova sat on the sofa and patted the cushion beside her. I went over and sat, then the officer joined us. She pulled out a business card and lay it on the wooden table. "Detective Jennifer Lopez. No, not that one. And I have some questions for you regarding a Denton Hatch, Zoe."

I blinked. "Denton Hatch?"

I hadn't been expecting that.

"Yes."

"Who is that?" Nova asked.

"The man who was on your property the other night," I said.

Nova looked at me. "And how do you know his name?"

"I found his wallet outside the front gate."

Nova frowned. "Why didn't you mention it?"

"I told Rose. She asked me to get the wallet back to him."

Detective Lopez met my eyes. "So you've met him before?"

"Not formally. But I saw him outside my bedroom. Spying, I guess. He scared me half to death."

Lopez's eyes sharpened. "You're certain it was Mr. Hatch?"

"The person I saw had the same orange hair as in his driver's license photo."

"We figured he was paparazzi," Nova said. "Chased him off."

Lopez tightened her jaw. She seemed as annoyed by Nova's presence as I was. "Is that true?"

I nodded. "He had a camera. Flashed it in my face."

Nova gestured to the windows. "We've had issues with photographers trespassing before. They're like mosquitoes. I'd prefer to swat them, but apparently that's against the law."

Detective Lopez pulled out a notebook and pen, jotted something down. "And where exactly outside the front gates did you find Mr. Hatch's wallet?"

"In the bushes. Below the *Starshine* sign."

She made another note. "If you don't mind, I'd like to see exactly where you encountered Mr. Hatch on the property."

Nova crossed her arms. "What exactly is this all about, Detective?"

Lopez fixed her eyes on me without responding, waiting for an answer.

I nodded and stood. "I can show you."

I led her down the hallway to my bedroom, then over to the glass sliding door. Nova trailed along after us.

I opened the doors, then pointed to the deck. "He was standing right there."

Lopez stepped outside, studying the area. "And this was at what time?"

"Late. After midnight."

"Last week?"

I nodded. "Tuesday."

"Detective, I really think we deserve to know what's going on here." Nova still looked annoyed that her earlier question had been ignored.

Lopez walked along the high wall surrounding the pool. "How exactly did he get onto the property?"

I gestured toward the left. "There was a palm tree behind the wall. I think he climbed up and over, then either fell or jumped into the pool. The splash is what woke me up."

Lopez glanced up at the wall. "There was a tree here?"

Nova nodded. "I had it cut down the next morning."

"What about security? I take it you have surveillance?"

"Of course," Nova said. "But the cameras cover the street and main gates, not the property itself."

"Why not?"

Nova stiffened. "Privacy. We don't need cameras watching our every move in our own backyard."

"I'd like to see your camera footage for the night of the intrusion."

"I can arrange that. But you won't find anything. It's like the man knew where all the cameras were."

"That's a bit odd, don't you think?"

Nova hesitated, then nodded. "Now that you mention it, I guess it is."

Lopez turned back to me. "What happened after you startled him?"

"He pulled out his camera and started taking pictures of me."

"And then?"

"I screamed. Locked myself in my room."

"We tried to find him," Nova said. "But he got out somehow. Left without a trace."

"And you didn't call the police?"

"What was the point?" Nova glared at Lopez like the paparazzi problem was her fault. "Even if he got arrested, he'd get a slap on the wrist. Or a fine. We've been down this road before many times."

Lopez turned back to me. "Do you still have the wallet?"

I nodded. "Yes, it's in my room. I can get it."

"I'd appreciate that."

I left them alone and went to my room. Once there, I opened my nightstand drawer, but the wallet was gone.

Anger roared through me. Someone had been in my room. *Again.*

I slammed the drawer shut, then retraced my steps back out onto the pool deck. "Someone took it."

"It's missing?" Lopez asked.

I nodded.

Her brows raised. "Where were you keeping it?"

"My bedside table."

"Maybe you moved it and forgot?"

I glared at Nova. "I didn't move it. I know exactly where I put it."

"Who has access to your room?" Lopez asked.

I shrugged. "Everybody, I guess. There's no exterior lock."

"Who would want to take the wallet?" Lopez asked.

"I don't know."

"Who knew you had it? Besides Rose?"

"Talon. Denton's receptionist."

"Because you stopped by his office to let him know where to find it?"

"That's right."

"Did any of those people tell anyone."

I glared at her. "You'll have to ask them."

Nova shielded her eyes from the sun. "What's so important about the wallet anyway Detective Lopez?"

"We're trying to trace Mr. Hatch's movements."

"Why?"

"We found Mr. Hatch's body washed up on Dockweiler beach yesterday morning. Near the jetty. He'd been in the water some time."

I stared at her. "His body? He's dead?"

"Yes."

"Suicide?" Nova asked.

"Not unless he put a bullet hole in the center of his own forehead."

Chapter Twenty-Five

I stared at Lopez. "Denton Hatch is dead?"

"Yes. When we informed his receptionist, she said you'd stopped by regarding his wallet."

My mouth went dry. "I just wanted to give it back."

"Mr. Hatch hasn't been seen since the night he was here at your property."

Nova shifted beside me. "What are you suggesting?"

"Nothing," Lopez replied with a smile. "But I was hoping you'd be able to tell me why he was here."

"Well, I have no idea," Nova said.

"According to his secretary, he mentioned he was leaving that day to meet with a client."

"Who?" Nova asked.

"Someone named R.E."

Nova shook her head. "There's no one at the house with those initials."

Lopez turned to me. "Is that right?"

I nodded.

Lopez scribbled in her notebook. "Did you speak with

Mr. Hatch when he was on the property? Any conversation at all?"

"No. I just opened the door and he was standing there, soaking wet. I screamed, slammed the door, and he ran off."

"So he wasn't coming to speak with you specifically?"

I shook my head. "Not that I know of."

Not unless my father hired someone to track me down. But then if Denton Hatch was looking for me, why did he run away? Why not introduce himself? And why sneak into the yard at all? He could have just gone to the front door.

No. Above all else, my father was cheap. He wouldn't spend money on a PI when he could do the job himself.

Lopez was still watching me.

"I have no idea why he was here," I said.

Lopez closed her notebook. "I'd like to speak with the rest of the family."

"Is that really necessary?" Nova asked.

"If it's too inconvenient here, I'd be pleased to speak with everyone down at the department. My office isn't as comfortable, however."

Nova pulled out her silver whistle and gave several sharp, piercing blasts.

I jumped.

"They'll be here in a minute," Nova said, tucking her whistle away. "Why don't we go down to the living room?"

We had to wait nearly half an hour for Rose and Caleb. When they finally walked through the front door, both looked slightly disheveled. They exchanged a quick glance before separating to stand on opposite sides of the room.

"What's this about?" Rose asked.

Talon poked his head around the corner.

"Go." Caleb pointed down the hallway.

He scowled but followed his father's order. Liam and Molly showed up shortly after that. Then Olivia, Willa, and Jaxon.

"Where's Gordon?" Nova asked.

"Walking the dogs," Willa reported.

Nova sighed.

"Is this everyone?" Lopez asked.

"Except the chef, the maids, and Maxwell."

"I'd like him to be here too," Lopez said.

Willa snorted. "Good luck. He doesn't get out of bed for less than a twenty-million-dollar payday."

"Don't be rude," Olivia said.

Nova eyed her. "Five bucks and you'd sell your soul."

Olivia flushed. "I would not!"

I slunk down against the couch cushions, wishing I could disappear.

"Why don't we get started?" Nova said. "It appears our trespasser from the other night was murdered."

Lopez stiffened. "I'm leading this investigation, Ms. Marlowe. Not you."

Nova shrugged, seemingly unrepentant.

"The photographer?" Rose blinked. "He's dead?"

"Who would want to kill a paparazzi?" Willa asked.

Caleb snorted. "Half of Hollywood."

Lopez raised her hand. "He wasn't a paparazzi. Mr. Hatch was a respected private investigator."

"Now there's two words I've never heard paired," Jaxon said.

Lopez glared at him. "He cracked the Telford case."

"Oh," Rose said.

I glanced at her. "What's that?"

"Daughter of a movie producer who was kidnapped thirty years ago. Everyone figured she was dead. Turned out she was stolen by the cook and had been living less than two miles away all that time."

"Did any of you have reason to hire a private investigator?" Lopez asked.

A chorus of "no" rippled around the room.

Gordon appeared, slightly out of breath. He held up his phone. "Sorry I'm late. Had to take the dogs out for their walk."

"It's all right if you don't want to sit in on this, Gordon." Nova waved a dismissive hand. "It's family business."

Lopez stepped forward. "I would like him to stay. Have you heard of a Denton Hatch, Mr.—"

"Falls."

"Mr. Falls."

Gordon nodded. "Yes, I know Denton. I hired him to do a job. Why?"

"He's been killed," Lopez said.

Gordon blanched. "Denton is dead?"

Lopez nodded.

Rose was staring at Gordon. "What did you say?"

He glanced at her. "I hired him."

Nova shot to her feet. "You hired a private investigator?"

Liam clapped his hands. "Good job, Gordon."

"Why the hell didn't you inform us?" Jaxon asked.

Gordon flushed, releasing the dogs from their leashes. "Because it was none of your damn business."

"Everything that happens to this family is my business."

Gordon leaned down and picked up Monaco—or Versailles—cradling the dog against his chest. "It was about Beth."

"Oh for Pete's sake," Willa said. "She's been dead for

years. Move on already!"

Nova whirled around to face her. "How dare you talk to my husband like that?"

Caleb stood. "Everyone needs to calm down."

"Oh, shut up," Willa said.

Lopez stuck two fingers in her mouth and blew. A sharp, ear-piercing whistle that sliced through the air. The room fell silent.

Liam pulled out a joint and lit it.

Lopez eyed him.

He shrugged.

Lopez turned back to Gordon. "Mr. Falls, how exactly do you know Mr. Hatch?"

Gordon ran his fingers over the dog's head. "I hired him to investigate my first wife's death."

Willa groaned. "Oh God, here we go again with the first wife nonsense."

Gordon flushed, his eyes filling with tears. "Beth deserves justice. Hit and run, tenth anniversary coming up. I hired Denton to solve her case. But finding him here surprised me, too."

Nova walked over and touched his arm. "I wish you would have told me about this, Gordon."

"I did," he said without meeting her eyes. "You didn't want to listen."

I remembered their argument in the hallway the other night. Nova saying something about leaving the investigating to her, Gordon insisting he was tired of waiting. I'd thought they were talking about tracking down Maxwell's supposed spy, but maybe they'd been talking about Beth.

Lopez pulled out her notebook again. "So you didn't have a scheduled meeting with Mr. Hatch that night?"

"No." Gordon shook his head. "But I did help him escape."

Lopez looked up at him. "What do you mean?"

"I joined the initial search party. Found him hiding by the side gate, soaking wet and shaking like a leaf. Poor bastard looked terrified. I opened the gate so he could slip out."

Nova stared at her husband. "You helped him escape? Why didn't you tell me?"

"Because I knew you'd be angry."

"And he didn't say why he was out here at the property?" Lopez asked.

"No. There wasn't really time." Gordon gestured to Caleb, Liam, and Jaxon. "They were still searching. He said he'd call me, tell me what he'd found out the next day. But the call never came."

"And did you try phoning him?" Lopez asked.

Gordon nodded. "Yeah. But I couldn't get a hold of him. I guess it's because he was…"

"Dead," Lopez finished.

He blanched. "Yes."

"Did anyone take Mr. Hatch's wallet? It's gone missing from Ms. Smith's room."

Everyone denied it. Hard to tell if anyone was lying. Acting ran in their blood.

Willa scrolled on her phone. "Maybe the carjackers killed him."

Silence. Nova went rigid. It looked like she might crack in two.

Lopez raised her brows. "Carjackers?"

"The ones who drove Talon and his nanny off the road the other day," Willa said.

"That's not *exactly* what happened," Nova said.

Liam took a long drag of his joint. "Close enough."

Lopez turned to look at me. "I wasn't aware of a report about a carjacking."

I opened my mouth, then closed it again. I didn't know what to say.

Jaxon cleared his throat. "I didn't feel it was necessary to file a report."

Lopez raised her brows. "You didn't feel it was necessary?"

"What are you talking about?" Rose asked. "You told me that you reported that to the police. My son was in the car!"

"He wasn't hurt," Nova said.

Rose whirled around. "No, he was fucking traumatized!"

"You're being very dramatic, Rose."

Rose launched herself at Nova.

Lopez bolted forward, getting between the two of them.

"You lied to me!" Rose exclaimed.

"I was protecting the family," Nova replied, holding her at arm's length. "Which is more than what anyone else does around here."

Voices rose, overlapping and getting louder. Liam watched his sisters fight with a goofy grin that kept getting wider. Willa scrolled on her phone, indifferent to the riot she'd unleashed. Olivia had found wine. Jaxon crept toward Maxwell's office.

I escaped to my room. Behind me, words flew like shrapnel.

Chapter Twenty-Six

I knocked on Talon's door.

"Come in."

He was still sitting on his bed with a book. "Still interested in that swim lesson?"

"Yes!" He was already off the bed.

"Great. Get your shorts on and meet me outside in ten minutes."

I changed into my swimsuit, then pulled my hair back into a ponytail. I grabbed a couple of towels from the bathroom, then went outside. I closed the door behind me to kill the yelling from the living room.

Talon looked nervous and excited, bouncing on his toes as he waited for me.

I set the towels on a chair. "We're going to take this really slow, okay? The first thing we need to do is get you comfortable being in the water. Swimming comes later."

"I understand."

I slipped into the water at the shallow end. "Come sit on the step here in the water."

The water came up to his waist.

"Now I want you to practice closing your eyes and putting your face in the water. Just for a second at first."

Talon hesitated, then leaned forward and dunked his face, popping back up a second later, water streaming down his cheeks.

"How was that?" I asked.

"Okay."

We spent an hour getting him comfortable with water on his face, then blowing bubbles, holding his breath.

I moved on to the next step once he seemed ready. "Now we're going to kneel on the bottom."

He lowered himself, then stood again. Then tried again. The water came up to his neck.

I knelt beside him. "I'm right here."

He nodded, then gradually relaxed. When he was ready, I got him to dunk his whole head underwater. Each time he came up sputtering and laughing.

Another hour. He grew increasingly more comfortable and soon was no longer afraid. He jumped into the deep end where I waited. Turned around and doggy paddled to the wall.

"What's the point of this?" he asked.

"If you were to fall in, the first thing you need to do is turn around and find the wall or edge."

He nodded and jumped in again, being sure to splash me.

I laughed, then saw movement at the glass sliding doors of my room. Rose, watching us.

I raised my hand and waved.

She nodded. Then disappeared.

Talon sat on deck.

"You tired?" I asked.

He nodded.

I swam over and hauled myself out, sitting beside him.

"Before we wrap up, there's one rule that's more important than anything else I've taught you today."

"Never swim alone."

I smiled. "You got it. Until you're really good, I don't care how comfortable you get in the water. You always need someone with you."

"Because of what happened to Isabella?"

"Because drowning can happen to anyone, even experienced swimmers like me. It's so easy to hit your head on a boat. Or get overwhelmed by a wave. Promise me."

"I promise."

I gave him a hug. "You did great. You're my best student ever."

"Really?"

I grinned. "You're also my only student."

He laughed. "Can we practice again tomorrow?"

"Of course."

We grabbed our towels, dried off, then went inside to get ready for dinner.

I stripped off my wet suit and stepped into the shower. Once finished, I washed out my suit and hung it to dry.

I heard raised voices from somewhere down the hallway as I dressed. Were they really still fighting?

I opened my door and peered out.

Talon was doing the same from his doorway. He glanced over at me. "I've never heard Uncle Gordon yell like that before."

Nova's voice, soothing but failing to calm whoever she was talking to.

"Should we go to dinner?" I asked.

Talon nodded.

We walked down the hallway together.

I spotted Nova at the door as we approached the front

entrance, blocking Gordon's path, her hands pressed against his chest.

"You've been drinking! You can't drive."

He pushed her away, his face flushed. "Get out of my way, Nova."

"Gordon, please—"

He shoved past her and stumbled out the front door, slamming it behind him. Nova stood for a moment, staring after him.

Then she bolted for the front closet. Grabbed her shoes, a green leather jacket, and her purse. She flung the door open, tearing after him. "Wait for me!"

I walked over to the door, intending to close it but she was back a second later. "He left without me."

"Calm down." Rose appeared in the living room. "Gordon will come back when he's cooled off. He always does."

Whatever animosity had been between the two sisters when Lopez was there appeared to have dissipated.

"I don't think so," Nova sniffed. "Not this time. He's incredibly angry."

"About what?" Rose asked.

Nova tightened her jaw. "It's personal."

"Nova—"

"I said it's personal."

Rose sighed. "You need to eat something. You'll feel better after you get some food in your stomach."

Nova nodded, pulling out her phone. A second later, she texted someone. Gordon, I assumed.

We all made our way into the dining room, where the usual elaborate spread had been laid out. But the atmosphere felt different tonight. Heavier. Tense.

Liam was already seated, drink in hand. "What's all the ruckus about?"

"None of your business," Nova replied, pacing behind him.

Liam raised his eyebrows.

Rose shook her head at him. He grinned but didn't push it.

Nova held her phone to her ear. "Gordon, answer the damn phone. Talk to me."

But he obviously didn't answer, because seconds later she rang him again.

"Sit down," Rose said. "Pacing isn't going to make him answer any quicker."

Nova ignored her, stopping at the sideboard and opening a drawer. Seconds later, she got out a pack of cigarettes and lit one up.

"Where did those come from?" Rose asked.

"I know all of Maxwell's stashes," Nova said, taking a deep puff.

Liam snapped his fingers, gestured for one.

"No," Rose said.

He grimaced at her. Slowly, the family gradually gathered around the table. Within minutes, Olivia was already deep into the wine.

Liam sat across from me, pushing his food around his plate without taking a single bite.

"You're getting too skinny," Rose said. "You need a better diet."

Liam shrugged but didn't lift the fork to his mouth.

Willa glanced at Nova. "Sit down. You're making me dizzy."

Nova shot her a withering look but finally dropped into her chair. She kept the phone in her lap, checking it every twenty seconds for messages.

"What's eating Gordon?" Jaxon asked. "I can't remember him ever missing a meal."

"I don't want to talk about it," Nova said, stabbing her chicken.

Liam looked up from his untouched plate. "He discovered who Maxwell's spy is. Maybe that's bothering him."

"We all know who it is." Jaxon aimed his fork at me. "Zoe."

Liam shook his head. "No. Zoe told me Gordon knew who it really was. Or at least he said he did."

All eyes turned to me. My cheeks reddened. I glared at Liam. Did no one in this family know how to keep a secret?

Rose leaned forward. "Is that true, Zoe? Gordon told you he knew who Father's spy was?"

I swallowed. "Yes. But he didn't tell me who it was. Not even a hint."

Nova dropped her fork on her plate. "Bullshit. If Gordon knew something that important, he would have told me. We don't keep secrets from each other."

"Well, if Denton Hatch were still alive, he might disagree about that," Liam said.

Nova picked up her fork and threw it at him.

Liam ducked. The fork landed somewhere in the wall of succulents.

"Please," Rose said. "Some semblance of civility?"

Nova pushed her chair back and left the table without a word. Liam started building what looked like a small fortress out of mashed potatoes.

"What did you and Caleb get up to today?" Jaxon asked, chewing on his chicken.

"Audition," Rose and Caleb said simultaneously, then looked at each other.

"Different auditions," clarified Rose.

Caleb nodded. "Different projects entirely."

"You're going to a hell of a lot of auditions lately," Willa said.

Rose glared at her, then turned to Talon. "How was your swimming lesson? Did you like it?"

His expression brightened. "I loved it. Zoe's a great teacher. I can put my whole face underwater now and even doggy paddle a little."

"That's wonderful, sweetheart."

A maid appeared in the doorway, hovering, looking like she wished to be anywhere else.

Rose turned to her. "Yes, Maria?"

"Mr. Marlowe would like to speak with Miss Zoe after she's finished with dinner."

Everyone at the table turned to stare at me like I'd just been called to the principal's office.

I pointed to my chest. "Me?"

She nodded.

Liam nudged me with his elbow, grinning. "I knew you were the spy."

"I am not the spy."

Nova reappeared in the dining room, phone pressed to her ear. "Pick up, Gordon. Please. We can figure this out together. Just call me back."

She ended the call, walked over to her chair, and slumped in it.

We ate, pretending not to watch her unravel.

Chapter Twenty-Seven

I BRUSHED MY TEETH, washed my face, and checked the sliding doors.

Patio lights glowed across the pool deck.

I made sure the door was locked and then lowered the blinds. I was keeping the outside lights on tonight.

A knock on my bedroom door.

I sighed, then walked over and answered it.

Rose stood in the hallway. "I want to apologize for dinner. Everyone's on edge tonight after that detective's visit. "

"That's alright. I understand."

"Are you ready to meet our father?"

I hesitated. "Did he say why he wants to talk to me?"

"No. But you're about to find out."

I followed Rose to the main entrance. Maybe I should ask about getting a lock. I might feel more secure.

But before I could, Nova appeared, pulling on her green jacket. Jaxon trailed behind her, car keys jangling in his hand.

Rose stopped. "Where are you two going?"

"Out to look for Gordon," Nova said, heading for the front door. "He's still not answering me."

"He'll come home when he's cooled off," Rose said.

"I'm not so sure."

Jaxon grabbed his sister's elbow and steered her toward the front door. "We'll be back later."

"You want help?" Rose asked.

Jaxon shook his head. "No. We got it."

A second later, they were gone.

Rose turned to me and shrugged. "Come on."

We headed toward the stairs.

Willa bumped into us. "I'm going to get some sparkling water. You want any?"

"You're going to float away on all those bubbles," Rose said.

Willa grunted, then made her way into the kitchen. I caught a glimpse of Bertie at the sink, washing up his dishes behind her. Rose was already halfway up the stairs. So I hurried to catch up. We made our way to the third floor.

Rose stopped at the last door at the end of hallway and knocked. "Everybody decent?"

The door opened and Olivia appeared, hair disheveled and makeup smeared. The aroma of wine clung to her like perfume. Not that I could really smell it, because the stench of cigarette smoke billowing out of the room was overwhelming enough to gag me.

Olivia spotted me, her eyes narrowing. "I knew it."

I raised my brows. "Knew what?"

Olivia ignored me, glancing at Rose. "You're plotting against me. All of you."

"And why would we do that?"

"Because you want to break up my marriage." Olivia

pointed at me with a quivering finger. "That's why you brought this one in. So she could take my spot."

I curled my lip. Ew. She couldn't honestly think I was interested in Maxwell, could she? Though I guess she was only a few years older than me.

"Don't be ridiculous," Rose said. "You're drunk."

"I am not." I recoiled at her breath. I didn't know how she was walking, let alone talking.

Rose pointed down the hallway. "Come back when you're sober."

Olivia's face crumpled. Then she pushed past us, stumbled down the hallway, and entered another room. She slammed the door hard enough to rattle the walls.

I wondered if that was her room.

Rose gestured for me to enter.

Maxwell was propped up in bed, looking like a scarecrow in silk pajamas. A lit cigarette smoldered between his fingers, the ash precariously long and threatening to rain down on the comforter. The room reeked of stale tobacco. Everything had a slightly yellow color, from the curtains to the bedding to the wallpaper. Even Maxwell himself. It was like being in swallowed an ashtray.

He glanced over at Rose. "Send Nova up."

"She's gone out."

He raised his brows. "At this time? Where?"

Rose shrugged. "I think Gordon's on a bender."

"What happened? The dogs shit on the carpet again and Willa yell at him?"

"I don't know."

He waved a hand. "Well, when she gets home, make sure she comes see me. It's time I start the divorce paperwork."

"Whose? Hers or yours?"

He scowled. "You know damn well I'm talking about Olivia."

Rose crossed her arms. "Are you going to tell Olivia first?"

He shrugged and ash drizzled down from his cigarette onto the bedsheets. "Does it matter?"

Rose tipped her head. "Probably not."

He waved his hand. "Get out."

Rose ignored him, walking over and kissing his forehead. "You don't scare me, you old monster."

He grunted.

She walked to the door, then paused. "Don't scare Zoe away. Talon likes this one. And so do I."

Then she stepped out, closing the door behind her.

Maxwell gestured toward the lamp on his nightstand. "Come over here to the light so I can get a good look at you."

I crossed my arms. "Say please."

His bushy eyebrows shot up to his hairline.

I flushed. "I'm—"

"Don't you dare say you're sorry. I like a straight shooter. You talk to my grandson that way?"

"No." I shook my head. "He has better manners than you."

Maxwell laughed, then gestured to the light. "Please."

I walked over and stood by the lamp, feeling more like a specimen under examination than a nanny. "I hope you're not thinking of me for wife number six. Because I'm not interested."

He snorted, peering up at me with the intensity of a casting director. "I'm done with marriage. At least for this year."

I did a little twirl. "Satisfied?"

He narrowed his eyes. "You must be smarter than you look, but I trust Madeline sent me the right person."

"Sent you? Rose hired me."

He took a long drag from his cigarette. "With my approval. So what do you think of my children?"

I blinked. "What do you mean?"

"You know." He laughed, then started coughing. I picked up the glass of water on his nightstand and handed it to him. He took it, sipping. Then cleared his throat and took another puff.

I picked up the ashtray and held it out. He glared at me, but he stubbed out his cigarette. I set it back down. "Why do you care what I think of your kids?"

"Because you're spying on them. Feeling out who's best to take over the business." He leaned back against his pillows. "It's obviously *not* going to be Rose. She's far too soft. But who among the others has the spine to uphold the Marlowe name?"

I stared at him. "I don't understand."

"Surely, you didn't think I was paying *that* amount of money for a nanny?" His eyes glittered. "Jesus Christ, the kid is thirteen. Why the hell does he need a goddamn babysitter?"

The room tilted. I reached out and touched the wall for support. "So I really am here to spy?"

"Of course you are, but I didn't want you to know right away. I wanted you to get the lay of the land. Make some first impressions of the rabble."

I swallowed. "Madeline wouldn't agree to this."

Maxwell laughed. "Madeline knows all about it. She approved it. Said you were a smart cookie who had your wits about you."

Smart cookie? I doubted Madeline used those words.

"I don't believe you."

"No?" Maxwell reached over to his nightstand and grabbed his phone. He dialed, then hit the speaker. "Let's ask her, shall we?"

The phone rang. Once. Twice.

And then—

"Maxwell?" It was Madeline.

"Hello, darling. I'm in bed but I've got Zoe with me," he wheezed. Then he added, "Not literally, of course."

"I hope not," she said.

"Madeline?" My voice sounded shaky.

"Has Maxwell updated you with the job requirements?" she asked.

I stared at the phone. "You knew about this?"

"Of course. And I assured him that—"

I turned on my heel and walked out of the room, not bothering to close the door behind me.

"Girl!"

I ignored him.

Madeline had lied to me. I had trusted her. And she had lied.

I made my way downstairs. Rose and Caleb were in the living room chatting.

"Zoe?"

I ignored Rose, running back to my bedroom. Then I closed and locked the door behind me. My hands were shaking. I clenched them into fists.

My phone rang. I pulled it out of my pocket.

Madeline's name flashed on the screen. I ignored the call.

She rang again. This time I answered. "How dare you!"

"Zoe—"

"You lied to me?" My voice cracked, I blinked back tears.

"As did you to me."

The blood drained from my face. I felt a cold chill down my back. "What? I've never lied to you."

"Your father, Zoe. He's not dead, is he?"

My vision blurred. The room spun. I couldn't catch my breath. Couldn't get any air to my lungs. My hands went ice cold and clammy. The phone nearly slipped from my grip. Everything was upside down and backward.

I dropped onto the bed.

"Zoe?"

I cleared my throat. "That's different."

"In what way?"

I couldn't think of an answer. My hand was so tight on my phone, I thought it might snap. "How long have you known?"

She laughed. "Oh, Zoe. I do extensive background checks on all my employees before I hire them."

Extensive?

So did that mean—

No. I wasn't going to ask if she knew *everything*.

"You are right about one thing," Madeline said. "I withheld information from you, and for that I am sorry."

"Why?" I sounded like a little kid.

"Maxwell offered to cover your first year's tuition at Columbia."

I blinked. "What?"

"I thought it'd be a nice bonus for you at the end of the job. Only I was the one who was supposed to inform you that the job switched. Bloody Marlowes. Always having to be in control."

Bloody Marlowes? She actually sounded irritated. Any nothing ever phased Madeline.

"But why me?" I asked.

"You're a keen observer of human nature, Zoe. Isn't

that why you want to be a writer? Why not put those skills to good use and get paid handsomely for it?"

I got up, pacing the floor. "I wouldn't have minded. But not being told in advance is a deal breaker. You should have asked me first."

"I understand. And if you don't want to do it, I'll arrange for your flight home. Put in someone else."

I hesitated. The tuition money. My future. Everything I'd been working toward.

"How long do I have to spy?"

"Maxwell wants his decision made within the month. You're to observe the family dynamics, assess each potential heir's capabilities, and provide a comprehensive report."

I stopped pacing. "And then he'd pay my first year at Columbia?"

"Plus your regular salary, of course."

I sank onto the bed. A year at Columbia. "Is this a bribe?"

She laughed. "We prefer bonus. What do you think?"

I sniffed, wiping my nose on my sleeve. "The family already suspects I'm a spy."

"Then you might as well get paid for it."

I stared at the floor. Stay with Talon? Or leave and be further from my dream?

"Can I sleep on it?"

"Of course, Zoe. Call me in the morning."

She disconnected. I stared at the phone.

Had I ever really known her?

Chapter Twenty-Eight

I TRIED SLEEPING.

But I couldn't shut off my brain. Instead, I tossed and turned for what felt like hours. I didn't know what to do. Stay? Go home?

My phone kept buzzing on the nightstand like an angry insect. Finally, I grabbed it and checked my messages. Madeline had texted: *Sweet dreams. We'll talk in the morning.*

I snorted.

How optimistic that she thought I would sleep after learning I had been hired as a family spy. I also had a voicemail from the unknown number.

I really shouldn't listen.

But how much worse could tonight get?

I hit play.

"Zo? It's me. Listen, I know you probably don't want to hear from me, but I've got an opportunity I think you'd be interested in. Tania told me all about what happened, and this could really help you out financially. Give me a call back when you—"

I disconnected.

Hit delete.

Fuck him.

And now I really wouldn't be able to sleep. What was my father up to? *None of your business, Zoe. NONE.*

That's how I'd wound up in trouble before. By trying to help him out. And he'd left me holding the bag.

I threw off the covers, pulled on a hoodie and headed out of my room and down the hallway. I needed something hot and soothing to calm my nerves.

Willa was curled up on the couch, phone in her hand, staring at the screen as I walked past the living room.

She started, looking over at me. "Have you seen Jaxon?"

"Not since he left with Nova. They're not back yet?"

"No. Not answering his phone either."

I gestured down the hallway. "I'm going to make some tea. Want some water?"

She didn't answer, already back engrossed in her phone.

I continued to the kitchen, filled the kettle, and plugged it in. I wondered how Elsa was doing. I glanced at the clock. Past midnight. 3 a.m. in New York. Too late for her advice, although I had a feeling I knew what she would say.

Stick around and earn that tuition.

Maybe Frenchie? But I had even less idea of what time it was where he was. And he might not even be in service range.

When the kettle boiled, I made my tea and headed back to my room. I changed into my bathing suit and grabbed a towel. Then I went out to the pool, dumped my towel on a chaise, and set my tea on the table to cool.

Hopefully being active would help me reach a decision.

At the very least, it would help me stop feeling like I

wanted to punch something. Or someone. Like my father. Or Maxwell. Or Madeline.

I jumped into the water. It was lovely and warm. Then I started doing laps. How could Madeline do that to me?

Throw me in the deep end and expect me to swim?

I snorted, coughing on water.

Maybe I was being too harsh. Didn't it mean something that she thought I was a keen observer? There was a reason she'd placed me in complex situations. She'd been upfront about that from the beginning: that my assignments might be challenging, that wealthy families often had complicated dynamics. In a way, she had trusted me more than I trusted her. Because I hadn't told her about my father. And when she found out, she hadn't fired me. Surely that had to mean something.

I reached the far end of the pool and pushed off the wall, gliding underwater before surfacing. The Stockports had been a nightmare, but I'd handled them. Lyon Island could have been even worse, but I'd survived there too. So what was a little spying? That was hardly comparable to my previous experiences.

I floated on my back, staring up at sky.

The tuition money could change everything. Give me a head start on the future my mother had stolen away.

I could invest it and let it grow while I earned the rest.

And everyone here thought I was a spy anyway.

I rolled over and continued swimming. The warm water and cool night air felt like a cocoon. It made me feel safe and protected.

A shadow moved at the far end of the pool.

I surfaced, treading water. "Hello?"

No response.

I swam down to the far end, pulling myself up on the edge to get a better look. But there was no one there. I listened, holding my breath. Nothing but the gentle lapping of water against the pool sides and those persistent insects chirping from beyond the walls.

Another shadow shifted.

I looked up. Clouds passed over the moon, sending shadows dancing across the concrete. I was spooking myself for no reason.

I got out and drank my tea. Then started shivering, so I dove back in, swimming along the bottom of the pool to the shallow end.

The deck lights went out.

I surfaced, looking around. Had a bulb burned out?

No. All the lights were off. The patio had plunged into complete darkness. There must be a secondary switch somewhere outside my bedroom. Maybe further along the balcony?

Oh well. Swimming in the dark didn't bother me. If anything, it felt more peaceful.

I took a deep breath and dove to the bottom, sitting cross-legged on the tiles, eyes closed, holding my breath. The water pressed against me from all sides, muffling any sound from the world above.

I still felt sad. I was used to betrayal from my father and Toxic Tania. They'd made a career out of disappointing me. But not Madeline. Madeline was supposed to be different. She was supposed to be the one person I could trust, the mentor who actually cared about my future.

Hot tears mixed with the water.

And then I heard a splash.

Dammit.

So much for this pool being "mine."

I pushed off the bottom, surfacing. I took a breath and opened my eyes. Someone had joined me in the pool.

Couldn't they use the main one? Why did they have to invade mine?

I snorted.

LA was getting to me. Entitlement was contagious in the Hills.

Whoever it was probably hadn't seen me sitting on the bottom of the pool.

"Hope I didn't scare you." I swam to the edge and climbed out, water streaming from my suit as I walked over to the lounge chairs and grabbed my towel, wrapping it around my shoulders. The night air felt cold against my wet skin.

I glanced back at the pool. The water was too still.

Except for a body floating face down, fully dressed in a man's dinner clothes. Dark liquid spread around him in the water like an oil slick.

"You spilled your wine."

No response.

And that wasn't wine.

Whoever this was must have hit his head on the bottom or the side of the pool when he jumped in.

I tossed my towel aside, jumped back into the water, and swam over to him. How come there was so much blood? Dark ribbons of it spread through the water like spilled ink.

There was much more than a simple head injury would cause, wasn't there?

I reached for him and rolled him over onto his back. Gordon stared up at me, his skin chalk white, his throat gaping open like a second mouth.

I screamed.

Then clamped my right hand over the wound. Blood seeped between my fingers, warm and sticky. Gordon's eyes flew open, wild and unfocused. He sputtered, sending droplets of blood across my face and into the water around us.

"Don't fight me," I said, treading water. "I'm trying to help you."

He was heavy. I hooked my arm under his chin and kicked toward the shallow end, fighting to keep both our heads above water. Blood continued to spill between my fingers.

Gordon grabbed my wrist with surprising strength, his fingers digging into my skin.

"What is it?"

He opened his mouth, trying to form words. Blood bubbled up instead. Then, with enormous effort, he managed one word.

"Nova."

Then his grip softened, his arm fell into the water, and his eyes rolled back, showing only white.

"Gordon? Gordon, stay with me!"

No response. He went limp in my arms.

"Help!" I screamed. "SOMEBODY HELP ME!"

The patio lights blazed on, flooding the area with harsh white light.

"Rose! Nova! Anyone!"

Talon appeared in pajamas, hair wild. His mouth dropped open. "Is Uncle Gordon okay?"

I shifted to block his view.

"I need you to call 911. Get an ambulance. The police. Now!"

He nodded and sprinted back toward the house.

I reached the pool steps but couldn't figure out how to drag Gordon out if I wanted to keep my hand pressed against his throat. My arms were shaking. He was so very heavy.

Footsteps.

A shadow appeared around the edge of the house. My heart was thunder.

What if was whoever did this to him? What if they were coming back?

Run, Zoe, Run.

I couldn't leave Gordon. Or drag him out alone.

I was trapped.

Chapter Twenty-Nine

Bᴜᴛ ɪᴛ ᴡᴀꜱ Rᴏꜱᴇ.

She appeared on the deck, in pristine white silk pajamas.

"It's Gordon!" I yelled. "His throat's been cut!"

Her eyes widened as she tore across the deck toward me, jumping into the pool and splashing over to me. She grabbed Gordon by the arms, then we steered him toward the pool steps, his body heavy and awkward between us. I tried to keep one hand against his throat—the gaping wound felt warm and slippery under my palm—and the other beneath his head so he wouldn't sink.

"Take him," I said when we hit the stairs.

She recoiled at the gash in his throat, her face going white. The wound was deeper than I thought, a jagged slice that went straight across his neck, exposing the dark red muscle underneath and the pale cartilage of his windpipe.

My stomach made somersaults.

I swallowed acid, then grabbed Rose's wrist and

yanked her arm forward. Seconds later, she was gripping the wound.

I scrambled up the stairs, my knees nearly buckling, and ran to the chaise. I grabbed my towel, twisting it into a tight knot. My bloody fingers left red smears on the white terry cloth.

I retraced my steps, joining Rose yet again, and bunched the towel under Gordon's throat, wrapping it around his neck as a pressure bandage.

Probably too late. The blood had almost slowed to a trickle.

Rose cradled his head in her lap. "Gordon? Can you hear me?"

His eyes were open, but he was having trouble focusing. His lips moved, but only wet gurgling sounds and bubbling pink foam bled out at the corners.

"Hush." Rose smoothed his hair back. "Don't try to talk. Help is on the way."

Liam appeared on the deck, wearing boxer shorts and a faded band T-shirt. "What the fuck is going on? Talon said there's an emergency—" He stopped when he saw us. "Jesus Christ. Is that Gordon?"

I nodded. "Is the ambulance coming?"

"Yeah. What happened to him?"

I gestured to my throat. "His throat—"

"It's been cut," Rose said.

Liam recoiled. "Was it an accident?"

I shook my head. "I don't know. I didn't see what happened. I was swimming. Then he was in the pool. I thought he jumped in, but maybe someone pushed him."

Liam glanced around "Who?"

"I don't know! It was dark. Someone turned the deck lights out."

He glanced over at the lights. "They're on now."

"Talon. He heard me screaming."

"You didn't see anyone?" Liam eyed me, maybe suspicious. "Hear anything odd before the splash?"

Why was he asking me so many questions? Had he hurt Gordon and wanted to make sure I didn't see or hear anything?

I pressed harder on the towel. "No."

Gordon gurgled again. His eyes rolled toward Rose, then back to me. He reached up and gripped my wrist again. There was barely any strength behind it.

"Stop moving," Rose said. "Help will be here soon. You're going to be okay."

I don't think any of us believed her.

A wet, rattling noise came from Gordon's throat. It made my skin crawl. I looked down at him. His eyes were still open, staring up at the star-scattered sky. But now they had a glassy, unfocused look.

Then his hand fell away from mine and splashed into the water.

I glanced down at his chest. It seemed awfully still. His hands floated at his sides.

I pressed my fingers to his neck, searching under the towel for a pulse, but I couldn't find one. Still, I didn't give up.

Willa stepped through the glass sliding doors. "What's all the yelling about—" She saw Gordon. "Oh my God!"

She started screaming.

"Willa!" Rose said. "Get back inside!"

The blood-curdling bellows continued. Everyone from Rodeo Drive to Malibu was going to know something was wrong at the Marlowe Estate.

"Liam, do something!" Rose said.

He walked over, grabbed her by the arm, and flung her into the pool. She shrieked a beat before the splash.

Her head burst out of the water. She was coughing and retching. "What was that for, asshole?"

"You needed to calm down," Liam said.

She splashed to the edge. "So one person drowning tonight wasn't enough for you?"

Liam crouched, holding out his hand. She hesitated a moment. Then took it and he hoisted her out.

"Gordon didn't drown," Rose said.

She turned to stare at us. "What?"

Sirens howled before Rose could elaborate. She turned to Liam. "Open the front gates. Now."

Liam hesitated, running a hand through his hair. "Shouldn't we tell Dad first? He's going to want to know—"

"Do it!"

"I'll go." Willa glanced over her shoulder, then disappeared into my bedroom.

Liam walked down to the other end of the deck and dropped into one of the chairs.

Rose leaned forward, nudging me. Her eyes were full of tears, and her lips trembled. "Is Gordon dead?"

I drew my hand out from under the towel and nodded. "I think so."

She gave a small cry. I leaned over Gordon to give her a hug. She rested her head on my shoulder.

Jaxon appeared, in pajamas like the rest of his family. He walked over and stood looking down at us.

"Jesus Christ. Willa said he was injured. Did he kill himself?"

I blinked. "You think this was suicide?"

He looked startled. "Don't you?"

I pulled the towel away from his throat. The wound smiled up at us.

Jaxon fell a step back. Then pulled out his phone.

Dialed. "This is Jaxon Marlowe. I need a security team at the house immediately. We've had an incident. Full perimeter sweep. Someone may still be on the property."

He disconnected. "Nobody leaves the house until security clears the grounds."

"Call the police," Rose said.

"Rose."

She bared her teeth. "*Now.*"

He nodded, then walked off and made another call.

Rose looked over at me. "I want to be with Talon."

I nodded, helping her lift Gordon's head from her lap, and rest him on the pool deck. Then she got to her feet and ran to the house in her blood-spattered pajamas. I hoped she'd change before seeing him.

I glanced back down at Gordon. The sirens were loud now. Help had arrived.

But Gordon was no longer bleeding, and his skin was turning waxy and pale, his lips tinged blue. Life had drained out of him along with the blood.

I set the towel aside. And then, because I didn't know what to do, I took his hand in mine and held it to my chest. Of course it was useless, but maybe it would comfort him.

Jaxon walked over, his phone still out. "Bertie. Check the entire property. We may have trespassers. Don't go alone. Take whoever you can find from the staff."

He rang off.

Willa returned with four EMTs in tow and I was shooed away from Gordon so they could get to work. My legs were shaking too much for proper walking, so I crawled to the lounge area where Liam sat.

He got up and helped me into a chair.

Then he left me, heading into my room, reappearing a minute later with a towel. He brought it over and wrapped it around me.

What was happening here?

Was this an accident? It had to be, right? Because why would anyone want to kill Gordon? He seemed like such a gentle man. What could he have possibly done to deserve this?

And who would have done such a thing? Someone in the family? The person who killed Denton Hatch? Or the attempted carjackers?

How had he ended up in my pool? Had he been trying to get to me to help him? Or had the killer not seen me down there in the dark water? It would have been awfully risky to push him in if they knew I was there.

And why this pool instead of the main one? Why my private courtyard?

I felt something soft envelope me. I opened my eyes. Caleb crouched beside me. He had draped a blanket over my shoulders.

"Rose thought you might be getting cold."

"Thank you," I said.

He squeezed my shoulder. "Police will be here shortly."

I was starting to shiver, partly from my wet bathing suit, but mostly from the adrenaline crash. My hands wouldn't stop trembling. Liam reached over and squeezed my shoulder.

The EMTs had Gordon on a stretcher and were wheeling him out. They didn't seem to be in a hurry. A few seconds later, Jaxon joined us. He held up his phone. "I still can't reach Nova. Calls are going straight to voicemail."

"What do you want us to do?" Caleb asked.

"Stay here and wait for the police."

Caleb nodded.

"I'm sending Willa to the hospital to stay with Gordon," Jaxon said. "Someone from the family should be there. I'm going to go back out and look for Nova."

I stared at him, confused. "She didn't come home with you?"

Jaxon shook his head. "No. We checked the bars he used to frequent. But didn't find him. I said it was getting late and that Gordon would come home eventually. But Nova was worried about him. She wanted to keep looking." He glanced at the pool. "Turns out she was right to be worried. Didn't think he was upset enough to take his own life."

I shivered, despite the blanket and towel. I wasn't buying suicide. Gordon had seemed terrified. And if he'd done it, where was the knife?

"Where is Nova now?" Caleb asked.

Jaxon shrugged. "Probably still barhopping. Whatever the reason, she's not picking up her phone. Probably pissed at me for leaving her."

"I'll come with you," Caleb said. "We can cover more ground together. Nova needs to know what happened."

"Handle the police, Liam?" Jaxon asked.

"Sure."

Liam pulled a joint from his pocket when Caleb and Jaxon left. He lit it, then took a long drag and held it out to me.

"Take a hit. I promise I won't narc."

I stared at it for a moment.

Then I took it from his fingers and inhaled. The smoke burned my lungs, making me cough. He grinned, patting me on the back. I felt a slight loosening in my chest, a dulling of the sharp edges of panic.

We sat in silence, passing the joint back and forth to the sound of more sirens and police arriving.

"Feeling better?" Liam asked.

"I guess so." I shrugged. "How come you're not more upset about Gordon?"

"We all die, right?"

I stared at him. "Not like this."

"Yeah. It's a bummer."

I glanced down at the water. The blood had already started to dissipate, the pool filter doing its thing.

Liam sighed, then took another drag. "Pool's ruined now."

Chapter Thirty

I CURLED up on the living room couch, knees to my chest. Rose's yoga pants were too short, leaving my ankles cold. The oversized cashmere sweatshirt hung loose and smelled like her perfume. I clutched the cream-colored throw, unable to get warm.

Police were everywhere.

Out by the pool. In my bedroom. Exploring the grounds. Searching the house.

The media were there, too.

At least that's what Rose said when she brought me the clothes. "The vultures have landed. Make sure to keep the blinds closed."

Detective Lopez was around here somewhere. I could hear her rubber-soled shoes squeaking against the marble floor.

Bertie had taken Rose and Talon to the Beverly Springs Hotel at 3 a.m. Lopez agreed a crime scene was no place for a thirteen-year-old. I wished I could have gone with them, but Lopez said she had questions for me.

So here I stayed, waiting.

I glanced down at my hands.

Even though I had spent twenty minutes scrubbing them, my fingernails still had dark crescents of blood beneath them. Gordon's blood.

I swallowed.

If I'd surfaced from the pool bottom ten seconds earlier, would I have seen who stabbed him? Could I have stopped it? Or would I have joined him, bleeding in the pool?

I had no idea.

And I didn't want to think about it.

I pulled the blanket over my head. Sleep came in fragments between the police radio static, until someone called my name.

I jerked awake and pulled the blanket down. Detective Lopez sat on the leather couch across from me, a steaming coffee of cup on the table before her. She balanced her notebook on her knee. I sat up, pulling the blanket tighter while stretching out my neck. I rubbed my throat, thinking of Gordon's wound.

Lopez didn't miss the gesture. "How are you doing?"

I shrugged. "Okay, I guess. I wish I could have done more for him."

"You did great. Gordon had already lost a significant amount of blood by the time he hit the water."

"Thanks." She was trying to make me feel better, but it didn't really register.

"I have some questions about tonight. Do you think you can answer them?"

The sooner I got this over with, the sooner I could get to bed and get some proper sleep. I nodded.

Liam wandered in and dropped onto the couch next to me.

Lopez tightened her jaw. "This is a private conversation."

He stretched his legs out, crossing his ankles. "It's my father's house."

"Not at the moment."

He raised his brows. "No?"

She bared her teeth. "No. It's mine. So unless you want to spend a night in jail for impeding an investigation, I suggest you skedaddle."

Liam turned to me. "You want a lawyer? If Nova's not available, we have more on speed dial. We tend to keep them fairly busy."

"I'll be fine," I said.

He shrugged and hauled himself up. Then he pulled out a joint and lit it. "Alright. But holler if you need me. I'll be in the kitchen having a smoke."

Lopez glared at him.

He took a long drag, exhaled in her direction, then strolled off to the kitchen.

Lopez watched him go, then looked back at me with a sigh. "Is everyone in this family as annoying as him?"

Despite everything, I laughed. "Maybe just him. And Nova. And Jaxon. And Willa. And maybe Maxwell. I like Talon and Rose."

"And Caleb?"

I shrugged. "I don't really know him. He seems alright."

She flipped to a fresh page in her notebook. "Alright, Zoe. Can you tell me what happened tonight? Start from the beginning."

"I made some tea and then decided to go for a night swim while it cooled. I needed to think."

"About what?"

I blinked. "Pardon?"

"Why did you need to think? Had something happened?"

I hesitated. I really didn't want to admit to the whole debacle with Maxwell and Madeline. "I got a phone call from my dad. It took me by surprise."

"What time was this?"

I reached for my phone, only to remember it was in my room. "I can't remember. I'll have to check."

"Your father will be able to confirm this?"

I pulled the blanket tighter. "I didn't talk to him. Just listened to his message."

"I'd like to hear it."

"I deleted it."

"I see." Lopez made a note. I wished I could see what she'd written. "Go on."

"I went for a swim."

"For how long?"

I shrugged. "I don't know. Long enough for my tea to cool. And then I got back in."

"You weren't cold?"

"The pool is heated."

"And then?"

"I thought I saw a shadow at one point. Then the lights went out."

"That didn't bother you?"

I shook my head. "No. I just figured there was a secondary switch and someone in the family turned them off for the night."

"And you didn't turn them back on?"

"It was peaceful. I dove down to the bottom of the pool and sat there for a bit. That's when I heard the splash."

"You were underwater when Gordon got in the pool?"

"At first, I guess I just thought someone else wanted to swim. So I got out."

Lopez looked up from her notebook. "You thought he was swimming fully clothed?"

"No. I don't know. They're a strange bunch."

"Then what?"

"I noticed—" I broke off. "At first, I thought it was wine. Then I realized it was blood. He was face down. I thought maybe he hit his head. So I got back in the water, flipped him over and saw…" I swallowed hard. "I saw it was Gordon. And I saw his throat."

"It was dark."

"Yes, but the moon was reflecting on the water. I screamed for help. Talon came running. I asked him to dial 911. And you know the rest."

"No one in the family knows how to swim."

"No."

"And yet…"

I shrugged. "What other reason would someone get in the water?"

Lopez met my eyes, tapping her pen against the notebook. "Did Gordon say anything to you before he passed?"

I nodded.

"What was that?"

"He said, 'Nova.'"

Lopez leaned forward. "He said his wife's name?"

I nodded. "Yes."

"You think he was trying to tell you something about her?"

I shook my head. "No, I just assumed he was asking for her. Like he wanted to see her before…" I trailed off.

"Did you see anyone else? Hear anyone?"

I thought for a moment, then shook my head. "No."

Lopez leaned back on the couch. "Do you usually swim at night?"

"No. First time."

"Hm." She flipped to another page in her notebook. "I'd like to ask you about the blood we found in your bathroom shower."

I blinked. "What?"

"We found blood in your shower. Like someone had gone in there to wash off."

Heat flashed through me, followed by a chill that made my hands shake. The living room suddenly felt too small, and too hot. "It wasn't me."

"I'm not saying it was."

"I haven't been anywhere near my bathroom since this whole thing started." My voice came out higher than normal, strained.

Lopez held up a hand. "Calm down, Zoe. I'm not accusing you of anything."

My heart was racing. Someone had used my bathroom. My private space. "Someone's trying to set me up. Otherwise, why use my bathroom? There are at least a dozen in this house."

"Maybe it was the most convenient. We found the murder weapon on the balcony outside your bedroom."

I stared at her, clutching the blanket. "Outside my room?"

"Yes. You didn't see anyone go in or out?"

"No. I'd closed the blinds. And the lights were out."

Lopez made another note. "What about sounds? Footsteps on the deck? A door opening or closing?"

I shook my head. "I was focused on Gordon. Trying to keep him alive. And afterward, everyone was going in and out of my room because it was the closest door to the pool."

She made another note.

Was it possible? That while I was fighting to save Gordon's life, his killer had been twenty feet away in my bathroom, washing blood off their hands?

"Anything else you can recall?" Lopez asked.

I looked at her expectant face. To hell with it. Someone in this family had tried to set me up, so why was I holding back?

"Gordon was upset about something earlier tonight. Nova said he'd relapsed. Started drinking. And then he went out."

Lopez leaned back against the couch. "Go on."

"Jaxon and Nova went after him, trying to find which bar they went to, but they couldn't."

"And why was Gordon still upset?"

I shrugged. "I don't know. I heard him and Nova arguing earlier. He was saying he couldn't believe it. She was trying to calm him down. But I don't know the details."

"And then he left?"

I nodded. "Jaxon came home when it started getting late, but Nova stayed out."

"And you didn't hear Gordon come home?"

"No."

Lopez tipped her head. "And Nova. Is she home now?"

I shook my head. "I don't think so."

Lopez closed her notebook and stood. She pulled out her phone and walked to the window overlooking the pool. I could hear her talking but couldn't make out the words. My brain was too scrambled to try.

She returned a few moments later and reclaimed her seat. "Given the circumstances, we're going to ping Nova's phone. Try to locate her."

I nodded.

"Tell me more about this argument between Gordon and Nova."

"I don't know anything aside from what I told you. He just sounded really upset."

"Do you think Nova is the type of person to hurt someone she's angry with?"

I thought of her chucking Liam's phone. The plates. The spoon. "I don't know."

"Tell me about Gordon. What was he like?"

"Nice. Gentle. He loved his dogs more than anything."

"Did he have any enemies? Anyone who might want to hurt him?"

"I haven't been here that long, but I can't imagine anyone not liking Gordon."

"What about his relationship with Nova?"

"They seemed happy together."

Her phone chimed. She pulled it out, then swiped it open, studying it for a beat. Then she got up and walked around to me, sitting on the couch. She held out her phone. There was a picture of a knife. Silver blade, black handle.

"Have you seen this knife before?"

I leaned forward to get a better look. "It looks like the steak knives we use at the dinner table."

She nodded.

Then her phone rang. "Lopez. Uh huh. Uh huh. I'll be in shortly."

Lopez hung up, then looked at me.

"We just found Nova."

I gripped the blanket. "Is she okay?"

Lopez tucked her notebook away. "Mrs. Marlowe has been spending the night in jail."

Chapter Thirty-One

I WOKE the next morning in the guest room.

My body ached from the unfamiliar mattress. Or the stress. I'd barely slept, one eye open all night. My suitcase sat on the floor.

Thank goodness.

Lopez had taken my bathing suit, Rose's clothes, and the blanket. I opened my suitcase. Everything had just been chucked inside.

I didn't bother with a shower. I'd had a long one before I'd gone to bed. I also wasn't that interested in being immersed in water so soon after last night's incident.

Incident. It was murder.

Poor Gordon.

I pulled on clean jeans and a sweater, tucked my phone in my pocket, and made my way downstairs. Monaco and Versailles lay on the front door mat, heads on their paws.

They both sat when they spotted me, but then lay down again in unison when they realized I wasn't Gordon.

I walked over and gave each a pet.

In the dining room, Liam and Willa were sitting at the

long wooden table. Both had a full plate of pastry and fruit, but neither seemed that interested in eating.

Shouting echoed from somewhere upstairs.

I slid into a chair. "What's that about?"

"Dad." Rose appeared in the doorway "He doesn't trust that the commie cops won't pin the murder on the family."

She walked over to the table and sat. I studied her.

She didn't believe that an outsider did this?

Liam stabbed a piece of cantaloupe with his fork. "Let's be honest. One of the family killed Gordon."

Rose's jaw fell open. "Liam Marlowe. Why would you say such a thing?"

"Because we're the only ones who were at the house last night."

"It could have been staff." Willa glanced at me. "No offense."

I raised my hands. "None taken."

Liam snorted. "Why the hell would the staff kill Gordon? He's the one who gave them bonuses at Christmas. Remembered their birthdays. Donated to their kid's college funds. The man was a goddamn saint."

Shouting grew louder upstairs. Something crashed. A lamp, maybe a vase.

"He's really upset," Willa said.

"We're all upset," Rose said. "But throwing things isn't going to bring Gordon back."

I got up and poured myself coffee from the silver carafe with shaking hands. As much as Liam was a scatter-brain, I believed his take on the situation over Rose's.

I headed back to the table with my coffee.

Rose held out her hand. "Thank you, Zoe."

I hesitated and then handed her the coffee, went back to the carafe and poured another. "Anyone else?"

No one answered.

I took my coffee back to my seat.

"Who do you think did it?" Willa asked, turning to Rose.

She took a sip, narrowing her eyes. "I don't. That's for the police to determine." She turned to me. "I apologize that you haven't been able to work very much since you arrived, Zoe. You seem to have arrived during a bit of a mess."

I forced a smile. "I've been through worse."

At least no one was trying to kill me. Yet.

My phone buzzed. I pulled it out. Madeline's name appeared on the screen. I pushed back my chair. "Excuse me. I should take this."

"Cops?" Liam asked.

I ignored him, stepped around the dogs, headed outside. Answered just before voicemail. "Hello, Madeline."

"Zoe. Rose called me this morning and told me what happened. Her brother-in-law was murdered?"

"Yeah."

There was a long moment of silence. "Do you want to come back to New York? I can arrange another position for you. Get you out of there today, as long as the police agree."

I looked back at the house and thought about Talon. "No. I'll stay on."

"Are you sure?"

"Yeah."

"And the secondary job?"

"I'll do it. But Madeline—you're never, ever to keep information from me again. About anything."

"Nor you, Zoe."

I flushed. "Agreed."

"Alright then. Be careful. And watch your back."

She disconnected. I stood there for a moment.

Be careful. Watch your back.

Like I had any choice.

I heard voices.

More cops, maybe.

I walked down the driveway toward the gates, weaving around a few police vehicles still parked on the property. Still collecting evidence. Or doing scene containment. I grimaced. I knew far too much about murder investigations.

Private security stood on the inside of the gate, although their presence wasn't doing much to deter anyone from getting too close.

Because outside was pure chaos. News vans crowded Mulholland Drive. Reporters clustered behind the police barriers. When they spotted me through the bars, a chorus of shouting started despite the officers trying to keep them back.

"Miss! Miss! Can you tell us what happened here last night?"

"Are you a family member? Do you work for the Marlowes?"

"What can you tell us about the police investigation?"

Cameras clicked like a swarm of insects. I raised my hand to block out the sun and hide my face.

"Can you confirm reports of a body being found?"

"Is the family making a statement?"

The questions came rapid-fire, voices overlapping.

I turned away, making my way back toward the house.

I heard a car honk. Loud and long. I stopped, glancing back.

A black and white police cruiser had pulled up to the

drive. One of the security guards hit the gate button, allowing the car to drive through.

I stepped aside. Nova sat in the back, a complete wreck. Her head slumped against the window, hair tangled and makeup smeared.

The officer parked, then got out and opened the back door. Nova got out, but then her kneed buckled.

The officer grabbed her before she hit the pavement.

I jogged over. "Let me help."

I slipped my arm around Nova's waist. The smell of alcohol and cigarettes clung to her clothes. I led her toward the front door.

"How am I going to live without Gordon?" Her voice was clogged with tears. "He was such a sweet man. Better than all of us."

"I'm so sorry, Nova."

We were a few feet from the front door when Jaxon appeared.

Nova's eyes flashed and she lunged at him. Punching his chest and shoulders. "This is all your fault! You shouldn't have stopped looking for him!"

"Nova, stop—" Jaxon tried to grab her wrists.

"If you'd kept looking, he'd still be alive!" She drew back and slammed her closed fist into his jaw. "It's your fault!"

Jaxon's head snapped to the side, a red mark blooming across his cheek.

The officer stepped between them. "Ma'am, you need to calm down."

"It's alright," Jaxon said, rubbing his face. "She's grieving."

Another cop car pulled up and parked. Lopez got out. "Get her inside. Now."

I steered her inside. Jaxon stayed put.

"He didn't deserve it." Tears trickled down Nova's face. "He didn't."

I patted her back. "I know."

I steered Nova into the living room, where she collapsed against the couch cushions like a broken doll.

"Can I get you something?" I asked. "Coffee? Tea?"

She wiped her nose with the back of her hand, leaving a streak of mucus across her cheek. "Water."

I nodded. "I'll be right back."

I headed to the kitchen and went straight to the cabinet for a glass. When I reached up to grab one, something flew at my head.

I ducked.

A glass water bottle sailed past my ear and shattered in a shower of glass and water against the wall. Shards scattered across the marble floor like diamonds.

I whirled around.

Willa stood by the kitchen island, her face bright red. "Oh my God, I'm so sorry, Zoe. I was throwing it at Bertie, not you."

I glanced behind me.

Bertie stood near the coffee machine, his face pale. Water dripped from his hair. A second later, he set down his coffee cup and walked out of the kitchen.

Willa opened her mouth like she was going to say something, but then seemed to think better of it. She turned and ran after Bertie.

I walked over to the window above the sink and looked out, watching Willa chase Bertie around the side of the house toward the back gardens, her arms gesticulating as she tried to catch up with him.

What the hell was that about?

Not that I cared.

I'd had enough drama for one day.

I grabbed a broom and dustpan from the utility closet and swept up the broken glass, dumping the shards into the garbage bin.

I opened the refrigerator and grabbed a bottle of water from the top shelf and headed back to the living room.

Lopez was seated across from Nova, her familiar notebook balanced on her knee. Nova had stopped crying, but her face was puffy, red, and streaked with mascara.

I held out the water. "Here you go."

Nova took it with trembling hands. "Thank you."

She tried to open it but didn't seem to have the strength, so I loosened the cap for her and passed it over.

"If there's nothing else…" I started to back away.

But Nova reached out and grabbed my wrist, looking up at me with red-rimmed eyes. "I want you to stay."

"Me?" I said.

She nodded.

"Are you sure you don't want Rose?"

She shook her head. "No family. I don't trust them right now."

I glanced over at Lopez. The detective nodded.

"Alright," I said.

Nova released my arm. I sat beside her.

She pressed against me, as if my presence alone might hold her together.

Chapter Thirty-Two

"Tell me about yesterday," Lopez said. "The last time you saw Gordon."

Nova twisted the bottle's cap. Unscrewing it. Screwing it back on. The metal made tiny clicking sounds in the silence. She cleared her throat. "We argued."

"Why is that?"

"Because of Denton Hatch."

"You were upset about that?"

Nova nodded.

"Why? You didn't want him looking into his wife's death?"

"No, that wasn't it."

Lopez opened her notepad. "Then why?"

Nova twisted the bottle cap again. I reached over and squeezed her hand. She gave me a smile. Set the bottle on the table. "Whenever he focused on Beth too much, he'd start drinking again. A drunk Gordon was never a good thing."

She reached out for the bottle, twisted off the cap, and

took a drink of water. "Last anniversary, he promised to let it go. Move on."

Lopez made a note. "Gordon was saying, 'he couldn't believe it.' What was that about?"

Nova's face crumpled. She set the water down, buried her face in her hands and started crying.

"Ms. Marlowe?"

"I'm so ashamed."

Lopez tapped her pen against her knee. "Of what?"

Nova opened her mouth, closed it again. "I called Hatch and canceled the job."

"You canceled the investigation into Beth's death?" Lopez asked.

Nova nodded.

"So you knew about it."

"I found a receipt in Gordon's papers. I figured that's why he came to the house." Nova wiped her nose against her sleeve. "To confront me. Or tell Gordon I'd interfered. It was stupid, I know."

"And how did Gordon find out you'd done that?"

"He called the company to pay an installment. I guess he talked to the receptionist. Found out it was already done. And that the contract had been canceled. He was pissed at me. Started drinking, and then left."

Lopez leaned forward. "And you followed him?"

"Jaxon and I went to all Gordon's former favorite bars, but there was no sign of him." She pressed her fingers to her eyes. "Jaxon wanted to go home, but I didn't. I knew I could find him if I just kept looking."

Lopez tapped her pen against her notepad. "Did Gordon have any problems with anyone else in the family?"

Nova looked up, her eyes hard. "Of course not. Everyone loved Gordon. Everyone."

"What about the carjackers that assaulted the family the other day?" Lopez asked. "Any chance they might have had something to do with his death?"

"No! He had nothing to do with that."

Lopez glanced at me.

I shrugged.

Lopez leaned back against the cushions, studying Nova's face. "Who do you think killed your husband?"

Nova's mouth opened. Closed. Opened again. Like a fish gasping on dry land. "I don't know. Everyone loved Gordon."

She was like a skipping CD, stuck on the same line. *Everyone loved Gordon. Everyone loved Gordon. Everyone loved Gordon.*

Nova started crying again.

Lopez closed her notepad. "That's all for now."

I nodded and touched Nova's arm. "Come on. Let's get you to bed."

I pulled her to her feet. She clung to my arm, her fingers digging in. We climbed to the second floor and stopped at the first door. "I can't go in there. It smells like Gordon."

I didn't blame her.

Another door opened further down the hallway.

Rose popped out. "Nova! I thought I heard your voice."

She darted toward us.

Nova let out a high-pitched wail and collapsed into Rose's arms.

I backed away, leaving them to it.

Rose let Nova along the hallway back to her door. Nova paused, looking back. "I left my jacket at the Glasshouse. Green leather. Gordon bought it for me last Christmas. I don't want to lose it."

"I can get it," I said.

"Take Bertie," Rose said.

They disappeared. It was odd seeing Nova vulnerable. Her iron will had seemed unbreakable. Until now.

I headed to Bertie's wing. TV voices leaked through his door. I knocked.

The door opened a crack and Bertie appeared. He stepped out into the hallway and pulled the door shut behind him.

"What's up?" he asked.

"Can you give me a lift to the Glasshouse? Nova left her jacket there last night."

"Sure." He nodded. "Give me five. I'll meet you at the car."

He slipped back into his room.

I got my hoodie, purse, and shoes from the guest room and went outside to the garage. I walked over to the tarp-covered car. Wondered what kind it was.

"That car belonged to Isabella. No one drives it anymore."

I turned around. Bertie stood behind me. He'd changed clothes. Dark jeans instead of khakis. A different shirt.

"Nova refused to get rid of it. Not that I blame her. It's a real beauty. Ferrari. Red. She loved that thing. Used to take it out on the weekends only. Drive up the coast. No one ever uses it now. Or at least, no one is allowed to."

"How strange."

"In what way?"

"I can see keeping a trinket to remember someone. But a car?"

He laughed. "Yeah, well, the wealthy do things differently, don't they?"

I nodded. "I guess so."

Bertie backed out the SUV. I joined him, and we drove around the cop cars.

"When do you think they'll leave?" he asked.

I glanced at the van. "When they finish gathering evidence, I expect."

"Lot of experience with murder?"

"Some."

He raised his brows.

I shook my head. "Don't ask."

He pulled around the last patrol car and we crawled downhill toward the gates. The reporters were still swarming outside them.

Only now there were a slew or major outlets with vans topped by satellite dishes. The security guard opened the gates and waved us through. Reporters rushed forward like a swarm of locusts.

Despite the bodies pressing against the windows, Bertie didn't seem the least bit fazed. I kept my head down so they couldn't see my face. Someone slammed their palm against my window.

Bertie tapped the horn. I glanced up. A man in a blue jacket stood in front of us. Bertie nudged him aside.

We cleared the crowd and he punched the gas. The SUV lurched forward.

Two cars pulled away from the cluster of vehicles behind us. A white sedan and a gray Honda, nearly colliding with one another while jockeying for position behind us. Bertie turned right, heading up Mulholland. The white sedan fell back at the first hairpin turn.

The Honda was still on our tail.

Bertie took another right, down a narrow street and then a left turn. Right turn. Up another hill.

The Honda finally vanished in the rearview mirror.

Bertie drove for ten more minutes, checking our mirrors and taking random turns.

Then he pulled over and killed the engine. Sinking back against his seat. "I want to explain the bottle incident."

I stared at him. "The what?"

"In the kitchen. When Willa threw the bottle. I want to explain."

Oh right. I had almost forgotten. "You really don't need to explain anything."

"But I do."

"It's obvious that you and Willa are having an affair," I said.

He paled. Gripped the steering wheel, then dropped his hands again. "Did she tell you?"

"No. But you're always together getting 'bottled water.'"

He slunk down in his seat. "Are you going to tell Jaxon?"

"No."

"Why not?"

"Because it's none of my business. But if it's obvious to me, it's probably obvious to someone else."

Bertie shook his head. "I doubt it. Jaxon wouldn't notice if the ceiling fell in on him. And everyone else is too self-involved."

I almost laughed. He might have a point. Besides most of the family was distracted by Caleb and Rose's antics.

"How long?"

"Six months. Maybe seven." He stared out the windshield. "We met when I drove for the studio. She helped me get the position with the family."

A car drove past. Then another. Normal people living normal lives. Or at least as possible in the Hollywood Hills.

"Are you in love with her?"

"Of course not."

Like that wasn't a lie.

He started the car, pulled away from the curb, then glanced over at me. "Besides no one is going to find out."

I hoped he was right. But I had a feeling that lies had a way of surfacing in this town. Much like bodies in swimming pools.

Chapter Thirty-Three

"Just drop me off here."

I didn't know what to expect from the Glasshouse. Maybe a sleek downtown bar with floor-to-ceiling windows, craft cocktails. Not this ramshackle corner building. The *G* was dark on the neon sign, so it read *lasshouse* in pink light. Paint peeled from stucco walls in long strips to reveal concrete like scars.

Bertie drove up the street and pulled into an empty parking spot. "I'll be waiting."

"Thanks."

I walked back to the bar. Solid black door with a small window covered in duct tape. Someone had spray-painted *CASH ONLY* in dripping silver letters.

I entered.

A few regulars hunched over drinks. Dim lighting hid sins or encouraged new ones. The bar ran along the far wall: scarred mahogany that had seen everything twice. Bottles lined the mirror behind it, liquor with names like *Kentucky's Finest* that had never so much as glanced at Kentucky.

A silver-haired woman polished perpetually dirty glasses.

I walked over to her. "I was hoping you could help me."

She raised her brows. "With?"

"A friend of mine was here last night. Left her coat behind. Green leather."

"That was your friend?"

I nodded.

She dropped her towel and crossed her arms. "She get home okay?"

Something in her tone made me pause. "Why wouldn't she have?"

The bartender shrugged. "Some guy was pouring drinks down her throat. Figured he was trying to get her drunk. I was about to go check on her when he left. Alone."

"Was he about my height, bit of a belly, thinning hair? Kind of looked like an accountant?"

"This guy was tall, good-looking. Dark hair, expensive clothes. Wore a Patek Philippe watch."

My stomach dropped. That was Jaxon. "He was buying her drinks?"

"Uh huh."

Maybe he was trying to get her to forget about the argument with Gordon.

"Did she leave with anyone?" I asked.

"I'll say. About twenty minutes later, cops showed up and arrested her for being drunk in public." The bartender leaned back against the cabinets behind her. "Dunno why. I was keeping my eye on her, and she wasn't being a pest. She was just upset about someone. Greg, I think."

"Gordon?"

"Yeah, that was it. Gordon. Figured she'd had a bad breakup or something. Who am I to intrude on someone when they want to drown their sorrows? That's the business model. Cops showed up and arrested her for drunk in public, but I don't know why. She wasn't causing trouble. Just upset."

I chewed on my finger. "Don't suppose you have security footage from last night?"

She narrowed her eyes. "Little young to be a cop, aren't you?"

"I'm just worried about her."

"That guy drug her?"

I hesitated.

"Shit." She jerked her head toward a door behind the bar. "Come on back, take a look."

I stepped around the bar and she led me through the door.

The back office: organized chaos. Empty bottles, invoice stacks, lost-and-found from the Carter administration. Nova's jacket on top.

I gestured to the jacket. "Do you mind?"

She waved her hand, squeezing past a filing cabinet that had seen better decades and settled behind the battered desk. "Go on."

The bartender switched on an ancient computer that wheezed to life like it was doing her a personal favor. The monitor flickered, then stabilized. She clicked through several menus, then stepped aside. "There we go. Take your time."

"Thank you," I said.

She nodded and left, closing the door behind her.

I went over and sat on the worn chair and looked at the screen. The timestamp showed last night at 9:47 p.m. I grabbed the mouse and scrolled forward, watching the bar fill with patrons.

Nova and Jaxon entered together at 11:23. She was clearly annoyed. Her posture was rigid and defensive as Jaxon gestured to the bar. *They definitely seem to be arguing about something.*

Jaxon pointed to an empty table in the corner. Nova went and sat, shrugging off her green leather jacket and draping it over the back of her chair.

Jaxon headed to the bar. I watched him order drinks. When he returned to the table, he set them both in front of Nova then took a seat. They leaned closed and started talking. Nova drank. Every now and then Jaxon would get up and fetch her another drink.

He nursed his drink while Nova downed hers.

Jaxon tapped his watched and pointed to the door. Nova grabbed his arm and shook her head. Even without sound, I could read her lips: *No, no, no.*

He shook her off, then pointed at her drink. She sat back in her seat, glaring at him. Jaxon took the moment to get up and walk to the exit.

Nova did the same, following him.

He stopped, glanced back. Looked pissed. Marched her back to the table, dropped her in the chair, and leaned his fists on the table.

Nova grabbed her drink, flung it at him. Whiskey splattered his face and shirt. He froze, alcohol dripping from his hair. Then he pulled out a handkerchief and wiped himself down. Nova collapsed, crying.

Jaxon stared down at her. Then he walked out, leaving her alone.

What had they been fighting about?

It certainly didn't look like Jaxon was trying to get her back home.

Maybe he had planned to check another bar but didn't want her to come? But why keep buying her drinks?

I kept watching, waiting to see if Jaxon came back. He never did. Nova remained at her table. She would occasionally stand, then seem to think better of it and sit right back down.

Then, just like the bartender had said, twenty-two minutes later, two uniformed cops walked through the door. They scanned the room and headed directly for Nova.

She tried to resist, clinging to her chair. They finally managed to shake her loose and marched her out. I waited to see if Jaxon came back.

He never did.

About an hour after Nova was taken out, the bartender collected her coat. I sat back, thinking.

Nova had wanted to go with Jaxon. That much was apparent, but he hadn't let her. Why? Maybe she had said or done something that upset him.

Maybe one of the other patrons had called the police. Several had been on their phones. I figured out how to download the footage and then emailed it to myself.

The bartender glanced over at me as I emerged from the office. "You see the guy who drugged your friend?"

I nodded, tucking Nova's jacket over my arm. "I did. Thanks again for letting me look."

She nodded.

I pulled out the card Detective Lopez had given me and forwarded the video file. She would probably be annoyed and accuse me of interfering or something. It really wasn't my business what Jaxon and Nova had been up to last night.

I walked to the SUV, knocked on the window. Bertie unlocked it. I climbed in.

"Took you long enough."

I held up Nova's coat. "They had trouble finding it."

Bertie pulled away from the curb. I rested my head back against the seat and closed my eyes. For the first time in a long while, I didn't keep watch for a gray car or black van.

Chapter Thirty-Four

BERTIE SLOWED the car as we approached the Marlowe estate. The police van and vehicles were finally leaving the property, but the reporters had multiplied like bacteria. Some of them even looked as though they were planning on camping out.

Wasn't there a law against this sort of harassment?

Bertie pulled up to the front gates and hit the button. I pulled Nova's green jacket over my head and ducked down.

I heard hands banging the SUV.

"It's Rose!"

"Any comment on the investigation?"

"Do you have some kind of statement?"

Someone tried my door handle and then they knocked on the window. Actually knocked. As though they expected me to roll down the window for an interview.

"Don't they know I'm a nobody?" I asked.

"Yeah, but one day you might be somebody," Bertie said.

I laughed. "I doubt it."

"Proximity to fame is a drug," he said, driving through the gates. I rested my cheek against my knees. Fame was supposed to be the pinnacle of success, but it was starting to feel more like a disease. Something that infected everyone in its path.

Anonymity was a blessing. The ability to walk down a street without anyone caring who you were. The freedom to make mistakes in private. Fame wasn't even something you had to earn anymore. Sometimes it just happened to you.

Bertie drove up the driveway, then he parked and killed the engine.

I sat up, pulling the jacket from over my head. "How did they get here so fast anyway? They were outside first thing this morning."

"They listen to police scanners for certain zip codes. Hunting for any drop of blood they can sniff out. Sharks with press passes."

"How long did it take you to get used to it?"

"I haven't, really. And I think that's for the best."

"I suppose so."

I opened the car door to get out, stopping when he leaned over and touched my shoulder.

"You promise you won't say anything about me and Willa, Zoe?"

I nodded. "But you need to consider doing it yourself. Before anyone finds out."

"I will. Things are just complicated at the moment."

Complicated. No kidding.

I entered the house through the front door, while Bertie went around to the alternate entrance. I hung up Nova's green jacket in the closet. It was quiet in the house. Maybe everyone had gone to bed.

Except I heard the TV in the living room. I walked down the hallway and spotted Rose sprawled on the couch, wrapped in the cream throw.

"I got Nova's jacket," I said.

"Mm hm." She patted the cushion beside her without moving her eyes from the screen. She was smoking a joint, the smoke curling up toward the vaulted ceiling.

I walked over and sat.

Rose passed me the joint. I held it like an assistant.

"Look." She nodded at the screen.

I watched a woman pacing her sunken living room in a halter-neck gown, cigarette in hand. Her hair was a perfect chestnut wave, her eyes defiant and glassy. She looked like a young Faye Dunaway.

Or a young Rose.

The woman on-screen clenched and unclenched her hands. "I won't put up with this."

Her pacing grew more aggressive. Like an animal testing its cage for weak spots. She stopped mid-stride and turned to the camera. "I'll get him. When he least expects it, I'll get him." The camera held on her face for a long moment. Rose paused the movie there, then reached out for the joint and I handed it back. She took a drag, exhaling slowly. The smoke drifted between us, but neither of us waved it away. "That's my mother."

"Isabella?"

Rose nodded. "Wasn't she beautiful?"

I studied the woman on the screen. Yes, she was beautiful. No wonder she became an actress. But it wasn't just her appearance. There was something magnetic about her performance, something that made it impossible to look away.

The camera obeyed her.

Rose took another drag, gestured to the screen. "I used

to study her films day in and day out, and yet I've never been able to hit that kind of emotional intensity and honesty. I wonder what I'm missing."

"I think you're good."

"Really?"

I nodded.

"Thanks." She blinked back tears. "I've made more than twice the films my mother ever did, but still I live in her shadow. Of course, it wouldn't be Hollywood if people weren't comparing women, right?"

"I guess not."

"I'm almost past my due date."

I frowned. "What do you mean?"

"I'm forty. That's like eighty for women in Hollywood years. The roles dry up. Unless you can somehow keep the public interested in you. And keep the tabloids tongues wagging."

"Did that happen to Isabella?"

"She died at thirty-eight. Her whole career happened before she hit forty." She took a long drag. "It's strange to think I've outlived her. And you know what's fucked up? I'm dealing with the same bullshit she did. Both of us called difficult when we asked for equal pay. Told we were divas for wanting script approval. Nothing ever changes in Hollywood. It just gets slapped with a new shade of lipstick."

"That's insane."

She grunted, leaning back against the couch. "You know what's insane? They're throwing away money. Proven box office draws, actresses who've spent decades perfecting their craft. Meanwhile, some guy gets to play action heroes and romantic leads until he's eighty. But a woman hits thirty-five and no one knows what to do with her."

She took another drag. Hit play.

The living room on the screen dissolved into a night scene; a pool surrounded by palm trees. Moody lighting, all blacks and silver highlights that gave everything an other-worldly quality.

A man stumbled into view, clutching his neck. He moved erratically, as if drunk or disoriented. His white shirt was pristine except for the dark red stain spreading from between his fingers.

Blood.

He stumbled along the edge of the pool, then stiffened and fell sideways. Landing in the water with a large splash. The camera lingered on the pool's surface while tendrils of blood spiraled outward from his floating body.

I got to my feet.

Rose looked over at me. "What?"

"That." I pointed to the screen. "Gordon was killed the same way."

Rose blinked, took another drag from her joint. "Not the same way. Not really."

"What do you mean? His throat is slashed. He fell in the pool."

"Yeah. I guess it is somewhat the same. Only he"—she gestured at the man with her joint—"was killed by his mother-in-law and Isabella is dead.

"Still. Don't you think we should tell Lopez?"

She shrugged. "It's just a coincidence."

I stared. A coincidence? Hollywood was its own world. I left Rose, headed to the guest room. Should I tell Lopez? Maybe it was just a movie.

I glanced over at my suitcase.

Had it been moved since I'd been out? I couldn't tell. I glanced around the room, then stuck out my tongue. If anyone was watching, I hope it gave them pause.

Then I pulled out my phone and started making notes, writing down everything I could remember about my stay with the Marlowes.

Chapter Thirty-Five

THE NEXT MORNING, I knocked on Talon's door. There was no response. I knocked again, a little harder this time. Still nothing. I inched the door open.

It was dark inside, the curtains still closed. I could make out a bundle in the bed, sheets pulled up high.

"Talon?"

"Yeah?"

"Want to go swimming? We can use the main pool."

"Don't feel good." His voice was thick, distant.

I frowned. "Some fresh air might help."

"No. I want to be left alone."

I hesitated. "I can grab a book? Read to you and—"

"No. Nothing. Just…please."

Leave me alone.

He didn't need to say it. I got the message. "Okay. But if you want to talk, let me know. You can even use your whistle."

He mumbled something I couldn't catch.

I went to see if I could find Rose, but she wasn't in the dining or living room, so I pulled out my phone and texted that Talon wasn't feeling well and that I was going to go for a short walk.

She responded with a thumbs up emoji.

I left the property, slipping out the side gate, keeping low so the reporters wouldn't see me. I rounded the corner and made my way up to Liam's spot. Then I hunkered down in the shade of a palm tree.

I pulled out my phone and dialed Elsa. It went straight to voicemail. I didn't bother leaving a message. She'd call me back when she had the chance.

I pulled up Frenchie's number next. Stared down at the digits for the longest time before I finally hit dial. The phone rang several times before going to voicemail. "Hey, it's me. I just…I just wanted to say that I miss you."

Then I disconnected.

Shit. Why did I say that?

I called back. "Sorry, ignore that last message. I'm just having a weird day. Everything's fine here. Call me back when you can. If you want. Or if you don't, that's okay too."

Oh my God.

I was making it worse.

I hung up, cringing, wishing I could take it all back.

I gazed out at the city. There were millions of people below, but I'd never felt so alone. Even Lyon Island hadn't been this lonely. At least there I'd had Frenchie.

My eyes started to feel heavy, so I made my way back to the house, sneaking in through the gate. Then I made my way to the guest room and took a nap.

Evening brought no improvement. Talon and Jaxon were missing from dinner. Gordon's empty chair. The dogs beneath it, catching chicken scraps from Willa.

Maxwell sat at the head of the table, his jaw working like he was chewing glass instead of lamb. "I'm going to find the bastard who killed Gordon. Offer a reward. Hundred thousand dollars."

Rose sighed. "Dad—"

"I liked the bastard," Maxwell said. "He was a good man. Solid. If someone wanted to kill one of us, why couldn't they have picked Olivia instead?"

Olivia cried out and grabbed the wine bottle, storming past the entering maid. The woman stumbled, nearly dropping her tray.

Willa rolled her eyes. "Well, that was rather dramatic."

"Or you," Maxwell said.

Willa glared at him.

Nova picked at her food.

Rose nudged her. "You need to eat something. You'll feel better." She turned to Liam. "You too. You're getting far too skinny."

"Stop changing the subject," Liam said.

Rose frowned. "What subject?"

"Which one of us killed Gordon. Because it was obviously one of us, right? I mean, who else has access to the house?"

"Liam…" Rose said.

"Come on. We all know this wasn't some random break-in. Someone in this family wanted Gordon dead and they made it happen."

"Don't be stupid," Willa said.

Maxwell waved his fork in the air. "The boy has a point. Which is surprising, given he's smoked nearly every brain cell away."

"Touché," Liam said.

"So are you confessing?" Willa asked.

Liam laughed. "It wasn't me. I was smoking pot in my room during the whole thing. High as a kite."

Willa took a sip of water. "That's not exactly an alibi,

Liam. Being stoned doesn't mean you couldn't have killed someone. And you don't have a witness."

"Neither do you."

"Actually, I was with Jaxon."

"Jaxon was out."

"He was home by then."

"Liar."

Rose chucked her fork onto the table. "Both of you stop it. Right now. Think of Nova."

I glanced over at Nova. She was staring at her plate. I couldn't actually tell if she were listening or not.

"What about you, Rose?" Willa asked. "Where were you?"

She recoiled in shock. "Caleb and I were asleep."

"Yeah, it's not like you were doing anything else with each other."

Rose flushed. "Excuse me?"

"Come on, Rose. Everyone knows your marriage is a sham."

"My marriage is none of your damn business."

"Everything in this family is everyone's business."

Rose raised her brows. "You want to talk about business? At least I have an actual job."

"My content has millions of followers."

"Your content is you being an asshole to your family for views."

"And you pretend to be other people, because being yourself doesn't pay the bills."

"It's called acting, Liam. It's an actual profession."

"So is mine."

"Filming yourself being a dick isn't a profession, it's a cry for help."

Nova picked up her plate and hurled it against the wall. It smashed into a thousand ceramic pieces.

We all sat silent, staring at her.

Then we heard yelling from somewhere deep in the house. Distant at first, then getting closer.

"Willa!"

The dining room door slammed against the wall. Jaxon stood there for a moment, wild-eyed before he locked onto Willa.

"Jaxon?" Willa half-rose from her chair. "What's wrong?"

Oh shit.

He'd discovered her and Bertie. That had to be it.

But Jaxon just crossed the room in three long strides and yanked her chair back from the table, dropping to his knees in front of her.

"Jaxon, you're scaring me—"

He wrapped his arms around her waist and pressed his face against her stomach. Then he started to cry.

Willa looked shell-shocked, her hands hovering over his head like she didn't know whether to push him away or offer him comfort.

"What the fuck is wrong with him?" Liam asked.

Willa patted his shoulders.

He pulled back and held out a small piece of paper. "Why didn't you tell me?"

Willa stared at the paper like it might bite her. "Jaxon…"

Liam reached over, snatched it from his hand, and glanced at it. "Oh shit."

Then Rose grabbed it from him.

"What is it?" Maxwell asked.

Rose blinked. "An ultrasound photo. Oh my God. Are you pregnant?"

Willa's face crumpled. Then she nodded, tears spilling down her cheeks.

Jaxon pulled away, patting at her like she was made of glass. "I never thought this day would happen. I can't believe it. Not after all those failed treatments. All those years of trying and losing hope and—God, I can't believe you didn't tell me."

I studied Willa's face.

Then a chill slithered down my back.

Bertie had said breaking up with Willa was complicated. Was he referring to this? Oh God. Was Jaxon even the father?

"Why didn't you tell us?" Rose asked.

Willa swallowed. "I guess I was too scared of miscarrying again. It happened so many times before, and I just…I honestly thought I had a stomach flu or something. I didn't want to get everyone's hopes up."

"How long have you known?" Jaxon asked.

Willa swallowed. "A few weeks. Maybe a month. I kept thinking it was stress, or maybe something I ate. I didn't want to take a test and be disappointed again."

Nova stood and stalked out of the room, slamming the door behind her.

Rose followed her out. "Nova?"

Jaxon grabbed Willa's hands. "I wish you'd told me earlier. We could have been celebrating this whole time."

"I'm sorry. I was just so scared after last time, and the time before that, and—"

"Don't apologize. We'll get you the best doctors, the best care. Nothing's going to happen to this baby."

Maxwell glanced over at her. "The last thing this family needs right now is another kid."

Willa paled.

I slouched down in my chair, wishing I had left with Rose. The temperature in the room plummeted ten degrees.

Jaxon got to his feet, glaring at his father. "Shut up."

Liam grinned.

Maxwell's face turned red. "What did you just say to me?"

Jaxon started. "Dad, I'm sorry. I didn't mean—I was just…the baby means everything to us, and you can't just—"

Maxwell stood, his chair scraping against the floor like nails on a chalkboard. "Don't you ever tell me what I can and can't say in my own house."

"Dad, please. I'm sorry. I shouldn't have said that."

Maxwell batted Caleb's arm. "Help me to my room."

Caleb nodded, taking the old man's arm and escorted him out of the dining room.

"Dad, wait." Jaxon scrambled after him. "Please. I was just being emotional. I didn't mean it."

The door slammed closed behind them both.

Willa sat there, staring at her hands. Then she got up without a word, picked up the ultrasound photo, and left.

Liam turned to me. We were the last two standing. Or sitting. "Well, that was fun."

A maid appeared in the doorway, looking nervous.

"What do you want?" Liam asked.

"The police are at the gate, sir."

"Again?"

"Yes, sir."

"Well, they might as well come in."

The maid nodded, then disappeared.

"Wonder what they want," Liam said.

I shrugged, looking down at my plate. I was hungry, but I didn't feel like eating. Still, I forced myself to eat a few bites of lamb.

The maid reappeared with Lopez.

"Sorry to interrupt," the detective said.

"Not at all," Liam replied. "We're getting used to it."

Lopez forced a smile, then turned to me. "Ms. Smith? I'd like to ask you to come with me down to the station."

"Is she under arrest?" Liam asked.

"Just some questions. And I'd prefer to ask them somewhere more private."

My stomach dropped. I followed her out, feeling Liam's eyes on my back.

Chapter Thirty-Six

I'm in the back of a police car again and I've never felt this tense before. Lopez ignored me, chatting with the driver about weekend plans. Her kid's birthday party. Mundane details that felt surreal.

We descended from the Hills, leaving the Marlowe fortress. The setting sun caught palm trees lining Mulholland, casting long shadows.

The Hollywood sign looked small from here. Smaller than it seemed in movies. Just white letters on a hillside, faded and unremarkable.

We turned onto Highland Avenue, descending into the Hollywood chaos. Tourist buses clogged the intersections. Street performers worked the corners. Along the Walk of Fame, I saw people taking photos with their favorite star.

We passed billboards advertising movies I'd never see. The officer driving made a comment about how Highland was always a nightmare this time of day.

I glanced out the window. People heading to dinner and shows. To whatever passed for nightlife in a city that never quite slept or fully woke up.

We hit Sunset Boulevard and turned east. There were fewer tourists now. More locals. The buildings got shorter. Neon signs more desperate. Tattoo parlors. Bail bondsmen. Check cashing stores with bars on the windows.

This was the Los Angeles they didn't put in movies. The version most tourists never saw. A city that existed between the dreams.

We turned south and the police station loomed ahead. Gray concrete. Flat windows reflecting the evening sky.

The sun was still hanging on but losing its battle with the night.

The cop parked around back.

The driver escorted me into the building, walking me along a hallway of interview rooms. The doors were closed but I heard crying behind one of them. Someone having the worst night of their life.

I was escorted to an interview room. Inside were two metal chairs and a table.

And then the cop left me. Not that I was alone. There was a camera mounted up high on the ceiling. Red light blinking like a warning. A poster on the wall let me know that the room was monitored.

No doubt Lopez was watching me.

I went and sat at the table. I could feel the cold metal chair through my jeans. I folded my hands in my lap. Linked my fingers together to keep them still. And waited.

I tried my best not to look like I was anxious or nervous.

But my heart was hammering against my ribs and my palms were damp. The fluorescent lights buzzed overhead, casting everything in that harsh institutional glow that made everyone look guilty of something.

The minutes crawled by. Each second felt like an hour.

I listened to the humming air conditioner. Footsteps in the hallway outside. Whoever had been crying had stopped.

I hoped that meant their day was getting better.

I tried to avoid looking at the camera.

The door finally opened.

Lopez entered with two cardboard cups of coffee and a file tucked under her arm. She settled into the opposite chair and set one of the cups in front of me.

Then she laid the file folder on the table. "How are you feeling, Zoe?"

"How do you think?"

Lopez took a sip of her coffee, ignoring the question. "I wanted to thank you for sending through the security footage. That was some smart thinking."

"Thanks." I picked up my cup and raised it to my lips. It was hot. Almost scalding. I set it down again.

"Do you know why you're here?"

"No."

Lopez flipped open her file folder. Inside was a photo of the knife she'd showed me the other day. The one with the carved handle. The one that killed Gordon.

She pushed it over to me. Then leaned back in her chair, sipping her coffee. Watching me over the rim of her cup like a cat eyeing a mouse.

"You already showed me that."

"Whose fingerprints do you think we found on it?"

"I don't know."

How could I know? It could be anyone's. The whole family had access to that kitchen.

"Yours."

I froze, looking up at her. "Mine?"

Lopez nodded and set down her coffee. "How do you explain that?"

"We used those knives at dinner the night Gordon

died. I guess someone took it then. It's not like I went through the utensil drawer grabbing knife handles."

"Don't you think it's a bit odd that out of all the knives in the house, that particular one was chosen?"

I thought back to the blood found in my shower. "Not if someone is setting me up."

"But why you, Zoe?"

I shrugged. "Maybe because I'm an outsider?"

She leaned back, studying my face. "Were you blackmailing Gordon?"

I gaped. "What?"

"Blackmail. Extortion."

"No!"

Lopez reached into her file folder. Pulled out another piece of paper and set it on the table in front of me.

I looked down at it. My whole world tilted and shifted.

"Fingerprints don't lie, do they?"

It was my mugshot. Fifteen years old. Staring out at me from across years of carefully constructed lies. There were bruises under my eyes. My hair was short and messy. Acne on my cheeks. I looked so small and scared. The kind of terror that comes from realizing the adults you trusted have thrown you to the wolves.

I glanced down at the name printed beneath the photo. *Zoe Smitts.*

Not Zoe Smith. Smitts. The identity I'd tried to leave behind. The girl who thought she was doing the right thing, only to find out she was making a terrible mistake. One that came with jail time.

"Do the Marlowes know who you really are?"

The detective's voice seemed to come from very far away. Like I was underwater. Like I was drowning.

I felt like I was going to cry. But I couldn't let the tears fall. Not here. Not in front of her. Not with that camera watching. I couldn't talk. My throat had closed up. The words were stuck somewhere between my chest and my mouth, refusing to come out.

I grabbed the coffee cup. Lifted it to my lips. Swallowed.

The bitter liquid burned all the way down, but I welcomed the pain. It was something to focus on that wasn't the photograph. That wasn't the name.

I was me. Zoe. Not the person in the picture. At least not anymore.

Lopez waited. Patient as a spider.

Because the fly was already in the web.

"No. They don't. No one does."

"The nanny service?"

I shook my head, clenching my teeth together. I didn't think so. Or had Madeline also uncovered this?

Lopez picked up another piece of paper. "Says here you were arrested for extortion. That you scammed a man out of ninety thousand dollars. You claimed he sexually assaulted you and he paid to keep you quiet. Only it turns out that he didn't do that, did he?"

I didn't say anything. What was there to say? Facts were facts. Court records didn't lie. The guilty plea was there in black and white, signed by me.

"Do you have anything to say?"

I shook my head.

It didn't matter that I was innocent. I had pled guilty to keep my father out of jail.

"Looks like you got thirteen months in juvenile detention."

I cleared my throat, nodding. "I did my time. And that has nothing to do with this."

"That's up to me to decide." She leaned forward and rested her elbows on the table. "Gordon hired that P.I. to investigate you, not his dead wife. New person in the house, close-knit family. Hatch dug up your record. Gordon confronted you."

I met her eyes. "And then I cut his throat and called for help?"

"Why not? It'd make an excellent alibi."

I felt cold. "So how did his blood get in the shower then?"

"Maybe it was put there earlier. Part of your story."

I pointed to her paperwork. "That's supposed to be sealed."

"Yes."

"Am I under arrest?"

"We're just having a conversation."

A conversation. Like we were old friends catching up over coffee. I put my coffee cup down. Then I got up and walked to the door with far more bravado than I was feeling. "I'd like to leave now. Please."

Lopez sighed, then got to her feet. "I'll have an officer drive you home."

"No. I'll find my own way."

I couldn't bear the thought of sitting another police car. I needed air. And space. Lopez opened the door, then led me back down the hallway to the reception area.

"I don't want you leaving LA for the next little while."

"Don't worry," I said. "I have nowhere else to go."

I made my way across the lobby and walked into the humid LA night.

Chapter Thirty-Seven

I stumbled out of the LAPD onto the sidewalk. Gray civic buildings loomed like tombstones. My phone rang. I ignored it.

I started running. Maybe trying to outrun the past? I wove around homeless camps sprawling between municipal buildings. Six years ago, Dad and I lived in his car. I still went to school somehow. He got me judo lessons. I think he promised my teacher something in exchange.

I hope he got paid. But probably not.

I slumped in the passenger seat, my judo gi still damp with sweat. All I wanted was to go to the community center, take a hot shower, and then go to the library and finish my algebra homework, but Dad had other plans.

"Just one quick stop, Zoe."

I crossed the road. Horn blared. A Tesla roared past, its driver flipping me off. I slowed down and forced myself to breathe.

"Dad."

"This is time-sensitive, kiddo. Big opportunity." His voice had

that edge it always got when he was working an angle. The same tone he used when talking to his "investors" on the phone.

I headed northwest past Echo Park's gentrified coffee shops. Industrial elements turned into expensive design choices. Sanitized hardship as lifestyle branding for people who'd never been poor.

I didn't bother to argue with him.

The sooner he saw his client, the sooner I'd get my shower. This wasn't his usual type of client. We were driving past sprawling estates with circular driveways and fountain features that probably cost more than most people's cars. Or at least our car.

Dad pulled into the driveway of a home that was all stone and glass and unnecessary columns.

New money.

He had a nose for it.

"Stay here." He checked his reflection in the rear-view mirror.

"Gladly." I had no intention of joining him.

I kept walking. Soon, Silver Lake's indie record stores and vintage boutiques gave way to East Hollywood's chaos. Taco trucks were parked next to nail salons, and Thai restaurants were wedged between check-cashing places. The traffic got denser, more aggressive.

I leaned into the backseat and got my algebra book. I watched Dad walk up to the front door, shoulders back, confident. He knocked, and after a moment, a man answered: middle-aged, soft around the middle. They shook hands.

Dad pointed toward the car. The man looked my way, then nodded and waved me over.

I swallowed bile. How naive I'd been back then.

Dad walked back over to the car.

"Good news," he said, opening my door. "Rick says you're welcome to come in. You can hang out in the kitchen and do your homework while we talk business."

I hesitated. "I really don't mind waiting here."

"You're gonna get cold, Zoe."

He was right about that, so I took my book and followed him the front door. Dad introduced us.

"Zoe, Rick. Rick, Zoe."

Rick shook my hand, barely gripping it. "Pleased to meet you."

Highland Avenue swarmed with tourists, phones out, snapping pictures. Hollywood Boulevard ahead—fame packaged for consumption.

Rick showed me into a kitchen that was bigger than any apartment I'd ever lived in: granite countertops, stainless steel appliances, an island in the center that could seat six people.

"Make yourself comfortable," Rick said. "There's drinks in the fridge, chips in the cupboard."

"Thanks."

Then he left. I listened for a moment, trying to hear if there was anyone else in this massive house. But it seemed to just be him. I walked over to the stainless-steel refrigerator, stuffed with food. Sushi, leftover chicken, potato salad, lasagna.

My stomach growled.

But it seemed weird to eat someone else's food. I took a Coke from the drinks holder (imagine having one of those!), then sat on a stool at the island.

The El Capitan Theater's marquee blazed against the dark sky, its vintage letters promising magic that had long since curdled. Slowing my pace didn't stop the memories from coming.

It was strange, sitting in a stranger's kitchen trying to do my homework.

I finished my Coke fast, still parched from judo.

I tried to focus on my homework, but my mind kept wandering. What did Dad really do? I had no idea. He was an investor, but that was about the extent of my knowledge. He'd never invited me to a job before.

I stopped in front of a street performer with her guitar

case open, hoping for spare change. Probably hoping to hit it big. Just like Dad.

After we'd been at Rick's for half an hour, Dad appeared in the kitchen. "How's it going, kiddo?"

"Can we go soon?"

He nodded. Checked his watch. "Another twenty minutes, and then we can get out of here."

He walked to the fridge, got out another Coke, cracked the can open, and handed it to me. "By the time you're done, I'll be ready to go."

I had thought about chugging it, but I had a feeling that's not what he meant.

I turned back to my algebra. Within minutes, the numbers on the page seemed to swim. I was more tired than I thought.

The dizziness got worse. The kitchen started to tilt, and the pencil felt impossibly heavy in my hand.

I walked along. And that's when I saw it. Isabella Marlowe's star, right there in the sidewalk between a souvenir shop selling "I ♥ LA" T-shirts and a museum showcasing wax figures from horror movies. I stopped, staring down at her name etched in the pink terrazzo.

"Dad?" I tried to stand, but my legs felt like they were made of concrete. I gripped the island and slid off the stool.

I needed to find Dad. Something was wrong. I stumbled down the hallway, using the wall for support. I didn't even know where I was going. Or where he was. I just needed to find him.

I made it to the living room and collapsed in the hallway, my knees hitting the hardwood floor. Rick lay sprawled on the Persian rug, motionless. Dad was standing over him, looking down at him.

"Dad."

He started and turned towards me. "Zo?"

"Dad?"

And then my world went black.

I stared down at Isabella's star. She'd drowned thirty

years ago, leaving behind a bunch of damaged children who wore whistles around their necks like talismans against tragedy. But someone had laid a rose atop her star. So not forgotten yet.

I woke up in the passenger seat of Dad's car, my head stuffed with cotton. A metallic taste in my mouth. We were parked in the community center parking lot.

"Hey, you're awake."

I sat, rubbing my head. The clock on the dashboard read midnight. That couldn't be right. Where had the last five hours gone?

"What happened?"

Dad reached out and took my hand. "That man—Rick—he drugged us. Both of us."

For a moment, the neon chaos around me felt like it belonged to another world. But no, it was this one. And it had just collided with my past.

"Why?" I asked.

"He wanted to take advantage of you, sweetheart. Thank God I came to before he could hurt you." He reached over and squeezed my hand. "I got you out of there as fast as I could."

A wave of gratitude washed over me. Dad had saved me from something terrible. Even though it didn't make sense. Because...

"Why was Rick on the floor?"

Dad shook out his hand, rubbed his fingers. "I punched him when I figured out what he did."

I froze. "You shouldn't have done that. What if he calls the cops on you?"

"He won't. He knows I'd expose him for being a pervert."

I stepped away from Isabella's star, looking around at the tourists posing for selfies, the costumed characters harassing people for tips, the street vendors hawking fake Rolex watches. Was any of this actually real?

Three weeks later, the police pulled us over on our way to judo. Took us into the station. Sent us into separate rooms. A detective displayed a series of photos in front of me like we were playing cards. Me unconscious, Rick lying over me.

I vomited.

"Mr. Hendricks says nothing actually happened. And that you've been extorting him for cash," the detective said.

I made my way to the cement wall outside the TCL Chinese Theater and sat.

I shook my head. "No."

"That's not what your father says," said the detective.

I stared at him. What?

"Says that he knew nothing about this. It must have been something you came up with to help pay the bills."

I couldn't talk.

And when I was finally released, Dad was waiting for me in the lobby. He tried to take my arm when we left, but I pulled away from him.

He ran after me, catching up. "You're a minor. You'll get a slap on the wrist, but I got priors. They'll throw the book at me."

I stopped. "What do you mean, you've got priors?"

"Come on, Zoe, you're not stupid."

And that's when I realized it. Dad was a con artist, not an investor. He'd used me.

"You drugged me."

He said nothing.

I punched him in the chest. "I could have died."

"No. I tested the dose."

"On who?"

And then I remembered I'd had no trouble falling asleep the past few weeks. Not that I felt rested. I woke feeling groggy each morning. I punched him again.

"I hate you!"

"Fair enough. But you need to plead guilty."

I walked away.

"Zoe?"

I ignored him.

But I did take the fall. I don't know. Maybe I thought it would help him out? Make him change his ways? Or maybe it was because at that point I still wanted him to love me. I still wanted a Dad.

I got thirteen months in juvenile detention, surrounded by kids who'd done things I couldn't even imagine. During that time, I learned that the only person I could trust was myself, because even the people who were supposed to love you would sell you out when it suited them.

It was a terrible lesson.

One I was still trying to undo.

But tonight, Detective Lopez had made it clear that some lessons never left you, no matter how far you ran or how much you tried to change.

Chapter Thirty-Eight

I PULLED out my phone to see who had called.

Frenchie.

I swallowed. Hit my messages. Sure enough, he'd left one. I pressed the voicemail button and put my phone to my ear.

"Zoe?" His voice came through crackling with static. "It's me…miss…next…okay?"

His voice faded in and out on the words, swallowed by interference and distance. I strained to hear, pressing the phone harder against my ear as if that could somehow sharpen his message. But it didn't.

I played it back, cranking the volume all the way up. It didn't sound any better. The static was only louder. I caught something that might have been "love" or "hope." Or maybe I was just imagining things.

I called him back.

The phone rang and rang. No answer. I tried again. This time it went straight to voicemail. I didn't bother to leave one.

What could he possibly do? He was thousands and thousands of miles away.

"You alright, love? Did you get some bad news?"

I blinked, looking up through my tears at a woman wearing a T-shirt with Wisconsin on it and reading, *curd nerd.*

I wiped my face with the back of my hand. "I'm fine."

"Are you sure? Do you need a lift somewhere?"

I shook my head. "I've got someone picking me up."

She looked unconvinced. I was an emotional wreck on a cement wall outside Mann's Chinese Theater. I forced a smile.

"Really, I'm fine. Someone's coming to get me any minute."

She nodded, but I could see she wasn't entirely buying it.

I lifted my phone, pretending to check it before waving my hand toward the cars lining the street. "Actually, there they are now."

She glanced over at the vehicles as though trying to figure out which one I was indicating. "Alright. You take care of yourself, love."

"Thank you," I said, and I meant it.

I got up from my perch and walked toward the street, heading for a brown car. I glanced back. She was still watching. I waved.

She waved back and turned to her friend.

I darted off when she looked away, running down Hollywood Boulevard until I found a quiet spot away from the main crowds.

I dialed Bertie's number. The phone rang twice before he picked up.

"Zoe? You okay? I heard the cops picked you up."

I swallowed. "Would you be able to come get me? I'm…" I looked around, for the street signs. "At Hollywood Boulevard and Orange Drive. Near Mann's Chinese Theater."

"Are you alright?"

"I'm fine. I just need a ride back to the house."

"Okay. Stay put. I'll be there in twenty minutes. I'll text you when I'm close."

I sat on the curb. LA's nightly performance continued around me, vibrant and alive. I felt like a ghost haunting the edges.

I hated that Detective Lopez had managed to drag my past all the way from New York to Los Angeles.

After I got sentenced, I didn't see Tania or my dad for thirteen months. They never once came to see me. Tania told me it would be too hard to see her baby in jail.

I snorted.

More likely she and Dad were enjoying the money they'd taken from Rich. I knew they had gone to Europe at least once. Who did that when their kid was behind bars?

I never spoke to Dad again. But Tania…well, I had to live somewhere.

I called Madeline.

"Zoe? What's wrong?" Her voice was thick with sleep.

"I'm sorry to call so late, but I need to ask you something. Did you give my phone number to anyone?"

A long pause, then, "Who would I give it to?"

"Anyone."

"Absolutely not. Client confidentiality is sacred, Zoe. You know that."

"Thanks. Sorry I woke you." I hung up before she could ask more questions.

But she texted: *Tell me what's going on.*

I typed back: *Getting a bunch of unknown calls. Guess they must be pranks.*

I pulled up Tania's number and unblocked it. Hit the green phone icon. It rang four times. I was about to disconnect when she answered.

"Zoe? Do you know what time it is?"

"How dare you."

She paused. "Excuse me?"

"How. Dare. You."

"Jesus Christ, Zoe. I already apologized about the damn money. I'd return it if I could, but—"

"This isn't about the money."

Tania sighed. She could probably give Rose a run for her acting money. "What then? I can't read your damn mind."

"Dad."

"What about him."

"You gave him my number."

"Oh." Her tone shifted to something nonchalant, almost bored. "What's the big deal?"

"What's the big deal?" I got to my feet. My voice rose, and several tourists turned to stare. I didn't care. "He nearly destroyed my life."

"Oh, come on, Zoe." I heard the TV in the background. She'd switched it on. "Don't be so dramatic. He made a mistake."

"He drugged me. Made me take the fall for him."

"That was years ago. People change."

"Not him."

"Now that's not fair, Zoe."

"Not fair?" I tightened my hold on the phone. "Do you want to know what's not fair?"

She sighed again. "I have a feeling you're about to tell me."

A horn honked. I looked up to see the black SUV

pulling up to the curb. Bertie rolled down the window and waved.

"You know what? Never mind. I hope you two are happy together."

I killed the call and walked over to the SUV. I got in up front next to Bertie, buckled my seatbelt, and he pulled away from the curb. We drove in silence for a few minutes, the city lights streaming past the windows.

My phone rang. I glanced at the screen. Tania. I needed to block her again. I hit decline.

It pinged almost immediately with a text. I swiped.

He seemed genuinely sorry about everything.

I typed back: *Fuck off.*

Then I blocked her number again.

"You okay?" Bertie asked.

"I'm fine now."

"You don't look fine. What did the police want?"

I shrugged. "More questions about the night of Gordon's murder."

"That it?"

"Yeah." I eyed him. "You reporting back to the family?"

He flushed. "No. Jesus."

I sniffed. "Sorry. I'm just a bit on edge."

I stared out the window at the twinkling lights of the city below. What the hell. I might as well tell him. I had a feeling the family was going to find out sooner or later.

"The cops found my fingerprints on the knife that killed Gordon."

He turned to me, staring. The SUV drifted left, crossing over the double yellow line. Headlights appeared in front of us.

I pointed. "Look out!"

He glanced up, then yanked the wheel hard, swerving

back into our lane. The driver of the oncoming car leaned on their horn until they'd passed. "Sorry about that. So … did you? Kill him, I mean?"

I glared at him. "No!"

He held up one hand. "Sorry, sorry. I was just kidding. Bad joke."

I crossed my arms. "Yeah, well, I'm not in a joking mood right now."

"I can see that." He continued to drive. "Besides, I know who really killed Gordon."

I stiffened. "What? Who?"

"Caleb."

"Caleb? Why?"

"I'm pretty sure Rose and Gordon were having an affair. Caleb found out and killed him."

"Rose and Gordon?"

"Yeah."

"Do you have proof?"

Bertie shook his head. "No, it's just a suspicion. But someone mentioned the possibility, and I thought it made sense."

"Who mentioned it?"

He shook his head. "It was just in passing."

"Well, I never saw Rose and Gordon even talk all that much."

"What better way to keep it under wraps? Avoid each other in public."

"Maybe."

He glanced at me. "Who do you think killed Gordon?"

I stared out at road. "No idea. But I don't appreciate being set up to take the fall."

Bertie turned onto Mulholland. "I can see why they might, though."

I turned to look at him. "Why?"

"Think about it. If you're supposedly Maxwell's spy, which is what everyone seems to think you are, then Caleb gets to kill two birds with one stone, getting rid of the guy who's sleeping with his wife while eliminating you and whatever secrets about him you've uncovered, leaving him free to take over the company."

"I don't know any secrets about Caleb."

"He doesn't know that though, does he?"

I frowned, considering. Twisted logic, but it felt forced. Like jamming puzzle pieces into place that didn't naturally fit together. "I don't know, Bertie. That sounds like a stretch."

"Does it?" Bertie navigated a hairpin turn. "You don't have any secrets about the family? Nothing you've overheard or seen that might be damaging? Make someone try and get rid of you?"

"I haven't been here long enough to discover anything worth killing someone over."

"You sure about that? Sometimes we notice things without realizing their importance."

Maybe Gordon found out about his affair with Willa. And Bertie had killed him to shut him up. That made more sense.

I pulled my jacket tighter, feeling alone despite Bertie beside me.

Chapter Thirty-Nine

THE WATER WAS warm against my skin. I'd been swimming laps and counting strokes. The chlorine smell disappeared, replaced by a metallic taste. I stopped mid-stroke and looked around, treading water. The pool had turned crimson.

Blood. I was swimming in blood.

I swam toward the edge of the pool. But no matter how fast I went, it stayed fixed in the distance like a cruel mirage, always out of reach.

I was getting tired. The blood was everywhere now. In my mouth, my nose, coating my skin like syrup.

I heard a splash behind me.

I twisted around.

Gordon.

He swam toward me. But something was wrong. His eyes were glassy, and he wasn't blinking. His skin was pale.

I kicked away, trying to put distance between the two of us.

But I couldn't get away.

He reached out and grabbed my ankle.

I tried to kick him off. "Let go!"

But he held tight.

The pool started to dissolve around us. The tiles, the concrete, the palm trees. They all melted away. And we were falling, into deep water, pressure building in my ears. Far above, the sun kept shrinking until light disappeared altogether.

And now it was pitch black.

I couldn't breathe. I couldn't breathe. I couldn't—

I jolted awake, my heart racing. The sheets were damp with sweat, twisted around my legs and pinning them in place. I kicked my feet free. My phone's blue glow cut through the pre-dawn darkness: 5:47.

Too early to be awake, but sleep felt impossible now.

A text notification blinked on my screen.

Elsa. *Thinking about you.*

I sent back a simple heart emoji, not trusting myself to form actual words yet. I shivered, pulling the blankets back over me, my forehead to my knees.

The nightmare clung like a second skin. I forced myself up, then into the shower. Hot water, trying to restore normalcy. Dressed and dried my hair.

I climbed back into bed and reviewed my notes. Typing up my suspicions about Bertie. Not that I really believe he had killed Gordon. But why all the questions? And who had brought up Gordon and Rose having an affair?

I stayed in my room until eight. Then I went and knocked on Talon's door. "Hey, it's me."

No response.

I cracked it open.

Talon was still in bed, covers pulled up to his chin, staring at the ceiling. Dark circles shadowed his eyes.

I walked over and sat on the edge of his bed. "Feeling any better?"

He shrugged.

"Do you want me to get your mom or dad?"

"No!"

I flinched.

He met my eyes. "Sorry. I'm fine, okay? I just want to be left alone right now."

"Talon—"

"Please, Zoe. I just need space."

I nodded. "Alright. But I'm going to tell Rose you're still not feeling well, okay?"

He frowned. "Do you have to?"

"Unless you want to do it."

He shook his head. I patted his leg, then left the bedroom and went downstairs. Rose was alone in the dining room, sipping on a cup of coffee.

"Rough night?" she asked.

I nodded, walking over to the coffee. "Nightmares. And I'm worried about Talon. He seems to be spiraling a bit."

"I know. I called his therapist. Got him an appointment this morning." She watched me pour out my coffee. "Maybe you should talk to someone too."

"Maybe." I took my seat at the table, wrapping my hands around the warm mug, letting the heat seep into my palms.

"If you need a recommendation, let me know."

"I will."

Family trickled in: Liam. Nova. Willa. I braced myself for questions.

"What did the police want?" Nova asked.

"To go over the night of Gordon's death."

She raised her brows. "Again?"

I nodded.

"And that was it?"

Did she know about my fingerprints being found on

the knife? About my criminal record? If she wanted direct answers, she could ask direct questions.

"That was it."

She grunted.

Liam looked pale.

"Where's Molly?" I asked. I couldn't remember the last time I saw her.

"No idea. We broke up."

"Oh. I'm sorry. I didn't realize."

He shrugged. "No big deal."

Had finding a dead body at the house cause them to split? Or did she suspect Liam of Gordon's murder?

Nobody seemed to have much of an appetite that morning. Nova picked at a piece of fruit, Willa stared at her cereal, and Rose barely touched her coffee.

Jaxon burst in through the door, stacking his plate with toast. "Beautiful morning, isn't it? I swear to God the sun seems brighter today."

Nova glared at him. "Could you not?"

His smile faltered. "Not what? Be happy? Be sorry that I'm not wallowing in misery like the rest of you?"

Nova slammed her fork down. "Gordon's dead."

"I haven't forgotten. But I'm going to be a father!" He tossed his butter knife on the table. "And I'm not going to apologize for being excited about something good happening in this house of doom."

Willa pushed back from the table and walked off.

"Now look what you've done," Jaxon said.

I finished my coffee, then excused myself.

A splitting headache built behind my eyes. Everything too bright and too loud. I collapsed on my bed, palms pressed to temples.

Half an hour later I heard voices in the hallway.

"But why does Dad have to come?" Talon asked.

"It's family therapy, sweetheart," Rose said. "*Family*."

Talon mumbled something. Footsteps faded. The house quieted and I started to doze…

I jerked awake and glanced at my phone. It was two hours later. Something had woken me.

I got out of bed and opened my bedroom door. I heard a scraping sound downstairs. Maybe one of the dogs needed to go out? Willa seemed to have taken charge of their feeding, but I had no idea if she was walking them regularly.

I headed down to the living room. And stopped.

Liam lay on the floor, convulsing. His arms and legs jerked against the floor, which explained the scraping sound. Foam gathered at the corners of his mouth.

"Liam!" I ran over and dropped to my knees, rolling him onto his side to protect his airway. I grabbed a throw pillow from the couch and wedged it under his head to stop him from hitting it.

"What's wrong?"

I glanced up. Nova stood in the hallway. "He's seizing. Call 911."

She dialed 911 and gave them the address.

I rested my hand on his shoulder. "It's okay," I told him. "You're going to be okay."

But I had no idea if he could hear me.

"They're on their way," Nova said, walking over to us. "I've texted the guards to let the ambulance in. My God. The vultures are going to have a field day with this. Stupid asshole. What a time to overdose."

"It's not that at all. He's epileptic."

Nova snorted. "No, he's not. Guarantee it's drugs. Some designer cocktail he invented for clicks. Idiot."

But then she sat with us, resting her hand on Liam's head.

The EMTs arrived. He'd stopped seizing but stayed unconscious.

"Bertie's out with Caleb, Rose, and Talon," Nova said. "And I don't drive. Take me to the hospital?"

She didn't drive?

"Of course. I'll just grab my shoes."

I ran to my room to get them and my purse, then met up with Nova in the front hallway, where she tossed me the fob to Gordon's Porsche.

Jaxon came down the stairs as we headed out. "What the hell is going on? I heard sirens."

Nova ignored him. "Get the car, Zoe."

"Will do." I ran to the garage, slid into Gordon's Porsche, adjusted the seat and mirrors, then threw the car into reverse. Nova got in and I gripped the wheel with trembling hands. How to get past the reporters?

Turned out, most of them had followed the ambulance. Vultures, indeed.

"Where am I going?" I asked, driving down the hill.

"Turn left at Laurel Canyon." Nova's phone rang. She glanced at the screen and let it go to voicemail. It rang again. And then again.

"Jesus, Jaxon." She switched it off.

"Don't you want to let him know what's happening?"

"He can go to hell."

I didn't press the point. Not my business.

"Why did you say Liam was epileptic?" she asked.

I glanced at her, before focusing back on the road. "He had a seizure the day we went to the observatory. He told me he was epileptic."

"He never mentioned that to anyone else." She gestured to the intersection. "East on Sunset."

Soon, the hospital came into view. I pulled up to the emergency entrance and Nova jumped out.

"You want me to wait?"

She nodded. "Meet me inside."

Finding a parking spot took forever. I locked the car and called Rose, but it went straight to voicemail.

"Rose, it's Zoe. We're at Cedars-Sinai. Liam had some kind of a seizure at the house. Nova's with him now and I know you're in therapy but call me back."

I hung up and sent her a text: *Left urgent voicemail. Liam at hospital.*

I headed for the emergency doors, wishing I'd gone back to New York when Madeline made the offer.

Chapter Forty

THE PLASTIC CHAIR bit into my spine. I'd been sitting in the same position for forty minutes, staring at medical posters that might as well have been written in hieroglyphics. F.A.S.T. for stroke symptoms. Cartoon soap bubbles demonstrating proper handwashing. Heart attack warnings in English and Spanish, because cardiac arrest was apparently bilingual.

The emergency room hallway stretched endlessly in both directions. Nova paced back and forth in front of me like a tiger, clutching her phone.

I checked my phone again. Still nothing from Rose. Where were they? The family therapy session couldn't still be going on, could it?

I leaned my head against the wall, staring up at the fluorescent lights.

Then I heard a commotion at the far end of the hall. I turned to see Rose, Talon, and Caleb all coming toward us.

"What happened?" Rose asked.

Nova shook her head. "Don't know. We're still waiting to see the doctor."

Talon sat beside me. "Is Liam okay?"

"I don't know," I replied with a frown.

We sat together for almost an hour before the emergency room doors swung open and a doctor emerged. She scanned the waiting area, then walked over to us.

"Liam Marlowe?" she asked, raising her brows.

"Yes," Nova nodded. "We're the family."

She glanced at Talon, hesitating.

I got to my feet. "Why don't I take Talon—"

Caleb stepped forward, reaching out for Talon's hand. "I'll do it."

He jerked away. "I want to know what's wrong with Liam!"

Rose eyed her son. "Go with your father."

"No!" He stamped his foot. "I'm old enough to know."

She clenched her teeth. "Talon."

Then he stormed off down the hallway. Caleb glanced at Rose, then followed after him.

The doctor looked from Rose to Nova. "Liam's brain tumor has shown significant growth since his last scan."

Nova paled.

Rose's mouth fell open. "Brain tumor?"

The doctor looked genuinely surprised by their reaction. "You didn't know?"

They both shook their heads.

She rubbed the back of her neck. "He has stage 4 Glioblastoma multiforme."

"What the fuck is that?" Nova asked.

"Cancer."

Rose's face crumpled. Her shoulders shook as tears spilled down her cheeks, and she pressed her hand to her mouth to stifle a sob.

"He'll need to stay for a few days while we stabilize him."

"What's his prognosis?" Nova asked.

The doctor hesitated.

Rose swallowed. "How long?"

"Maybe two to three months."

The hallway seemed to tilt around me. Months. Not years, not even a full season.

Rose broke into tears again. "That asshole."

"Can we go in and visit him?" Nova asked.

The doctor nodded, pointing to the door she'd just come through. "Of course. He's in room five. Just don't tire him out."

Rose wiped her eyes with the back of her hand, trying to compose herself. Nova took her hand and gave it a squeeze.

"Zoe," Nova said. "You might as well come in too."

I hesitated at the threshold. This wasn't my family. It wasn't my grief to witness. But Nova gestured me forward, and something in her expression said she needed witnesses to this moment. So I followed them through the sterile corridor, past rooms where other families held their own vigils, until we reached room five.

Liam's skin had taken on the waxy pallor of old candles. The IV line snaked from his left arm like a lifeline he didn't want, and the heart monitor's steady beeping counted down something none of us wanted to measure. But his ridiculous grin still stretched across his face, as if dying was just another prank he was pulling on the world.

"I guess the gig is up, hey?" he said.

Rose pulled away from Nova and walked over to him. "Cancer?"

"Seems so."

She punched him lightly on the arm. "How dare you not tell us!"

"Ow!" He clutched his arm, wincing.

She recoiled. "I'm so sorry, Liam."

He laughed. "Just kidding."

Nova glared at him. "Cut the shit."

His grin flickered and then died like a candle in wind. For the first time since I'd known him, Liam looked his age. Fragile, mortal, afraid. "I thought about telling you. But it's not like anyone could help me. Besides, it was too late by the time I found out."

"When?" Nova asked.

"Three months ago. Just thought it was headaches from the drinking. So I stopped. But the pain continued."

Rose leaned down and hugged him.

He shrugged. "I probably deserve it."

"Don't say that," Rose said, her eyes filling with fresh tears.

What could Liam have possibly done to make him think he deserved to die?

Kill Gordon?

"Does Molly know?" Nova asked.

"I suppose now is the time to tell you she's not my girlfriend."

"What?" Nova said.

"Molly is my nurse. She was trying to keep me comfortable at home. Because there's no way in hell I'm dying in a hospital. She wanted me to tell the family. And I refused. So she quit." He glanced over at me. "Bet you would never have taken the job if you'd known what a shit show this family was."

I forced a smile. "I've had worse."

A weak chuckle escaped his lips, barely more than a wheeze. The sound seemed to take everything he had. His head dropped back against the pillows and a coughing fit seized him, each hack sending tremors through his thin frame. Rose reached for the glass of water on the bedside table and held it to his lips. He swallowed. "Thanks."

She brushed the hair back from his forehead. "What am I going to do with you, Liam?"

His eyes softened. "You have a lovely family. You'll be just fine."

Rose's smile was all surface, like ice over deep water. Her eyes confessed that she was already grieving.

The door opened, and Caleb entered with Talon. His face was red, blotchy from crying. He ran straight to the bed and threw his arms around Liam.

"Are you going to be okay?" Talon asked.

Liam's hand came up to rest on his back. "No, I'm not kid, but you'll be alright. You got the best mom and dad on the planet and they'll take great care of you."

Talon burst into tears.

I walked over to Rose. "I could take Talon home if you'd like."

She nodded. "That might be a good idea."

"No!" Talon pulled back from Liam. "I don't want to leave!"

"Hey, I'll be home in a couple of days, okay?"

Talon studied Liam's face. "You're not just saying that to get rid of me?"

"I swear. And soon as I get home again, we're going back to that damn observatory and anywhere else you want to go. We'll do all the things before we can't do any of them."

Talon gripped his hand. "Okay."

Rose touched my arm. "Bertie is bringing Jaxon and Maxwell if you want to wait for a ride."

I showed her the fob to Gordon's Porsche. "I brought Nova."

She nodded, then gave Talon a big hug. "We'll see you at home."

He hung onto her for a moment, then let go. I held out my hand. At first, I thought he'd refuse to take it, but then he did. He kept looking back at Liam until I led him out the door.

We made our way out of the emergency room and into the lobby.

Talon stopped. "What's wrong with Uncle Liam?"

I looked down at him. His face was drawn, scared. More than anything, I wanted to take the pain away. To lie. But I told him the truth. "He has a brain tumor."

He blinked up at me. "Cancer?"

I nodded.

His fingers tightened in mine.

We walked outside to the parking lot. I stopped beside the Porsche.

A man in a dark jacket emerged from behind a white SUV. Tall, in his forties, with thick lips. I'd see him before. But where?

One of the paparazzi outside the Marlowes?

No, it was the Russian who'd talked to me on the street. What was he doing here?

Was he paparazzi as well? Hoping to get photos of… what?

A black van screeched up alongside us, its side door already sliding open. A hooded man crouched inside.

Oh shit.

The Russian man lunged, grabbing my upper arms, his fingers digging into my flesh.

I shoved Talon toward the hospital entrance. "Run!"

I reached into my purse and yanked out the taser. My hands shook as I jammed it against the Russian's ribs and pulled the trigger.

He bellowed, then convulsed, his grip loosening as he dropped to the pavement, twitching.

I turned to run after Talon, but another man had already jumped from the van. His hands clamped around my waist, lifting me off my feet.

I kicked and screamed.

Talon glanced back over his shoulder, meeting my eyes.

"Hey!" He whirled around and charged like a tiny bull, sneakers slapping against asphalt, glasses bouncing on his nose, thirteen-year-old fury and desperation driving him forward.

The hooded man vaulted down from the van. Scooped Talon up mid-charge and hurled him away.

Talon's small body slammed into the car door with a thud that echoed off the concrete.

"Don't touch him!" I screamed.

Hands seized me and hurled me into the van's darkness.

I hit the far wall shoulder-first, my knees cracking against the metal floor. Pain shot through my body like lightning.

The driver vaulted out and dragged the still-twitching Russian by his armpits, heaving his dead weight into the van beside me. The man's head lolled at an unnatural angle.

I scrambled toward the open door on hands and knees, my fingers stretching for freedom, for air, for Talon.

The door slammed shut like coffin lid.

Darkness swallowed me. The engine roared to life and we rocketed forward, tires shrieking against the concrete. Through the van's thin walls, I heard Talon screaming my name, his voice growing smaller and smaller until the hospital parking lot, and any hope of rescue, disappeared behind us.

Chapter Forty-One

I THRASHED like a hooked fish in the back of the van, my screams bouncing off metal walls and coming back to mock me. The Russian rolled on the floor, moaning. The hooded man grabbed my hands and zip-tied them behind me.

I fell forward onto my belly while he secured my ankles. Then a black cloth bag was thrown over my head.

"Quiet," a voice said.

I tried to calm my breathing, but panic clawed at my chest. The cloth bag over my head made everything worse: the suffocating darkness, the musty smell of old fabric, my own trapped breath muggy against my face.

"What do you want?" I asked.

The men ignored me, starting up a conversation as if I hadn't spoken. I struggled against the restraints, testing their strength.

Then one of the men nudged by shoulder. "Chill, lady."

"You chill."

He laughed.

God, I sounded like an idiot.

Rough hands grabbed my shoulders and hauled me upright against the van's wall. My spine pressed into corrugated metal, but sitting up instead of sprawled on the floor made me feel less like cargo and more like a person who might survive this.

I recoiled when one of the men touched my thigh.

"Nyet, nyet." A second later, he'd taken out my phone.

Damnit. But not unexpected.

The vehicle continued to drive.

I tried to keep track of the directional changes—right, left, left, right—but I was far too disoriented with the bag over my head. And there were several times when we seemed to go in circles. They were probably trying to make sure we weren't being followed.

Time lost all meaning. I had no idea if we were driving for minutes or hours.

"Where are you taking me?" I asked.

"You'll see soon enough."

I forced myself to focus on what I could control. My breathing. Staying alert. Listening for any clues about where we were going or what they wanted. But the few words they spoke all sounded Russian.

One thing was clear: this wasn't random. They'd known where to find me and had obviously followed us to the hospital. This was connected to the Marlowe family somehow. But they hadn't wanted Talon, only me.

Their conversation shifted, then they all burst into laughter. I caught the faint sound of cheering, excited voices. It took me a moment to realize what I was hearing.

They were watching sports. Some kind of a game.

I twisted my wrists against the plastic ties, feeling them bite into my skin. They were way too tight to slip through. I kept working at them anyway, turning my hands different ways, stretching my fingers, testing every angle for some kind of weakness or give.

But no luck.

I needed to try something different.

I explored the space behind me, searching for anything useful. I felt along the edges where the van floor met its sides, looking for a loose bolt or sharp edge, anything that could cut through my restraints. But there was nothing.

The men cheered again—someone had scored.

I forced myself to think. They hadn't killed me immediately, which meant they needed me alive for something. Information, maybe? Or leverage against the Marlowe family? But what could I possibly know that would be valuable to them?

My mind raced through everything I'd witnessed since arriving at the estate. There had to be something bigger at play here, something I'd stumbled into without realizing.

The van whipped around another corner without warning. My body slammed into the metal wall, my skull cracking against the unforgiving surface. Stars exploded behind my eyelids. I bit my tongue to keep from crying out —showing weakness felt dangerous here.

My head throbbed, but I forced myself to focus. Every turn, every stop, every voice might be the key to getting out of this alive. Whatever these men wanted, whatever warehouse or basement they were dragging me toward, I had a sinking certainty that once we arrived, the bag over my head would be the least of my problems.

"My family will be looking for me. They'll know I'm missing."

Silence.

I kicked my leg out, my foot connecting with the wall. The sound echoed through the interior and everything went silent. Even the game. "What's going on?"

"Soon enough," a man said. "So stay quiet, else we'll have to make sure you're quiet."

"Is Talon okay?"

"Who?"

"The kid I was with."

"Kid fine. Ran away."

I hoped that was true. Hopefully he'd gotten the license plate and raised the alarm.

What could they possibly want with me? I was a nobody—

Unless…

"Does my dad have anything to do with this?" I asked.

"Dad?"

"Victor."

"No Victor."

Okay. So nothing to do with my family.

Their game resumed.

The van began to slow, brakes squealing as we took a sharp right turn. Then another turn, this one slower.

I had a feeling we were nearing our destination.

I started to breathe more heavily.

A hand patted my back. "Alexi wants to talk."

Having a name made this real in a way I didn't want it to be.

The van came to a complete stop. The engine shut off.

The side door slid open with a metallic scrape and I started shaking.

Sound echoed around us. We were inside a warehouse or some kind of large building. Cool air rushed in, carrying the smell of motor oil and dust. I felt hands grab my ankles, then a sharp tugging sensation. Then my feet were loose. They'd cut me free.

Hands grabbed my arms, hauling me out of the van.

Conversation swirled around me in Russian. I heard at

least four or five different voices, maybe more. How many people were here? It sounded like a lot. Footsteps echoed off what sounded like high ceilings.

They walked me forward like a blind woman, my feet shuffling across smooth concrete, then over a raised thresh-old. Each step felt like walking toward my own grave. The warehouse floor felt smooth, then I felt a slight rise—a threshold. We entered what seemed like a smaller space from the way the sound of our footsteps changed.

"Sit," someone said.

I lowered myself onto a heavy wooden chair.

A hand grabbed my ankles. "Stay still."

Zip ties were fastened to my ankles, binding them to the chair legs.

The footsteps left. A door closed. Silence.

I was alone.

Or was I?

"Hello?"

No response.

I whipped my head side to side, trying to shake the bag loose, but it clung to me like skin. I rubbed my face against my shoulder, trying to push it up, but whoever put it on knew their business.

I tested the chair. It was solid. Even if I could tip it over, I'd still be trapped. Only I'd be lying on the floor. I twisted my wrists against the plastic ties behind my back. No luck.

So I waited.

And waited.

I heard the door finally open. Footsteps approached. The cloth bag was yanked off my head.

I squeezed my eyes shut. If I couldn't identify them, maybe they'd let me go.

A voice sounded in front of me; thick Russian consonants followed by silence. The man cleared his throat and spoke again.

A blade touched my ankle, sharp and deliberate. The zip tie snapped, then blood rushed back to my feet in a cascade of pins and needles. The knife moved to my wrists. One slice, and my hands fell forward, clumsy and numb.

I rubbed circulation back into my fingers while someone laughed at my covered eyes.

"Look," said a voice. Not a request.

I dropped my hands and opened my eyes.

The man standing before me could have stepped out of a corporate boardroom, if corporate boardrooms specialized in kidnapping. Expensive charcoal suit, crisp white shirt, no tie. Salt-and-pepper hair slicked back, his blue eyes studying me like I was a spreadsheet that didn't add up.

"Alexi?"

"Da."

"Why did you kidnap me?"

The man—Alexi—spread his hands wide. "I apologize for the manner of delivery. Was supposed to be invitation for friendly chat, but you got spooked."

I stared at him. "Spooked? Your men attacked me. Scared me half to death! Talon too!"

His brow furrowed. "What is Talon?"

"Not important. What do you want with me?"

He looked genuinely confused, as if I should already know. "The movie."

"What movie?"

"*Marvelous Devils 3.*"

What the fuck was he talking about?

Chapter Forty-Two

"*Marvelous Devils 3?*"

"Da."

"Wasn't it in theaters last year? "

Alexi nodded.

Some superhero trainwreck that died faster than a mayfly. I'd seen the trailers. Video game CGI and dialogue written by someone who could only approximate conversation. The kind of franchise-killing disaster that made studios pretend they'd never heard of sequels.

Alexi adjusted his Rolex. "I put seventeen million into project. I want my money back."

Seventeen million dollars. "Okay."

"Jaxon tell me he double whatever I invest. Safe franchise. Guaranteed returns."

"I'm not sure what this has to do with me. I don't know what Jaxon does with the business."

Alexi folded his arms across his barrel chest. "Jaxon say spy in papa's house. Watching. Until she backs off, no money. Papa doesn't like Russian rubles."

The spy.

Me.

Not that Jaxon knew it. Or did he?

I glanced toward the door. Two men in jogging suits stood on either side of it. One was picking his teeth with a toothpick. The other was watching his phone.

"So," Alexi said. "You back fuck off, da? Then I get money."

I stared at him. "I'm not a spy. I'm the nanny."

Alexi's face went blank, like his brain had just blue-screened. "*Shto?*"

I gestured toward the door. "I was with a kid when your men picked me up. That's my charge."

Alexi looked over his shoulder at the men at the door. "Nanny?"

The one with the toothpick shook his head. "Is not possible. Kid was taller than her."

"He's thirteen. Growth spurt." Besides, most thirteen-year-olds were taller than me. I wasn't exactly imposing. I spread my arms wide. "Do I look like a spy?"

Alexi tilted his head, studying me. "Spy never look like spy. Everybody knows, da?"

I held out my hand, waggled my fingers. "I can prove it. Give me my phone."

Alexi hesitated. Then nodded to one of his men.

The toothpick man tossed me my phone. The screen was cracked. Great. Something else to spend money on. I swiped open and pulled up Google.

It's hard to type when your fingers are shaky and sweaty. I had to wipe them on my jeans twice. Then I typed: *Hamptons, Darren, deceased,* and a bunch of other words.

Several articles popped up. Thankfully, the internet never forgot anything. I clicked on the first one from News 12 Long Island.

Man Attacks Nanny, Killed in Truck Collision.

There was a photo of the road blocked off by crime scene tape. Police cars. An ambulance with its doors hanging open.

It felt like a lifetime ago.

I scrolled down.

And there it was. A smaller photo embedded in the article. Me, looking a complete disaster, face streaked with dirt and tears.

I held out my phone. "That was me. My previous charge before this one."

Alexi took the phone from my hands, reading the article. Then he turned around and started yelling.

It was quite spectacular. Rapid-fire Russian with what I could only assume were some truly creative curse words based on the way his two men cowered. Alexi's face turned an alarming shade of crimson as spittle flew from his mouth. He gestured at the phone, then at me, then at his men.

I kept my head low. I didn't want to get caught in the crossfire. Alexi turned back to me. "Then tell me—why I still wait for money?"

I shrugged. "Maybe because the movie bombed."

He clenched his teeth. "Movie bomb?"

I shrugged. "I don't know. Talk to Jaxon."

He waved a finger in my face. "You tell Jaxon Marlowe he have twenty-four hours. Bring my money, or I make problem. Big problem."

I swallowed. "Okay."

Alexi tossed me my phone, then turned and walked out of the room. The door slammed shut behind him.

The toothpick man gestured to me. "Come on."

I stood. "Where are we going."

"Home."

I stared at him. "What?"

He laughed. "You think we kill you?"

The thought had crossed my mind. More than once. "I was picked up and thrown in the back of a van. What was I supposed to think?"

"We investors, not killers. Alexi wants his money back. He is…how you say…behind on child support."

Child support. Jesus. Even Russian mobsters had normal life problems.

"What about that stuff about making a bigger problem?" I asked.

He laughed. "Alexi only means he bring lawyers."

I wasn't sure I bought that.

The toothpick man held out the cloth bag. "Please. Office location is secret."

I tucked my phone in my pocket, then walked over and grabbed it. My hands were still shaking. I stuck the bag over my head, then he took my arm.

"We walk."

He steered me through a labyrinth of echoing corridors. Muffled voices drifted from behind closed doors. Russian syllables I couldn't decode. Somewhere an engine coughed to life, its rumble vibrating through the floor.

We stopped. I heard the van door slide open.

"Step up," the Russian said.

I stepped up into familiar metal darkness. At least this time my hands were free, my head uncovered. Small victories.

I heard the front passenger door close. And then we were on our way.

I held my breath, listening for breathing, shifting fabric, anything that would tell me I had company back here. Silence. I eased the hood off my head. Empty metal walls stared back at me.

I was alone. The two men were sitting up front.

Through the windshield: strip malls bleeding into fast food chains, a nail salon with Korean lettering, a tire shop advertising deals in English and Spanish.

We stopped at a red light.

I inched toward the door.

Ahead stretched LA's daily punishment: eight lanes of brake lights painting the asphalt red, bumper-to-bumper purgatory that could turn a five-minute drive into an hour-long vehicular prison sentence.

The driver threw up his hands. "*Yebúchie próbki!*"

"Da, da," said toothpick man.

The vehicle slowed. And then stopped because of the traffic.

I lunged, grabbing the van door handle and yanked. Bolting out of the van and hitting the pavement hard. A car horn blared.

I ran.

Straight into traffic.

A sedan swerved around me, the driver laying on the horn. A pickup truck slammed on its brakes. I could smell the burning rubber.

I glanced behind me.

Toothpick man stood beside the van, arms spread in genuine bewilderment. "Hey! Where you go? You don't want ride home?" He sounded hurt, like I'd rejected his grandmother's cooking.

I kept running. Weaving between cars. Dodging mirrors. Someone threw a water bottle at me.

I made it across the first four lanes by pure adrenaline and dumb luck. A Honda Civic missed me by inches. The driver—a middle-aged woman with mirrored sunglasses—swore at me. I couldn't hear her over the traffic noise, but I could read her lips well enough.

The median strip was just a few feet of concrete and some scraggly plants that had probably never been watered. I paused there for maybe two seconds before plunging into the second half of my suicide run.

A delivery truck laid on its air horn. A motorcycle swerved around me.

"Get off the fucking road!" someone yelled.

I kept running. Sweat pouring down my face. But finally I made it to the other side. I stumbled onto the narrow shoulder, my legs shaking so hard I could barely stay standing.

And still I kept following the highway's curve. The shoulder was barely three feet wide—just enough room to walk if you didn't mind the risk to life and limb.

I heard a door slam. Was that the men?

I glanced back. Oh shit. White van. But there was a woman driving. Not the Russians.

I turned back around.

My foot caught a chunk of broken concrete and I tripped.

And then I was falling.

I tumbled over the edge and down the hillside. Gravity took over and I became a human pinball, bouncing off rocks and bushes and chunks of debris that had probably been accumulating in this spot since the freeway was built.

A branch whipped across my face, leaving a burning line of pain. Something glass or metal tore through my shirt and scraped along my ribs.

I tried to grab onto something, anything, to stop my fall. But everything I touched just came loose in my hands. Dry grass. Brittle twigs. Handfuls of dirt.

The world spun around me in a nauseating kaleido-scope of brown earth and blue sky and the cacophony of traffic. I hit the bottom with a pounding thud that rattled my teeth and knocked every molecule of air from my lungs.

For a long moment, I just lay there in the dirt. Staring up at the strip of cerulean sky visible between the canyon's edges.

My phone was somewhere nearby. I could hear it buzzing against a rock.

Above me, the traffic continued its endless rush.

Chapter Forty-Three

FLUORESCENT LIGHTS HUMMED their dental-office song overhead, draining all warmth from my reflection. The mirror showed me a stranger: hollow-eyed, scraped raw, wearing exhaustion like poorly applied makeup.

Half my face looked like I'd used sandpaper as a washcloth, the worst of it hidden under white medical tape and gauze. My knuckles were wrapped like a boxer's, and my right knee bulged under layers of bandages that made my leg look deformed.

X-rays at the hospital had shown nothing broken. Small mercy.

The hospital had given me a generic gray T-shirt that hung on me like a tent. My original shirt had apparently been turned into confetti by my tumble down the hillside. I couldn't remember losing it, but pain had a way of editing memories.

I washed my hands best as I could, looking down at my forearm. A bruise was already forming, dark purple against my pale skin.

The washroom door opened. A cop peered in. "Miss Smith?"

"I'm coming."

I followed her down the corridor to an interview room. This one was nothing like the one I'd been in before. This one had leather chairs. Toys scattered on a small table in the corner. A hamper full of blankets. It looked like a therapist's office.

A basket of chocolate bars sat beside a box of water to my left. She gestured to it. "Help yourself."

Then she left.

I walked over to the table and stared at the basket. My stomach growled. I hadn't eaten since breakfast. I grabbed a chocolate bar and tore it open. I devoured it like I'd been stranded for weeks, then grabbed another before I'd finished swallowing.

The sugar helped. My hands stopped shaking. I took a water bottle, then I sank into one of the leather chairs.

I was halfway through my second Snickers when someone knocked on the door. I swallowed. "Come in."

Detective Lopez entered. "Zoe."

"Hi."

She took the leather chair next to mine. "You scared the hell out of the Marlowes."

I uncapped the water and took a long drink. "Is Talon okay?"

"Shaken up but unharmed. He wanted you to know that he called the police as soon as you were taken."

I smiled.

Lopez leaned back in her chair. "Would you like to tell me what happened?"

"I think it was a business dispute between the family and someone else. For some reason, they thought I was involved."

Lopez pulled out a small notebook. "Why is that?"

I fiddled with the bottle of water. "They thought I was the spy."

She blinked. "*The* spy?"

"Keeping tabs on the family for Maxwell."

"Why would Maxwell want to spy on his family?"

"He's thinking of turning the business over to one of them, so he wanted to see who was most worthy. At least that's what they told me."

"And you're not this spy?"

I hesitated. "Not at first. I really was hired to be the nanny."

"But?"

"It changed. Maxwell wanted me to observe his kids while I was there."

"And you agreed to this?"

I thought about the tuition money. "Yes."

Lopez made a note. "Tell me about the kidnapping."

I rubbed my head and winced. A lump was already forming. "They were Russian. I didn't get the plate on the van."

"That's alright. The hospital cameras caught it."

"They did?"

She nodded. "It was stolen."

"Oh. Well, after they grabbed me outside the hospital, they threw me into a van. Zip-tied my hands and feet. Put a cloth bag over my head." I took another sip of water. My throat felt raw.

"Did you get their names?"

"Just one. Alexi. He wasn't one of the van guys. He was later."

"Alexi. No last name?"

I shook my head.

"And then what happened?"

"They drove me to some warehouse where we met Alexi. He wanted to know why Jaxon wouldn't pay back his seventeen-million-dollar investment in *Marvelous Devils 3*."

Lopez blinked. "*Marvelous Devils 3*, the movie?"

I nodded.

"Jaxon told them he couldn't pay until after the spy left."

"And you got away how?"

"I convinced them I was just the nanny and they offered me a ride home. but I didn't believe them. I got out on the freeway and ran. Fell down a hillside trying to get away."

We went over the incident four more times. Lopez asked me questions about their appearances, the location, the vehicle. Would I be able to recognize the van? The location? The men?

I did my best to answer every question, but I was getting tired. And then a commotion erupted in the hallway outside the door. Voices. Running footsteps.

The door burst open, then Talon ran into the room, followed by a cop who glanced over at Lopez. "Sorry, Ma'am."

She waved her hand: no problem.

Talon came over and wrapped his arms around me, trembling. "I called the cops."

I held on tight. "You did good. You saved me."

"Why don't you go home," Lopez said to me. "I'll be in touch if I have further questions."

I nodded. "Thanks."

The cop escorted us through the station's maze of corridors and out to the parking lot, where Rose paced beside Bertie's SUV like a caged panther.

She ran over and pulled me into a hug. "You brave girl."

Then she set me back and looked into my eyes. Hers were filled with tears. "You saved my son."

I forced a smile. "That's what you pay me for."

She hugged me again.

Then she tucked me into the back seat and got into the front beside Bertie. Talon clambered in beside me, grabbing my hand, holding it tight.

"I'll keep watch for gray cars," he said.

"Thanks. But I don't think they'll be coming after me anymore."

Bertie started the engine. Rose twisted around to face me. "Who were those men?"

"Russian investors. Or at least that's what they said."

"Russian?"

I nodded.

Rose stilled. "One wasn't named Alexi Orlov by chance?"

I started. "I don't know his last name, but his first name was Alexi. You know them?"

Rose clenched her teeth. "They were nosing around a couple of years ago. Jaxon wanted to have them invest, and I told him under no circumstances were we funding a movie with Russian mob money. I can't believe he took it."

"Well, they want it back."

"Not before I kill that asshole."

Every muscle in my body began broadcasting its own personal pain report. I sank into the seat, eyes closed, feeling like I'd been run through a cement mixer. Paparazzi still swarmed the gates like antibodies attacking an infection.

This time, I didn't bother hiding. Let them take their

pictures. Bertie navigated the chaos, and we were inside the compound before I knew it.

Jaxon met us in the foyer. "Thank God, you're okay."

Rose punched him. Hard. Right in the face.

He stumbled backward, hand flying to his nose. Talon's mouth fell open, and he stared at his mother like she'd just sprouted wings.

Rose shook out her hand. "Ah! I broke my fingers."

Jason felt his nose. "What the fuck did you do that for?"

"You put Talon in danger."

"How?"

"Alexi Orlov."

He blanched. "What about him?"

"He fucking kidnapped Zoe. His men put their hands on Talon."

"Shit. Rose, I'm sorry. I didn't mean to let it get this far."

"What does that mean?"

"The company was hemorrhaging money. What was I supposed to do?"

Rose threw her hands wide. "I don't know. Try making movies that make money instead of these putrid remakes and sequels."

"You think it's that easy?" His voice cracked. "I'm trying to save the company Dad built."

She planted her hands on her hips. "I bring in more revenue than your entire slate of disasters."

"Box office receipts say otherwise."

"Fuck you. *Marvelous Devils 3*? Seriously? You green-lit *garbage*."

"The first two made money."

"The first two had decent scripts. The third one had sixteen writers."

Jaxon grabbed tissues from a side table, pressing them

to his nose, stemming the flow of blood. "The investors wanted a franchise. Something reliable."

"Reliable?" Rose laughed. "You borrowed seventeen million from Russian mobsters for a superhero movie that made twelve dollars opening weekend."

"They're not mobsters, they're investors."

"I don't give a shit what they call themselves." Rose bunched her hand into a fist. "They kidnapped my nanny. Terrorized my son."

"I was protecting the family business."

"You were protecting your own incompetent ass."

I glanced at Talon, then left them to it and headed down the hallway to my room. My body felt heavy. Exhausted. The adrenaline was finally wearing off.

I entered my room, closed the door behind me, kicked off my shoes, and dropped onto the bed.

There was a knock on the door.

"Come in."

Talon appeared in the doorway, looking smaller and younger than his thirteen years. I opened my bedside drawer and pulled out the silver whistle. The chain caught the light from the lamp. "I think I'm gonna wear this from now on."

"Wait a minute." Then he disappeared, returning moments later, whistle in hand.

We looked at each other. Then we both put them on at the same time.

"I was really scared," he said.

"Me too."

"Really?"

"Really."

He walked over and gave me another hug. "I'll let you get some sleep."

I nodded.

Then he left and I lay down, closing my eyes.

The house settled around me. Footsteps in the hallway. A door closing somewhere upstairs. I pulled the blankets up to my chin. The whistle lay heavy on my chest.

I clutched it, feeling safer.

Help was only three sharp blasts away.

If only Isabella had been so lucky.

Chapter Forty-Four

SOMEONE WAS KNOCKING on my door.

I peeled myself out of bed like old wallpaper. My ribs felt cracked, my shoulder throbbed, and my scraped face pulled tight when I tried to open my eyes fully.

Rose stood in the hallway outside my door. Her hair was pulled back in a messy ponytail. Dark circles shadowed her eyes.

Her perfect facade had cracked. Mascara smudged beneath her eyes, hair escaping its ponytail in rebellious strands, silk blouse wrinkled like she'd slept in it. "We're vacating the house."

"You're leaving?"

She nodded. "I'm not keeping Talon here until after Jaxon has figured out how to repay the Russians. Maxwell and Nova aren't going, but we're not staying and you're coming with us."

"I should probably tell Madeline."

"I already did. We're going to move to the yacht. Temporarily. We never use it anymore."

Like the car.

"So no one should think of looking for us there," she continued. "Not even the paparazzi. Meet us out front in half an hour?"

I nodded.

She made her way down the hall.

I closed the door behind her. Grabbed my carry-on from the closet and threw in my jeans, underwear, T-shirt, purse and phone charger.

I caught sight of myself in the mirror. Hair sticking up. Face scratched to shit. I went to the bathroom and checked beneath the sink for the first aid kit. Added a bunch of bandages to my bag.

Quickly changed and went and downstairs to the living room.

Jaxon paced the living room. His face red with rage, phone pressed to his ear. "That fucking bitch!"

Rose appeared. "Now what's happened?"

"Willa and Bertie," Jaxon said.

"What about them?"

"They've run off together."

I swallowed. I guess Bertie and Willa had decided to uncomplicate the situation.

Rose stared at him. "Willa and Bertie?"

"Apparently." Jaxon scowled. "They left sometime last night. Her clothes are gone. So is he. Along with fifty thousand from the safe."

"What about the baby?"

"Apparently not mine." Jaxon strode off to the stairs. "And good riddance."

Rose glanced at me, then shrugged. "Do you mind driving us to the marina?"

"No, I can do it."

We made our way outside. I put my bag in the back of

the SUV, then circled around to the driver's side. The keys were already in the ignition.

Caleb appeared with Talon. He had a single backpack slung over his shoulder and was carrying two suitcases.

Caleb reached for the bags. "I can get those."

Talon pulled away. "I'm fine."

"Talon—"

"I said I've got it."

He loaded the luggage into the back of the SUV, then climbed into the back seat, slamming the door behind him.

Rose got in beside him. Caleb leaned in and gave her a kiss.

Olivia appeared with a bag. "I'm coming too."

Rose shook her head. "No. You're staying with Maxwell. I don't want him to be alone."

"But the staff are here. Plus Nova. And Jaxon."

"If you leave my father," Rose said, "I'll make sure you won't get anything in the divorce."

Olivia paled. "What divorce?"

Rose slammed the door. "Let's go. Caleb will meet us there tonight."

The engine roared to life. Then I made my way down the driveway, and was surprised to see the paparazzi were gone.

Rose glanced at me. "Mandy Peters murdered her agent last night."

"And?"

"Fresh blood."

Right.

I navigated down Mulholland's serpentine curves, then merged onto Sunset, where billboards for streaming shows towered over manicured palms like digital gods presiding over paradise.

"Stay on this road for a while," Rose said.

The morning commute hadn't started yet—just a scattering of early risers in luxury cars or luxury jogging gear. A food truck dispensing overpriced coffee to people who could afford both rent and avocado toast. Easily the most relaxing car trip I'd had since coming to the city.

We drove past a Whole Foods. A Tesla charging station. A boutique selling thousand-dollar handbags to women who collected them like trophies.

Talon's head dropped back against the headrest. Dark circles rimmed his eyes. He looked as tired as I felt.

"Now right. Toward the coast."

I hit the blinker and turned.

The neighborhoods shifted again. Mansions behind gates. Then condos. Then nothing but scrub brush and the occasional coyote warning sign. I could smell the ocean before I could see it.

"That's it up ahead," Rose said.

Marina del Rey spread out below us like a city on water. Thousands of boats organized in perfect rows, hundreds of masts swaying like a forest. The parking lot was smooth asphalt marked with crisp white lines. A security booth sat at the entrance, manned by a guard in a pressed uniform who waved us through at the sight of Rose.

I headed for the parking lot and pulled in between a Bentley and a Maserati, then we climbed out and retrieved our luggage.

"This way." Rose led us over to the marina entrance. A white building made of glass. Marble floors and crystal chandeliers.

We bypassed the reception area and walked out through another set of doors. The main dock was wide as a street. Built on concrete pilings that disappeared into the dark water. Lamp posts lined the path, bases bolted to the planking.

We passed a motor yacht, its name painted in silver script: *Tax Write-Off.* A sailboat with a mast that stretched up to the sky like a telephone pole beside it.

The slips got larger as we walked. Forty-footers became sixty-footers. Then eighty.

A crew in matching polo shirts washed down a yacht named *Merger & Acquisition.*

And then I saw it.

The yacht rose out of the water like a wedding cake. Four decks stacked on top of each other. Maybe more.

"Welcome to the *Reel Escape,*" Rose said.

Gold letters curved across the stern. Below them, smaller text: *Marina del Rey.*

The *Reel Escape* made the neighboring yachts look like dinghies. A gleaming white hull and tinted glass rose from the water like a floating mansion, its twin exhaust stacks reaching skyward like chrome exclamation points. It may have been old, but the ship was pristine. The cost of maintenance alone must be staggering.

I followed Rose and Talon onto the vessel.

Rose opened a glass door the size of a storefront window. "Come on in."

The white leather furniture looked museum pristine. A dining table stretched along one wall. Mahogany, maybe, dark enough to see my reflection.

Eight chairs surrounded it. White leather with chrome legs.

The flat screen dominated the wall like a portal to another dimension. A hundred inches of black glass. The kind you saw in sports bars, not living rooms.

Movie posters hung in gold frames. Rose's face smiled

down from two of them. *Summer's Child* and *Midnight in Morocco*. The others showed actors I didn't recognize.

"Come," Rose said, leading us downstairs and along a hallway lined with doors. My feet sank into the cream-colored carpet as we walked.

Rose stopped at a door and opened it. "This is your room, Zoe."

I looked inside. A queen bed with white sheets stretched tight enough to bounce a quarter off. A porthole looked out onto the marina.

"Talon is beside you."

He pushed past us without a word. Then slammed his door.

Rose sighed. "He's not thrilled about leaving the house."

"I can tell."

"Caleb and I will be upstairs. Let me know if you need anything."

I nodded, setting my bag down.

"Anything else?"

"Actually, I have a question."

She gripped the doorframe. "Are you quitting?"

"What?"

"I wouldn't blame you. This whole situation…" She released the door and gestured toward the window. "It's not exactly what you signed up for."

"No, I'm not quitting."

"Ah. You're wondering if I still want to keep you on."

I nodded. "I've barely nannied Talon at all. Between the hospital and the Russians and Gordon…"

Rose stepped into my cabin and closed the door behind her. "Things will calm down. And then you and Talon can spend some time together."

"He's such a competent kid. He doesn't really need a babysitter, Rose."

"No, he doesn't."

"Then why?"

She paused. Then let out a long sigh. "I wanted Talon to have a friend."

I blinked. "A friend?"

She nodded. "I grew up on movie sets. Never had any real friends my age. Just other child actors, and that's not the same thing at all. It was all competition and stage mothers and bullshit."

"Don't you think kids his own age would be better for him?"

She laughed. "I tried that. But he finds them boring. They can't keep up with him intellectually."

Then she met my eyes. "Do you think I'm a bad mother for hiring you? Be honest."

I shook my head. "No. I think you're amazing."

She smiled for the first time since knocking on my door that morning. "Thank you, Zoe."

I nodded.

She squeezed my arm. "I'll let you get settled in."

Then she left me alone in the cabin.

I unpacked my few things into the built-in dresser. Everything fit in one drawer. I even had my own bathroom. Marble countertop. Gold fixtures. A shower with enough water pressure to strip paint.

I splashed water on my face and looked in the mirror. Peeled off the largest Band-Aid.

The scrape stretched from my cheekbone to my jaw in an angry red line. I traced the weeping line with my fingertip, wondering if I'd carry this reminder of my tumble down the hillside for the rest of my life.

I went into the bedroom and looked out the porthole. I

was on the starboard side with a view to the horizon. The ocean rolled in gentle swells that caught the afternoon light and threw it back in scattered diamonds. A pelican skimmed the surface, wings barely moving. Behind it, the wake of some distant boat cut a white line across the blue.

Next to the window, attached to the wall, was an emergency flare kit.

There was a knock on my door. I walked over and answered it.

Talon stood there, holding a chess set. He glanced at my cheek, then averted his eyes. "Want to play?"

"Sure."

We climbed to the main deck where afternoon sun warmed my battered face. The marina stretched around us like a moat of privilege, each yacht an island of wealth.

Talon arranged the chess pieces on a teak table that had been bolted down with marine-grade hardware: even board games required engineering when you were floating. We played all afternoon.

Rose brought us snacks. "Don't get too full. Dinner in an hour."

We nodded but dove into the potato chips anyway.

When we finished our sixth game, Talon gestured to the board. "Another?"

"You'll just beat me again."

"Probably." He grinned, then started resetting the pieces. "But you lasted longer that time."

I laughed.

Footsteps sounded on the deck behind us. I turned around. Caleb stepped onto the deck, looking like he'd fought his way through a windstorm, a duffel bag slung over one shoulder, dark stubble shadowing his jaw.

"Hey, buddy." He reached out to ruffle his son's hair, but Talon ducked away.

"Don't."

Caleb held up a hand. "Sorry. I just—"

Talon stood, gathering the chess game. "I'm going to get ready for dinner."

Then he walked off.

Caleb turned to me. "Did he say what's bothering him?"

I shook my head. "The carjacking. Gordon's murder. Liam's illness. It's been a pick your trauma kind of week for him."

Caleb nodded. "Yeah. It's just—it feels like something else. If you find out anything, let me know?"

I hesitated, then said, "I'll do my best."

"Thank you, Zoe."

I headed below to wash up, already regretting my promise to Caleb. The last thing I wanted was to turn Talon into another surveillance target. He had enough problems without his nanny becoming his spy.

Chapter Forty-Five

ROSE HAD WHIPPED up grilled halibut with herbed crust. Rice pilaf. Steamed vegetables. We ate in the small dining area off the galley.

I could see other yachts in the marina through the windows, their lights twinkling in the gathering dusk.

Talon picked at his fish.

Caleb cleared his throat. "So. You excited about starting your PhD?"

Talon didn't respond.

Caleb glanced at Rose. She shrugged.

"I saw something on the news about a new planet they discovered. In the Kepler system?"

Talon paused, his fork halfway to his mouth. "Kepler's not a system. It's a space telescope."

"Oh. Right."

"And they don't discover planets anymore. They detect exoplanets using transit photometry. The last major discovery was TOI-715 b, but that was months ago."

"I just thought—"

"You thought wrong."

"Talon," Rose said.

He set down his fork. "I'm not hungry. I'll be in my room."

Caleb's face crumpled as Talon disappeared. "I was just trying to engage with him."

Rose leaned over and patted his hand. "It's not your fault. It's been a hell of a week. And he's losing his best friend."

Caleb nodded. "Of course. You're right."

We finished eating in silence, me feeling like a third wheel the whole time.

I helped Rose clear the dishes after dinner, then washed up while the two of them went outside and sat on the deck. Their heads were close together as they talked in low voices.

No apparent animosity between them.

I didn't bother saying goodnight after I finished cleaning up, instead heading straight to my bedroom. I checked my messages. No response from Frenchie.

I texted Elsa. *We're staying on a yacht for the next few days. Feels surreal after everything that happened*

Ooh, luxury! Living that rich girl life now! Are you okay though?? That kidnapping thing sounds terrifying

Trying to enjoy it Miss you

I changed into my pajamas and switched out the bandages on my hands.

Then I curled up on the bed, staring out the porthole and watched the sun, a perfect orange ball, sinking into the water. The sky caught fire. Clouds turned pink, then gold, then deep purple.

The water reflected it all back, like watching the sunset twice.

It took twenty minutes for the sun to disappear

completely. Then the sky faded to deep blue. Stars appeared. A few at first, then more.

The yacht swayed. I closed my eyes.

The mattress was perfect. The sheets were a cool Egyptian cotton. But every sound seemed amplified. Water lapping against the hull. Footsteps on the deck above. The distant sound of laughter.

Around midnight, I gave up trying to sleep.

I grabbed my hoodie, then slipped out of the cabin and made my way upstairs and outside onto the deck.

Rose sat on a bench near the bow, looking out at the water. A joint glowed orange between her fingers. She glanced around, caught my eyes.

"Sorry, I didn't mean to interrupt," I said.

"Can't sleep?"

"Not used to the motion."

"It takes getting used to."

"I'll leave you."

"No. No. Grab the champagne from the fridge, would you? Bring a couple of glasses."

I made my way to the galley, opened the refrigerator, and found a bottle of Dom Pérignon on the top shelf. Embossed gold label, and cold to the touch.

I returned to the deck with bottle and two champagne flutes from the cabinet. Rose stubbed out her joint in an ashtray as I handed her the bottle.

Rose peeled away the wire cage with ease and then gripped the cork while rotating the bottle: the technique of someone who'd opened enough champagne to stock a wedding. The cork came out with a soft pop, flying out over the edge of the boat and disappearing into the dark.

I sat beside her and held the glasses while she poured.

She set the bottle aside, took one of the glasses, and

raised it in a toast. "To surviving another day in the Marlowe family."

We clinked. The champagne was cold and crisp. Tiny bubbles burst on my tongue. I sat beside her.

"You like LA, Zoe?" she asked.

"I do."

"But you wouldn't want to live here, not full time?"

"No. I like the seasons."

"Yeah. I understand that."

Stars punctured the darkness like scattered sequins. Away from the city's glow, the night sky revealed its full arsenal of light.

"Sometimes I feel like running away. It's hard to figure out when I'm supposed to perform and when I'm supposed to be real."

Her honesty caught me off guard. I had no roadmap for conversations about the performance of being human. She changed the subject.

"What do you want to be when you grow up, Zoe? I can't imagine it's a nanny."

I took a sip of champagne. "A journalist. Well, maybe not any longer. A writer. Novelist. Not that I've started writing yet."

"Why the switch?"

"Madeline says I'm good at observation."

"Madeline is right."

"Thanks."

Rose drained her champagne and sparked another joint, the flame illuminating her face for a brief moment before she held the joint toward me like an offering.

I shook my head, looking out at the marina lights reflecting on the water. "It's beautiful here."

"Maybe. But I hate this yacht. It's full of terrible

memories." She took another drag. Held it in. Then let the smoke out slowly.

"So why do you keep it?"

Rose leaned back, looking up at the sky. "Because Nova won't get rid of anything that belonged to Isabella."

"Your mother owned this?"

"She owned everything. The houses, the cars, the yacht. The studio." Rose leaned over the edge of the boat and flicked her ash into the water. "She was a control freak. Had to own and possess everything she touched."

"Including her husband and children?" I took a sip of champagne.

Rose looked over at me. "Especially her children."

"That can't have been easy."

She shook her head. "If we annoyed her, she'd take anything that we loved and throw it out. Liam's toys, Nova's books, my scripts, Jaxon's money."

"That's terrible."

"Liam had this vintage toy robot when he was five. This little mechanical thing that walked around and made beeping sounds. Some director gave it to him."

She took another puff of her joint. "Isabella hated that damn thing. Said it was too noisy. She threatened to throw it overboard. Right off this deck."

She gestured toward the railing. "Liam was crying, begging her not to. But she held it over the water. Taunting him. Telling him maybe if he was a better boy, she'd let him keep his toys."

"I'm sorry."

"Liam tried to grab it back. He was so little. He just wanted his robot." Another drag. "He pushed her out of the way. And then she was gone."

A chill went down my back. I stared at her. "What?"

"Yeah." Rose pointed to a spot about twenty feet from where we sat. "She went right under like a stone."

"You're saying Liam is the one who knocked her overboard?"

She nodded. "But he didn't know she couldn't swim. He was five."

"And no one else saw?"

She shook her head. "We were all downstairs. I had gone to check on him, saw he was missing and went to find him. Met him on the stairs. He simply said that he went to get his robot."

She took another drag. "I tucked him to bed, kissed him goodnight. Then went to bed myself. No one knew she was missing until morning."

Her words drifted between us like smoke that couldn't be waved away.

She smiled. "I don't think Liam really knew what he had done. I tried to do my best to reassure him that she'd just fallen over, but for some reason in his teens, he started remembering. And then came the drugs and the drinking as he tried to forget."

She blew out a breath and looked over at me. "We weren't sorry she was gone, Zoe. God, that sounds horrible, doesn't it? But it's true. We were relieved."

I fingered my glass.

"She was a monster through and through. She would have thrown us away too if she thought she could have gotten away with it. Chucked us overboard and sailed away."

Rose stubbed out her joint. Picked up her glass and held it out. I topped it up. She took a sip. "Nova was the only one who mourned her. But then she always worshipped Isabella. Thought she could do no wrong."

We sat in silence for a while. The lights from shore twinkled across the water.

"I trust you won't tell anyone that sordid little family tale?" Rose asked.

I shook my head. "Never."

"Thanks."

"Is that why Liam said he deserved to die?"

She nodded. "Yeah. Poor bastard."

I heard footsteps behind us and turned.

Caleb appeared, clutching his phone. "Jaxon called. Liam's taken a turn for the worse."

Rose was on her feet in an instant. "How bad?"

"He wants us at the hospital. Now."

I stood. "You should go. Talon and I will be fine here."

Rose looked uncertain. "Are you sure?"

"Positive."

Caleb was already heading toward the gangplank. Rose grabbed my hand and squeezed it. "Thank you, Zoe. I'm sorry if my story upset you."

"Thank you for trusting me with that." What else could I say?

I walked them to the gangplank.

"Pull it up behind us." Caleb pointed to a small metal box mounted on the hull. "Red button retracts it."

"But how will you get back up?"

"We've got remotes."

I watched them walk down the aluminum plank, their footsteps echoing against the metal. Caleb looked back when they reached the dock, giving me a thumbs up.

I found the control panel and hit the button.

The gangplank shuddered, then slid up, sections telescoping into each other like a collapsing antenna. Thirty seconds later, it had disappeared into the hull.

I walked to the stern and stared at the spot where Isabella Marlowe had vanished thirty years ago. The water looked innocent now, reflecting the marina lights like scattered coins. But some secrets never stayed buried.

They just waited for the right tide to wash them back to shore.

Chapter Forty-Six

ROSE AND CALEB disappeared into the maze of docks, their footsteps swallowed by distance.

I walked back to the stern, my bare feet silent on the teak decking. The marina breathed around me: water kissing hulls with gentle slaps, rigging chiming like wind chimes in the salt breeze, the distant arterial hum of PCH.

Even the city's restless energy felt muted out here, filtered through money and distance.

I pulled my hoodie closer, the fabric damp from ocean spray.

Then turned around and froze.

Staring at the name of the boat: *Reel Escape.*

RE.

My pulse quickened. Lopez had said Hatch was meeting someone with the initials RE. Everyone assumed it was a person. But what if it wasn't?

What if RE was a place?

This place?

And Gordon was supposed to meet him here?

Everyone assumed the meeting never happened, that

Hatch died before he could deliver whatever bombshell he'd uncovered. But what if they had connected? What if Hatch had revealed his wife's killer, sending Gordon spiraling back into the bottle?

But why didn't Hatch simply call the police?

Unless Hatch and Gordon hadn't met up.

And Hatch met someone else here.

But who?

I went into the main cabin. Hatch's body had washed up on shore. Was it possible he'd been on the boat? Killed here, taken out to sea, then tossed overboard? That would have been far easier than killing him elsewhere and driving him to the ocean like everyone seemed to think.

I scanned the room. The living area was pristine. Too pristine.

Maybe it had just recently been cleaned.

But no.

That couldn't be possible. Could it?

I started searching for any sign that Hatch had been here. If he'd been on board as a guest meeting with Gordon or someone else, it would probably have been in the kitchen, the dining area, or one of the seating areas. Somewhere they could sit and talk. Somewhere private where he could share whatever news Hatch had uncovered about Beth's death.

I walked through the galley first, glancing around. I opened a few cupboards, but I had no idea what I was looking for. Evidence of some kind of fight? There weren't any broken dishes.

I opened drawers. All the cutlery seemed to be there.

The knife block was full. I went to the dining area. Maybe they would have met here? Except that it was kind of formal.

I stepped outside and flipped on the deck lights, their

harsh LED glow turning the teak white as bone. I methodically checked each lounge area. The aft section was tucked away from the marina's main thoroughfare. Private enough for clandestine meetings, close enough to the water for easy body disposal.

I examined the area.

The cushions sat plump and undisturbed. No overturned glasses or scattered papers. Everything looked like it had been styled for a yacht broker's photo shoot.

I dropped onto the bench. I was being ridiculous. I picked up a throw cushion and hugged it to my chest.

A dark fleck caught my eye: rust, maybe, or old wine. I brushed at it with my finger. The spot flaked away like dried blood, leaving a rusty smear under my nail. My hand froze. I looked closer at the bench's white surface.

A constellation of dark droplets decorated the wall behind the bench—tiny, almost artistic in their spray pattern. The kind of delicate spatter that comes from arterial pressure meeting sharp steel.

So small they'd be easy to miss unless you were specifically looking for them. Like someone had tried to clean up but hadn't been thorough.

Shit.

Maybe it was just rust.

But I knew it was blood spray.

If it belonged to Hatch, someone from the family had killed him.

I needed to call Lopez.

My phone was charging in my cabin. I circled around the yacht's starboard side, my heart hammering against my ribs. I took the stairs two at a time inside, my feet silent on the carpeted steps.

Then I heard the gangplank screech. Someone was

coming aboard. Surely, Rose and Caleb weren't back already? Maybe they had forgotten something?

I checked my phone when I got to my cabin. A text from Rose: *arrived at the hospital. I'll text you an update.*

My blood turned to ice water. They'd just arrived at the hospital. So who was prowling around upstairs?

I stepped into the corridor and knocked on Talon's door. Silence.

I slipped inside, moonlight streaming through the port-hole like liquid mercury, painting everything in shades of silver and shadow.

His bed was empty. Sheets twisted, still warm.

Where was he? Had he gone upstairs? Was he trying to escape?

A floorboard creaked behind me.

I spun around just as something whistled through the darkness toward my skull. I threw my hands up defensively. Wood cracked against bone, my forearm absorbing the blow meant for my head.

Pain shot up my arm like electricity.

I stumbled backward. "What the fuck?"

"Oh shit! Zoe?"

Talon emerged from the cabin's darkest corner, a wooden baseball bat trembling in his white-knuckled grip. Moonlight turned his face into a porcelain mask of terror, his usually neat hair sticking up in panicked tufts.

He dropped the bat.

"Where did you get that?" I asked.

"I brought it with me."

"Why?"

He blanched. "Because I thought Caleb might come after me."

I rubbed my forearm where the bat had connected. It

was already starting to throb and swell. That was going to leave a hell of a bruise. But what was one more?

I gaped at him, my forearm throbbing. "Why would he do that?"

"Because he saw me."

"When?"

Talon looked miserable. "The night of Uncle Gordon's murder."

Every muscle in my body locked. "What?"

He sniffed. "I saw him come out of your room. All wet. A towel around his head and shoulders."

I sank onto his bed. Caleb had killed Gordon? And Talon was a witness? No wonder he'd been acting so strange. Then I rubbed my head. It still didn't make sense. "But why would he kill Gordon?"

Talon shrugged. "I don't know. Bertie said maybe Mom was having an affair with him."

I frowned. "I don't believe it."

"Why not?"

"I know this is going to sound stupid, but I think your parents are having an affair with each other."

He stared at me. "What?"

"They always leave together. They're on their phones at the same time. I don't think Rose was following Caleb that day we ran into them at the restaurant. I think she was meeting him there."

"But why would they do that?"

"I don't know why your family does half the things it does."

"But if she wasn't having an affair with Gordon, Dad had no reason to kill him."

"Exactly. So how well did you see your dad that night?"

He pursed his lips. "It was dark and … maybe I just assumed it was him."

Assumptions. They had a way of getting people killed. I heard the boat's engine rumble beneath us. The vibration traveled through the hull, through our feet, into our bones. Then it began to move.

"Where are we going?" Talon asked.

I got to my feet. "I don't know."

I spotted a movie poster on the wall above Talon's bed. *The Last Witness.* The movie Rose was watching the other night. The poster showed her in shadow, looking back over her shoulder with terror in her eyes.

I walked over and read the credits.

Isabella Marlowe … and Jaxon Marlowe. My heart nearly stopped. What had Rose said? That Jaxon had only ever been in one movie. This one. The one where the man had his throat slit. Wound up in a pool.

"Is it possible you saw your uncle Jaxon that night? He and Caleb are the same height."

Talon paled. "Maybe."

I glanced up at the ceiling. I needed to stop the boat from leaving the marina. I gave him my phone. "Dial 911 and ask for Detective Lopez. Tell her where we are."

He nodded, then made the call.

I ran to the door and grabbed the handle.

But it wouldn't turn.

I tried again. Pulled harder. Twisted it both ways.

Nothing.

Someone had locked it.

Fuck.

We were trapped on a boat heading out to sea. And I was pretty sure Gordon's killer was our captain.

Chapter Forty-Seven

I POUNDED on the door with both fists.

"Open the door! Let us out!"

No response.

The engines roared to life beneath us, twin diesels churning water into foam. Vibrations traveled up through the hull, through the floor, into my bones. We were picking up speed. I pounded again, ignoring the pain in my knuckles.

"Open the damn door!"

Nothing.

I tried kicking it. All I did was leave smudges on the wood.

Talon touched my arm, held out my phone.

I took it from him. "Detective Lopez?"

"Zoe? What's happening?"

"We're on the family yacht. *The Reel Escape*. Being taken out to sea. Talon and I have been locked in a cabin below deck."

"I'm notifying the Coast Guard right now. Police boat too. Sit tight."

I laughed. Even if we could get out, where we were supposed to go? We were on a bloody boat.

I swallowed. "I think it's Jaxon. Talon saw him coming out of my room the night of the murder. He lured Caleb and Rose away."

"We finally found Hatch's car. It had been towed from the marina. Found hidden documentation that the vehicle that killed Gordon's first wife Beth belonged to Isabella Marlowe."

"But she would have been dead at the time."

"Yes. It was being driven by Nova Marlowe at the time of the accident."

I swallowed. "Nova killed Beth?"

"Yes. And we believe that's what Hatch told Gordon."

Everything clicked into place. Jaxon getting Nova drunk at the bar that night. Making sure she had a solid alibi for when he murdered her husband that night. Killing to protect his sister from being charged with manslaughter. The family needed to be protected. Even from family.

I felt the yacht's acceleration in my stomach. I glanced over at Talon. His eyes were wide and black.

"You need to hurry," I said.

"Coast Guard's mobilizing now. Stay on the line with me. Don't hang up."

"I'm going to hand the phone to Talon. I'll try to block the door somehow so he can't get in."

"Alright."

I passed the phone back to Talon. He clutched it to his chest. I looked around the small cabin. The bed and side tables were bolted to the floor. The portholes were too small for us to climb out.

"What's Uncle Jaxon going to do to us?"

"I don't know."

His eyes filled with tears. "Don't lie."

"You're his flesh and blood. I refuse to believe he wants to hurt you," I said. But my voice was shaking.

"Then why did he lock us in?"

"Maybe he just wants to scare us. Make sure you won't tell anyone you saw him."

He sniffed, nodding.

I searched the cabin. Yanked open every cupboard. Pulled the cushions off the built-in seating. Checked under the bed.

Nothing that could block the door.

The boat hit a large wave. Salt spray splattered against the porthole.

I walked over and picked up the baseball bat. At least we had this.

And then I smelled it.

Something strange. Sweet and chemical. Like cleaning fluid mixed with something medicinal.

I turned to look at Talon. "Do you smell that?"

He nodded, pointing.

A thin haze drifted down from the air vents near the ceiling. I got to my feet. Smoke? Were we on fire?

No.

Gas.

I grabbed the phone from Talon. Tried to keep my voice calm. "He's pumping some kind of gas into the cabin."

"What kind of gas?" Lopez asked.

"I don't know."

"Try and keep it from entering the cabin."

I handed Talon the phone and stripped the bedding. Then I climbed onto the small bedside table. The boat swayed, I lost my balance and tumbled down onto the mattress.

Talon cried out.

I forced a smile. "I'm okay."

I climbed back onto the table, wobbling as the yacht pitched.

The chemical smell invaded my lungs with each breath, making the world tilt sideways.

Plus there were three other vents.

I got back down, took the phone. "I can't cover the vents."

"Don't panic. We'll find you."

My mind raced. How long had we been moving? The marina could be miles behind us now. The Coast Guard would have to search thousands of square miles of dark ocean.

"Get down on the floor," Lopez said. "Gas tends to accumulate along the ceiling first."

I gestured frantically for Talon to drop down beside me.

I collapsed beside him, grabbing the fitted sheet and tearing at it with my teeth like a wild animal. The fabric finally gave way with a satisfying rip. I fashioned a makeshift mask, knotting it tight behind my head.

It was almost as bad as that hood the Russians had thrown over my head. But at least this time I could see. I tore another strip. Wrapped it around Talon's head and tied it off. "Can you still breathe?"

He nodded.

I got a notification on my phone. Two percent battery remaining.

"My phone's dying."

"Alright," Lopez said. "Keep it on as long as you can."

I set it aside, then lay down beside Talon, taking his hand.

My eyes began to burn.

Talon whimpered.

"I'm right here," I said.

Chemical fire spread through my tear ducts. Water poured from my eyes, turning the improvised mask soggy and useless. Even with my lids clamped shut, the gas found every nerve ending, turning my face into a map of pain.

Talon tried to shake me loose. "It burns."

"Don't rub them. You'll make it worse."

Talon tightened his grip on my hand. I opened my eyes. I could see him blinking through my blurred vision, his eyes red and streaming.

The haze grew dense as fog, each breath like swallowing poison. My stomach rebelled violently. I clawed the useless mask away just as bile erupted from my throat, splattering across the cabin floor.

Talon was retching as well. I untied his mask so he wouldn't choke.

He doubled over, throwing up Rose's dinner all over the floor.

Now we had no protection at all. The full force of the gas hit our lungs.

Talon closed his eyes tight, his face scrunched in pain.

I curled up around him. "Talon?"

He didn't respond.

His breathing was labored. The burning in my eyes was so intense I could barely keep them open. Everything blurred together through my tears and the thickening haze.

The cabin felt smaller. Darker. The gas continued to seep in.

"Talon, you've got to stay awake."

I pressed my fingers to his neck, searching for a pulse. Found it. Weak but steady. I shook him again. "Come on, wake up."

But he was unconscious.

The boat's engine noise changed. Slowed to an idle. The gas stop pumping in the room.

My heart thudded against my ribs.

I covered my mouth with one hand, tried to haul Talon toward the bed with the other. I wasn't sure what I was planning. There was nowhere to go.

But I was too woozy.

I collapsed onto the floor, fighting to stay conscious.

The door lock clicked.

Jaxon stepped inside, wearing a full gas mask. Black rubber face. Round goggle eyes. Clear plastic breathing apparatus. He looked like something from an apocalyptic nightmare.

He stood looking down at us.

I threw myself across Talon.

A grunt escaped his mask, irritation at my defiance. His boot connected with my ribs, a precise kick that drove the air from my lungs and sent lightning through my torso. Pain exploded through my body. I recoiled.

He leaned down and grabbed Talon by the ankles. Then dragged him out of the room.

"Don't touch him!" Saliva poured down my chin. My voice came out slurred and strange. Words were slurry in my mouth. I might not have said them out loud.

I tried to follow. But my limbs were rubber.

He pulled Talon into the hallway. Then slammed the door behind them.

The turning lock was like thunder.

But some of the gas escaped when he opened the door. I still couldn't see well, but I could think better.

I crawled over to the door, forced myself to stand.

Then I started kicking.

Again and again. Throwing my body weight behind

each blow. I backed up, took a running start, and hit the door with my shoulder.

The impact jarred my teeth.

I almost tripped on the bat. Picked it up and struck the polished brass door handle. The metal rang like a bell. I swung harder, denting the mechanism. Again and again, hitting the decorative cover, cracking then splitting.

On the fifth strike, something inside the lock gave way with a satisfying *snap*.

I grabbed the handle and twisted, throwing my shoulder against the door one more time.

It flew open and I stumbled out into the corridor, gasping for air that didn't taste like chemicals.

The corridor spun around me. My vision went black for several seconds. When it came back, I was lying on my side in a puddle of my own drool.

"Get up, Zoe," I told myself. I crawled back into the room, grabbing my phone. Jaxon didn't know it was dead. I crept along the passage on my hands and knees, feeling like I was swimming through syrup.

I found the stairs and pulled myself up one step at a time. Then made my way across the living room and into the galley. Straight for the fridge. I grabbed a bottle of water, uncapped it, tilted my face up, forced my eyes open, and poured out the water.

It was cold and it stung, but it helped clear my vision. I grabbed a steak knife from the drawer, then made my way outside into the stern lounge area. The ocean breeze hit my face like a blessing. I gulped down the fresh ocean air.

We were a long way from shore and it was dark. Thank God for the moon. Across the deck, I spotted Jaxon dragging Talon toward the boat's rail.

"Hey! Asshole!"

His head snapped around.

I held up my phone. "Just called the cops on you. They're coming."

His gaze flicked between Talon's limp form and me. Decision made, he abandoned his nephew and stalked toward me with predatory focus.

I backed away, clutching the knife behind my back.

"Might as well deal with you first. Thank you for saving me the trouble of hauling you up here."

"The cops know everything. That you killed Hatch. And Gordon."

He laughed. "The cops know shit. I didn't kill Hatch. Nova did that."

I stumbled back. "What?"

"Nova has always been too emotional for her own good. I told her a million times to leave Gordon alone after his wife's death."

I stared at him. "You mean after she killed her?"

He hesitated. "Exactly. But Nova felt too guilty. She couldn't live with what she'd done. So she went to that AA meeting intending to apologize. Offer him money to shut him up. Support him. I don't know. Instead, the idiot fell in love."

I took another step back, clutching the knife. He continued to track me.

"And when Gordon found out, you had to kill him."

"Of course. No one else was going to do it. I'm the protector of this family. I keep our secrets buried. Maintain our reputation."

"And Talon?" I asked.

Jaxon frowned. "The boy saw too much. Knows too much."

"Rose will never forgive you."

Jaxon glared at me. "Rose will never know the truth.

She'll think you both fell overboard. Another tragic family accident."

"She won't believe it."

He smiled. "I'm very persuasive."

Then he lunged.

And I stabbed. Striking him in the chest, but only barely.

He bellowed, punching me in the head. "You little bitch."

Stars whirled in front of my eyes. I hit the side of the cabin, collapsed onto the deck.

He grabbed the knife and tossed it over the side. Then he leaned down and hoisted me up. Pressing my back against the metal deck rail. The steel was cold through my thin shirt.

I braced myself. Gripping the rail behind me with both hands.

He tried to lift me.

I kicked at his legs and tried to knee him in the groin while hanging on to the railing for my life.

Behind him, Talon stirred.

He sat, shaking his head like he was trying to clear cobwebs.

He met my eyes.

"Run!"

Jaxon turned his head. I grabbed him around the neck and held on, but Talon didn't flee. Instead he ran toward us.

"Get away from her!"

Jaxon spun around, slamming me backward into the side of the cabin.

My spine hit the hard fiberglass wall. Volcanic pain erupted through my back and shoulders. The impact knocked the wind out of me, I lost my grip on him.

He grabbed Talon by the hips, hoisted him up and lunged forward.

Talon's eyes met mine. "Zoe!"

Talon's body arced through the moonlight and vanished. The splash when he hit the water might as well have been a gunshot.

"No!" The scream tore from my throat.

Jaxon turned back to me, wiping his hands like he'd just taken out the trash. "Now. Where were we?"

I sprinted toward the bow, my feet pounding against wet fiberglass. I vaulted over the rail without hesitation, launching myself into the void.

For a heartbeat, I was suspended between the boat and the ocean, between life and death.

Then gravity claimed me, and I plummeted toward the hungry Pacific below.

Chapter Forty-Eight

THE OCEAN HIT me like a frozen fist, driving every molecule of air from my lungs. Salt water rushed into my mouth and nose, darkness closing over my head like a lid.

Sound became muffled and strange. The yacht's engines a distant throb, water gurgling in my ears like a death rattle. Panic spiked through me as I imagined getting chopped up by the propellers, but I kicked hard against the churning wake.

My chest felt like I'd inhaled napalm. The gas had left my lungs raw as hamburger, every breath a symphony of broken glass. I surfaced, gasping, saltwater streaming from my hair.

The yacht's lights were already distant, leaving me alone in an ocean of black ink.

Where was Talon?

The water slapped against my face in irregular waves. I raised my head, treading water. Navigation lights blinked red and green in the distance, but they might as well have been stars for all the help they offered.

I tried to get my bearings. The coastline was a thin line of lights about two miles away.

"Talon!"

The yacht was dark.

And then a beam of light. Jaxon. Looking for me with a flashlight. The light came closer. I dove under the water, swam off. Surfaced again.

"Talon!"

And then I heard it.

A whistle.

Three sharp blasts.

"Keep blowing!" I shouted, grabbing my whistle, raising it to my lips, and blowing three sharp blasts in response.

I treaded water, waiting.

He responded again.

The sound came from my left.

I swam as fast as I could. The cold had knocked some sense back into me, but my limbs still felt like lead weights. I had to find Talon before the cold got to him.

Or he drowned.

Or Jaxon found us.

I blasted my whistle again.

And so did he.

Only it cut off.

I blew mine again.

No response.

Shit.

"Talon!"

Water splashed into my mouth. I choked, coughing.

And then I heard his whistle again. Closer now. I swam toward the sound. My clothes dragged at me. I rolled over and kicked off my shoes.

My legs felt lighter, more responsive. I could actually make progress now.

Something white bobbed in the water ahead.

A channel marker buoy.

And Talon was clinging to it.

Moonlight caught the white of his t-shirt and the gleam of his glasses, miraculously still clinging to his face despite the chaos. He'd wrapped himself around the metal pole like a koala, his thin arms barely able to encircle its girth.

Thank God.

Jaxon caught me with the flashlight as I swam toward Talon.

I froze, looking up at him.

Then he disappeared.

Whatever game Jaxon was playing could wait. I headed straight for Talon. Then I heard the yacht's engines.

The boat started circling us, moving in a wide arc around our position, engines churning the dark water. Each pass brought it closer, the wake growing more violent as it expanded.

Waves were hitting me hard. The buoy rocked. Water sloshed on Talon's head.

"Hold on!"

The yacht completed another circle, this one tighter. The wash was getting worse. Rolling waves that lifted Talon up and hurled him down in sickening lurches.

The buoy groaned against its anchor chain.

He was struggling to keep his head above water. Each wave that hit us sent spray flying.

I swam harder, fighting against the turbulence. The yacht came around again. Closer still. The wake was now a churning wall of white water that slammed into the buoy like a battering ram.

I reached Talon just as another massive wave hit. I grabbed onto the buoy with one hand and him with the other.

"I've got you!"

His whole body was shaking, either from cold or terror or both.

"Can you hold on?" I asked.

He nodded, but I could see he was barely managing.

Another wave hit. It knocked me back. He slipped from my grasp and went under like a stone.

"Talon!"

I dove deep, searching the dark water. The ocean was murky even in daylight. At night, it was like swimming through black coffee. I couldn't even see my own hands in front of my face.

I windmilled my arms through the black water, praying to connect with fabric, flesh, anything human. The cold was already getting to me. My muscles cramped. My lungs screamed for air.

Nothing.

I surfaced, sucked back oxygen, dove again.

This time my fingers brushed fabric. An arm hit me in the face. I grabbed hold of his shirt and hauled him up, breaking the surface in an explosion of spray.

He sputtered, coughing, and the he panicked.

He grabbed at me, his hands clawing at my shoulders and arms, pushing me under and using me as a flotation device.

I pulled out of his grasp and swam backwards. I had to. He would have drowned us both.

I circled back, approaching him from behind. Grabbed him under the arms in a rescue hold.

"No more struggling," I said into his ear, "or we'll both drown."

He continued to flap about.

"Talon! Listen to me."

He stilled.

"That's it. I've got you. And I'm not gonna let you drown, okay?"

He burst into tears.

I treaded water, holding him tight. "I'm not lying, okay?"

He nodded, his body was vibrating like a tuning fork.

I swam us back to the buoy. Linked his arms around the pole. Then hooked myself on as well, holding onto him with my free hand.

He was breathing too fast.

"Slow down. We'll be fine. Police and coast guard are looking for us."

The Pacific water was maybe fifty-five degrees, cold enough to kill in hours, not days. Talon's thin frame was already betraying him, violent shivers wracking his body as hypothermia began its deadly work. How long before the Coast Guard found two corpses floating in the dark?

Twin diesels roared across the water, growing louder by the second.

I positioned myself at Talon's back, covering him, then looked over at the yacht. Jaxon was bringing the boat back around, trying to find us.

Then he was back on the deck with his flashlight.

Sweeping its beam across the water.

I ducked behind the buoy, pulling Talon with me. It was barely wide enough to hide both of us, and all we had.

The flashlight beam passed over our hiding spot. Moved on.

Thank God.

I lifted my head.

The beam snapped back, shining directly in my eyes.

Shit.

Then it snapped off.

"What's he gonna do?" Talon was barely audible, teeth chattering so hard he could barely get the words out.

"I don't know. But whatever happens, don't you let go of me."

He nodded.

The engines changed pitch. Jaxon brought the yacht around again, and I could see what he was planning.

The prow was headed right for us.

He was going to run us over. Use the yacht as a weapon. If we were ever found, it would look like an accident.

"Talon, get on my back. But be loose with your arms so you don't strangle me."

He wrapped his arms around my shoulders and his legs around my waist. I could feel his heart hammering against my spine.

I waited, watching the boat.

The yacht bore down on us like some prehistoric sea monster. Its running lights blazed in the darkness. White water peeled back from the bow like the ocean was being unzipped.

The engine noise was deafening now, echoing across the open water.

I waited until the last possible second, preparing to kick hard to the right.

But then a loud scraping sound split the night.

A *CRACK* like a tree falling.

The boat stopped dead in the water and tilted to the side, its bow lifting up out of the ocean.

It had run aground.

Jaxon had misjudged the depth, and the yacht had hit a submerged outcropping. It listed heavily to starboard, its hull grinding against whatever obstruction had stopped it.

"What happened?" Talon asked.

"It's run aground. Take a breath."

"Why?"

"Because we're going underwater."

"I'm scared, Zoe."

"I know. So am I. But I got you, okay? And whatever you do, don't let go."

His fingers dug into my shoulders. "I won't."

"Count of three. One. Two."

I heard him take a deep breath. And then I dove.

I swam toward the yacht, Talon clinging to my back. The vessel was in serious trouble, listing so far to one side that its deck was only a few feet above the waterline.

I swam to the lowest side, where the rail was closest to the water.

One of the dock lines had fallen into the ocean, still attached to a cleat on deck. Thick white rope that looked strong enough to hold our combined weight.

My fingers were numb from the cold, but I caught it in both hands, treading water.

Then I knotted it around Talon's waist.

"What are you doing?" he asked.

"Getting you out of here."

The knot was clumsy, but it would hold. I gave it a test tug, then looked up at the yacht's tilted deck.

"I'm gonna climb up, then pull you out."

"No. Don't leave me."

"Stay strong, Talon, okay?"

He nodded.

I lunged for the railing. Still inches short. The yacht groaned and settled deeper, bringing salvation within reach.

I exploded out of the water, fingers locking onto cold metal, hauling myself up and over the rail. Water poured from my clothes like I was a broken fountain.

I grabbed the rope and hauled Talon up.

I was exhausted. My arms shook from the effort, but he was almost within reach—

Something slammed into me. Jaxon. All two hundred pounds of him.

I lost my hold on the rope. The impact drove the air from my lungs and sent me sprawling across the wet deck.

Talon fell back into the water with a splash.

"Hold on!" I screamed.

Jaxon scrambled over to me, his hands finding my throat, thumbs pressing into my windpipe. His face was a mask of rage. "You should have gone quietly."

I couldn't breathe. Black spots danced at the edges of my vision.

I punched him. A wild, desperate swing that connected with his nose. The exact spot where Rose had hit him. Cartilage crunched under my knuckles and warm blood spattered across my hand.

He bellowed, his grip loosening.

I kicked him in the groin. Hard as I could.

He grunted, doubling over, and lost his hold.

I scrambled to my feet and ran back to where I'd left Talon. He was still in the water, clinging to the rope.

I glanced back. Jaxon was charging after me.

I ran.

Down toward the stern. My feet slipped on the wet fiberglass, but I managed to keep my balance.

He followed. I could hear his footsteps behind me, his ragged breathing.

The yacht was listing more now. Whatever damage it had sustained below the waterline was letting in serious water. The boat groaned and creaked as metal stressed against metal. I needed to buy time so Talon could climb up the rope on his own, or so the coast guard could find us.

But Jaxon was faster than me. Stronger. And he wasn't weakened by whatever gas he'd used in that cabin.

I reached the stern and spun around.

He was ten feet away. Blood streamed from his broken nose. His shirt was torn.

Coastline lights twinkling in the distance, about two miles away.

Jaxon lunged at me.

The yacht shuddered and listed farther to starboard.

He stumbled, missing me.

I feinted left, then dodged right. But we were sinking. I was about to run out of deck to retreat to.

I fled back toward the bow, along the port side where the deck slanted upward at a crazy angle. I slipped on the wet fiberglass and went down hard, my palms scraping against the surface.

Jaxon was right behind me.

His hand closed around my ankle.

I kicked back with my free foot. Felt it connect with something solid.

He grunted and his grip loosened just enough for me to pull free.

I scrambled forward on hands and knees, then regained my footing.

The bow was only twenty feet away, but I could hear Jaxon getting closer.

The yacht groaned like a living thing in pain as the boat slowly gave up its fight against the ocean. I had maybe minutes before the whole thing went under.

And Jaxon was still coming after me.

Chapter Forty-Nine

Jaxon's footsteps pounded on the deck behind me.

"There's nowhere to run." His voice was calm. Almost conversational. "Give up, Zoe."

"No way."

Something flew past my head. A deck cushion. It hit the rail and bounced into the sea. I glanced back. He reached for a fire extinguisher.

He was throwing debris at me.

I dodged left as the extinguisher struck the side of the ship where I had been. It clattered across the deck and disappeared over the side.

I ran along the slanted deck, my socks slipping on the wet surface. The yacht was listing badly now. Maybe thirty degrees. I spotted a large deck locker near the stern rail. Maybe I could hide in there?

I flung open the lid and saw a stack of orange life jackets.

I grabbed one, shoving my arms through the armholes and pulled it over my head. Thick padding pressed against my ribs. My fingers fumbled with the buckles across my chest. Cold had stolen most of the feeling from my fingertips.

I grabbed an armful of the remaining jackets and ran down to where Talon was hanging in the water, still holding tight to the rope.

"Heads up!" I chucked the life jackets over the side, then crept toward the bow, using deck furniture for cover. The game was simple: keep Jaxon focused on me, not on the kid dying of hypothermia in the water.

Metal screamed against rock somewhere below, the yacht's death throes vibrating up through the deck. The list was getting worse by the minute. I could hear Jaxon moving around on deck, his footsteps were getting closer.

"Come out, come out, wherever you are, Zoe."

"I will if you let Talon go. He's just a kid. He won't say anything."

"But children remember everything eventually. Puberty was the end of everything for Liam. I spent years keeping him stoned out of his mind so he wouldn't spill the beans. Just imagine having to turn your sibling into an addict to keep the family secrets."

I grimaced.

"It was hell."

For Liam too, I imagined.

"I'm not doing that again."

I belly-crawled along the yacht's tilted deck, saltwater soaking through my clothes. Searchlights carved through the darkness like lightsabers in the distance.

I needed to get their attention. They were too far away to hear me shouting and it was too dark to see me waving.

Flares.

There were some in my room. And there had been a white box on the wall next to the lifejacket locker. Maybe there were some in there.

A loud *thunk* sounded from behind him.

Something long and sharp embedded itself in the cabin wall inches from where I crouched. I glanced up. A fishing spear, its barbed tip buried deep in the fiberglass, its aluminum shaft vibrating from impact.

I turned.

Jaxon was braced against the railing, ten feet away, loading another spear.

I bolted for the life jacket locker, my feet sliding on the treacherous deck. I pried the white emergency box open. Inside was coiled rope, a whistle, some kind of repair putty, but no flares.

But there were some in my cabin.

I ran inside and hit the stairs. They were flooded. I hesitated.

Then something hit me from behind.

I tumbled down the stairs into the flooded hallway below.

The Pacific rushed over my head in a frigid embrace. I surfaced, gasping in what used to be the yacht's hallway, now a vertical swimming pool lit by emergency strobes that painted everything in hellish red.

Jaxon looked down at me, aiming his spear gun from the top of the stairs.

I ducked deep.

The spear sliced through the water, grazing my upper arm with a line of fire across my skin.

I surfaced, blood mixing with salt water.

He slammed the hatch down. The bang echoed through the flooded space.

I splashed up the stairs, water and blood streaming from my hair and clothes. I pressed my shoulder against the heavy hatch and pushed. It didn't budge. He'd locked it from outside.

I continued down into the flooded hallway. Although now it was sideways. Water was up to my waist and rising fast, the bedrooms now above me.

I hoisted myself up and through the angled doorway and climbed over to the window where I found the emergency kit mounted on the wall. I opened it and took out the flare gun alongside three cartridges in waterproof packaging.

I grabbed a spare shirt from the dresser, fashioning it into a makeshift bag for the flares and gun, then tucked the whole bundle against my chest.

I couldn't get out the hatch, but I could go out through the same hole that was sinking us.

I filled my lungs with recycled air and let gravity pull me down into the flooded bedroom below. It was fully under water. The gash in the hull was visible in the red emergency lighting. It was narrow, and jagged fiberglass edges stuck out like broken teeth. Beyond it was nothing but black water.

I surfaced and undid the buckles on the life jacket, wrestling it off my head.

I drew a deep breath and dove down, squeezing into the opening.

Sharp fiberglass scraped my shoulders, cut into my arms.

I twisted sideways, trying to make myself smaller. A jagged piece caught my shirt. I yanked harder. The fabric tore.

I was halfway through when my hips wedged against the sides. Stuck.

Panic shot through me. My lungs were already burning. I pushed against the hull with my feet, trying to force myself through. The edges cut deeper. More blood in the water. I twisted again, forcing my way forward inch by inch.

Then I tumbled through. Free. For a moment, I didn't know which way was up. I let myself float. My body wanted to rise, so I kicked toward what I hoped was the surface. My chest felt like it was going to explode. My vision tunneled, the world shrinking to a pinprick of red light.

I finally broke through the water, gasping for air.

A scream split the night.

Talon.

I swam around to the other side of the boat as fast as I could. The yacht was listing so badly now that the deck was almost vertical.

Jaxon had cut the rope.

Talon was in the water, splashing and sputtering. Without the rope to hold onto. His head disappeared beneath the surface before he managed to struggle back up, coughing salt water.

I swam over to him, grabbed one of the lifejackets I'd thrown earlier, and took hold of him.

He bellowed until he saw it was me and burst into tears.

I forced a smile. "Told you I was going to save us."

I worked his thin arms through the holes, pulling the orange padding over his shoulders. Then I clipped the buckles closed.

Treading water, I pulled the flare gun out of my shirt.

The soaked fabric had turned the knots into concrete. I gnawed at them like a rabid animal until they finally surrendered. Then I pulled out the flare gun and a cartridge.

"Hold this." I handed Talon the shirt with the other two cartridges.

I tore open the package. Pulled out the red cartridge. Cracked the gun open and slid it into the chamber. The cylinder clicked into place. I snapped it closed.

"Ready?" I asked.

He nodded, his eyes wide.

I held onto his life jacket with one hand and pointed the gun into the night sky with the other. Then I squeezed the trigger.

The flare shot out with a loud pop and a shower of sparks. A brilliant red streak arced up into the darkness like a meteor. High enough to be seen for miles, it exploded at the top of its trajectory in a burst of crimson light that painted the water red.

Jaxon leaned over the edge of the tilted deck. "You bitch!"

The flare's crimson glow turned him into something from a nightmare. Blood streaming from his shattered nose, shirt hanging in tatters, eyes blazing with the kind of fury that comes from watching your world burn.

I reached into my shirt and got another cartridge, loaded it into the gun, and aimed it right at him.

He froze, raising the speargun. "Don't you fucking dare."

I pulled the trigger.

The flare streaked across the water trailing sparks and smoke. Hit him square in the chest with a shower of ruby red fire.

His scream split the night as magnesium fire ate through fabric and into flesh, the flare's chemicals turning his chest into a constellation of burning wounds. He stumbled backward for a minute, dropping the speargun, beating at the burning flare with his hands, trying to smother the flames. Then he charged forward, diving into the water.

Landing beside us.

The boat lurched and made a sound like a dying whale. Air bubbled up from somewhere deep in the hull as the last pockets of trapped air escaped.

The *Reel Escape* was going down.

The stern sank first, bow rising higher and higher out of the water.

Jaxon surfaced near us, his clothes still smoking. Patches of his shirt had burned away completely. Red burns covered his chest and arms. He tried to grab me. "I can't swim!"

I kicked away, pulling Talon with me.

We stroked toward the navigation buoy that had saved us before. The *Reel Escape* surrendered to the Pacific with surprising dignity. No explosions or dramatic death throes, just a quiet slide into the abyss. Within seconds, only bubbles marked where millions of dollars in Marlowe family history had vanished forever.

I was exhausted.

Every stroke was agony. My muscles had nothing left to give. The cold had sapped what little strength I had left.

The buoy was fifty yards away. Might as well have been fifty miles.

The flare dissipated high above us, flames surrendering to the dark.

"Hold on." Talon sounded stronger now that he had the lifejacket keeping him afloat. "Boats are coming."

The searchlights were definitely closer now. I did my best to keep swimming. But I was so cold. And so tired. The hypothermia was setting in. Making my thoughts sluggish. Turning my movements clumsy.

My strokes became weaker. More erratic.

The buoy seemed to get farther away instead of closer.

"Zoe?"

I grunted. Unable to speak.

And then I heard a splash nearby.

A woman in a bathing suit popped up beside us. For a moment I almost thought she was a mermaid. "Hey, sweetheart. How are you both doing?"

"Take Talon," I said, pushing him toward her.

Then I couldn't hold on anymore and I slipped under the water.

Chapter Fifty

I OPENED MY EYES.

Staring up at white ceiling tiles.

The room stunk of hospital.

I blinked, trying to focus. Everything felt fuzzy around the edges, like looking through dirty glass. My throat was raw.

I heard a rustling sound to my right.

I rolled my head to the side. Talon sat propped against white pillows, his nose buried in a paperback. The hospital gown swallowed his thin frame, making him look more like ten than thirteen.

He glanced over and saw me watching him. His face broke into a smile. "You're awake."

I tried to speak but could only croak.

He pointed. "There's water on your bedside table."

I glanced to my left, spotting a plastic cup with a straw. My arm felt like it weighed a hundred pounds, but I managed to grab it. Then I sat back on my elbow and took a difficult drink.

I set my cup down and lay back against the pillows. "Where are we?"

"Cedars-Sinai. Two floors down from Liam."

"How did we get here?"

"Coast Guard. You were kind of out of it." His eyes grew watery. "I thought you died, Zoe."

My entire body ached. "I kind of feel like I did. How long have I been out?"

"Two days."

"Jeez."

I stared at the ceiling. Thinking back to the *Reel Escape*. The cold water. Jaxon's hands around my throat. Being trapped in downstairs. Forcing my way out. Surfacing near Talon.

Then nothing.

"Are you going to pass out again?"

I laughed. "No. I'm awake."

He ducked his head, pretending to read, but I caught him stealing glances over the pages every few seconds. I pinched my arm. It hurt, and I was glad to know this wasn't a dream.

I heard voices in the hallway.

Rose entered the room, holding the door open wide. Then Caleb pushed Liam's wheelchair through the doorway.

I waved.

Rose gasped, then ran to my bed, hauled me into her arms and burst into tears. Full on crying, soaking my hair.

"Stop it, Mom," Talon said.

"I can't," she wailed.

I patted her back.

Caleb parked Liam's wheelchair at the foot of my bed.

"Good job, saving the brat, Nanny Zoe," Liam said.

Talon stuck out his tongue.

Liam grinned. Then his laughter bubbled up: pure and bright and utterly alive.

Rose pulled back. Her mascara had smudged all over her cheeks and probably mine as well. "Thank you for bringing my baby back to me."

"I'm just glad I was there."

Inadequate words, but honest ones.

Rose dragged her hand across her cheeks, creating abstract art with her mascara. For once, she didn't give a damn about her appearance. Caleb walked over and took my hand. His mouth trembled and I could tell he was trying not to cry. I gave it a squeeze.

There was a knock on the door. Lopez entered without waiting for an answer.

Rose stiffened. "Did you find my brother's body?"

She shook her head. "No, but he'll wash up sooner or later. The ocean might be deep, but the currents around Los Angeles are predictable."

"Well, as far as I'm concerned, the fishes can eat him," Rose said.

Lopez walked over to us. "However, I did want to let you Nova's been arrested for the death of Beth Falls, and Denton Hatch's murder. Turns out she did find out that Gordon hired him. Killing him was her way of canceling the contract. Too late. Hatch had already told Gordon that she was responsible for Beth's death."

"Jesus Christ," Rose said. "The press is going to have a field day."

"Nova had no idea Jaxon planned Gordon's murder. He'd told her they'd just talk things through like civilized people. When Gordon's throat was cut, Jaxon assumed he was dead. But Gordon managed to crawl to your pool, probably hoping you'd save him, Zoe."

"And Talon?" Rose asked. "Did Nova know what Jaxon had planned for him?"

Lopez shook her head.

Rose tightened her lips. "Well, I guess that's a small mercy."

The detective's phone chirped. She checked the screen, frowning. "I need to take this, but I'll be back shortly to take your statement, Zoe."

I nodded.

"Speaking of phones," Rose said, taking one from her purse and setting it on the bedside table. "Caleb picked you up a new one. I got your number from Madeline. Liam set it up for you."

"Thanks."

She nodded. "There's someone else that wants to see you. If you're up to it?"

I couldn't imagine who. I was beginning to feel overwhelmed. But I nodded. Might as well get all the visiting over with.

She walked to the door and opened it.

Maxwell walked in, with Olivia trailing behind him.

He came over to my bed. "Looks like Madeline sent me the right one after all." His voice was hoarse. I could tell he was trying not to cry. "Thank you for saving my grandson."

"You're welcome."

Maxwell's eyes crinkled with something like amusement. "I'm afraid you're out of a job, though. Only got one heir left worth a damn."

I laughed. "That's okay. I'm kind of ready to be done."

Maxwell gripped my hand, gave it a squeeze. Then he turned to Olivia. "My wife has something to tell you. Something Liam discovered."

I glanced at Liam. His eyes were on Olivia.

Olivia's wedding ring spun around her finger like a prayer wheel, faster and faster as her panic mounted. "I'm sorry about the cameras. I put them there."

I blinked. "You did?"

Maxwell gestured to me. "Tell her the rest."

She looked down at the floor. "I also drugged your tea that night so I could gain access to your room."

The pieces clicked into place. No wonder I'd crashed so hard that night, exhaustion was only the start.

"I was concerned that you and Maxwell … well." She glanced at her husband.

Once again. Ew.

Maxwell turned towards the door. "She only did it because if I cheat, she gets more money in the divorce. Now I need a cigarette."

Olivia stared after him. "We're getting divorced?"

But Maxwell was already gone.

Olivia glanced at Rose. "We're getting divorced?"

"Ask him," Rose said.

"Maxwell, wait!" Olivia ran to the door, following him out.

The room fell quiet again.

I looked at Rose. "Did she take Hatch's wallet as well?"

She shook her head. "That was found in Jaxon's office."

Their voices became background noise as exhaustion pulled me under like an undertow. I opened my eyes again to find it was just me and Talon in the room.

I rolled over and reached for the phone. I had several missed calls and a text from Elsa.

Flight to Los Angeles on Friday. ✈️ *Can't wait to see you!* 😊 🖤

I smiled. Texted: *Me either.*

My phone buzzed.

Elsa again. *Heard about the boat rescue on the news. Are you okay?*

I typed back slowly. My fingers felt clumsy. *I'm okay. Long story. Tell you when you get here.*

Can't wait. Love you.

Love you too.

I set the phone aside. Glanced over at Talon. "What are you reading?"

"Hardy Boys."

"The Hardy Boys? Isn't that a little basic?"

He shrugged. "I like the mystery."

I laughed, then closed my eyes, and drifted off to sleep.

The nightmare was over.

Time to figure out what came next.

Chapter Fifty-One

I FOUND Talon in the living room, sitting on the couch with a box, wrapped in white paper with a large silver bow. I set my suitcase and carry-on bag in the front doorway.

Every muscle in my body felt like it had been tenderized with a meat mallet.

The cuts on my arms from the fiberglass were still tender. My shoulder ached where I'd wrenched it swimming. My cheek was still bandaged. I was trying my very best not to cry.

I walked over to Talon, forcing myself to smile.

He picked up the box. "I have something for you."

I sat on the couch beside him. "Let me guess. A really big whistle."

He laughed.

I took the box. It was heavier than I expected. I tore the paper off. A MacBook Pro. The latest model. I stared at the laptop, then at him.

"Talon, I can't accept this."

"You can."

"But it's too much."

"You said you wanted to write a novel. You need a laptop for that."

I pulled him into a hug, blinking back tears. "Thank you."

He hugged me back, his thin arms wrapping around my shoulders.

When we pulled apart, I studied his face. "I know it was you."

He blinked. "What was me?"

"The one who was spying for Maxwell. That's why you took a year off school, isn't it? So you could watch your family."

Talon went statue-still. Then his mouth twitched, fighting a smile that eventually conquered his entire face.

"Gordon figured it out?" I asked.

"Yeah. It was my idea to have Maxwell 'hire' you as backup, so no one would suspect me."

I laughed. "You little mastermind. I want an invite to your PhD graduation."

"Deal."

I clutched the laptop to my chest. "I'm gonna miss you, Talon. But I'll look for you in the stars."

"I'll be there. Discovering new ones."

I sniffed, wiping my eyes.

He squeezed my hand. "Thank you for being my friend, Zoe. You know when you said it must be lonely being smart?"

I nodded.

"You were right. But this is the first time ever I haven't been."

I hugged him again. "I'll always be your friend. No matter how old."

I heard movement on the stairs and turned to see Rose and Caleb joining us. I got up and walked over to them.

"You've been a godsend, Zoe," Rose said. "Truly."

Caleb nodded. "We'll never be able to thank you enough."

"Do you mind if I ask a personal question?"

"Go on," Rose said.

"Are you pretending to have affairs with other people, but it's really just yourselves?"

Rose went beet red. Caleb stared at his shoes.

"Just trying to rekindle some of the magic we once had," Rose admitted.

"And Lana Ferris?"

Caleb laughed. "She and her husband were the ones that suggested it. Said it worked for them. She was meeting up with us to see how it was going."

I flushed. "Sorry, I didn't mean to pry."

"Nonsense," Rose said. "You're family."

I almost believed her. "Good luck running the company."

"Actually, I'm thinking of selling." Rose replied, pulling me into a hug. "It's time for a fresh start. Take care of yourself, Zoe."

"You too."

Caleb stepped forward and gave me a brief hug as well. "Keep in touch."

I nodded.

Then grabbed the whistle around my neck. "I nearly forgot this."

Rose grabbed my hand, tucking it around the whistle. "You keep that. You never know when you might need it."

"Thank you, Rose."

"Now are you sure we can't give you a ride to the airport?"

"No, I'm good. The Uber will be here any minute."

They formed an honor guard to the front door, none

of them wanting this moment to end. I secured the laptop in my carry-on while Caleb hefted my suitcase, playing the gentleman one last time. I heard a vehicle coming up the drive. It was my ride.

Talon grabbed me from behind, wrapping his arms around me and burying his face against my shoulder. I held him tight, feeling him shake. "I'm going to miss you."

"Me too," I said.

The car stopped and the driver popped the trunk.

Caleb lifted my suitcases inside and then opened the back door. I was shaking. And couldn't get in.

"Zoe?" Rose asked.

I blinked back tears. "If I could have any mom in the world, I would choose you, Rose. I want you to know that."

Her face crumpled. She pressed her hand to her mouth, trying to hold back her own tears. "Oh, Zoe."

"I mean it. You're just so loving and accepting." My voice cracked. "I never imagined a mother could be like that."

Rose pulled me close again, her arms tight around me. "You know you can call me anytime if you need anything. You got it?"

I nodded against her shoulder.

"Open door policy. You're not the nanny anymore, Zoe. You're family."

This time, I did believe it. Even if it was just for this moment, I felt it. Really felt it. "Thank you."

She pulled back, wiping her eyes. "Now you'll be late to pick up your friend. Have fun at the Beverly Springs Hotel. Order room service. Go shopping on us. Have fun, okay?"

I could barely speak. "Thank you."

"Now get in the car before we all start crying again."

I laughed.

I slid into the Honda's back seat, already missing them. But before I closed the door, I poked my head out. "Could I ask one favor?"

"Of course," Rose said.

"Could you send a bunch of autographed photos to Madeline for the nannies?"

She laughed. "Consider it done."

I smiled, then closed the door, watching them out the back window, waving until they disappeared from view. Then I burst into tears.

Thankfully my driver didn't ask any questions.

The vultures had moved on to fresher carrion, leaving Mulholland Drive peaceful for once. My phone pinged. I figured it was Elsa, but nope.

It was from Bertie.

A photo filled my screen: Bertie and Willa on white sand under blue sky, both glowing with new love and vitamin D. She looked radiant with her hair loose and wild, while he looked like a man who'd won the lottery and couldn't believe his luck.

I typed: *Congratulations!*

Then hit send.

I opened a new message to Elsa: *In the car now!* 🚗 *Should be at LAX in about 45 minutes. I'll be waiting at the curb in arrivals. Black Honda Civic. Can't wait to see you!* 😊✈️💜

I sent the text, then leaned back against the head rest and closed my eyes. I would miss the Marlowes. A lot.

When we were ten minutes from the airport, I checked Elsa's flight status on the airline app. They were early. Her flight from JFK had landed twenty minutes ago.

I checked the message I'd sent her.

It showed delivered but not read.

We pulled up in arrivals, joining the long line of cars at

the curb, exhaust vomiting from engines. Stinking up the already hot air.

I glanced at my driver. "She should be here soon."

But fifteen minutes later she still wasn't. I sent another text: *I'm here! Are you getting your luggage?*

Still nothing.

Maybe her phone died. That happened sometimes on long flights. But it was only five hours. I tried calling. It went straight to voicemail.

"I can't wait," the driver said.

"I know." I paid him and climbed out, dragging my suitcase and carry-on.

LAX's afternoon heat hit like opening an oven door. I escaped into the terminal's air-conditioned sanctuary.

The arrivals board confirmed what the app had told me. Her flight had landed over half an hour ago.

I walked to arrivals and waited for almost an hour. But there was still no sign of Elsa. So I went to airline desk, getting in line behind a family arguing about lost luggage. When it was my turn, I approached the counter.

"I'm looking for a friend on the flight from JFK that landed almost two hours ago. Can you tell me if she was on board?"

She shook her head. "I'm sorry, I can't provide passenger information due to confidentiality policies."

Right. Of course. "Thanks."

I walked away, a knot of worry starting to form in my stomach.

A cop lounged near security, middle-aged and radiating the enthusiasm of someone counting minutes until retirement.

"Excuse me, I'm looking for my friend. Her flight landed two hours ago but I can't find her anywhere."

"Maybe she flaked off. Happens all the time."

"No, she wouldn't do that. We had plans."

"Did you check the restaurants? Bathrooms? Why don't you do that, then come back and check with me. She's probably just fixing her makeup."

I clenched my teeth. Asshole.

I swallowed my irritation and played dutiful tourist, methodically checking every Starbucks and Hudson News, every bathroom and restaurant. I sent more text messages to Elsa's phone. Nothing. I called her number, and it went straight to voicemail.

The knot in my stomach had grown teeth, gnawing at me with increasing hunger.

Where was she?

I was standing near the Hudson News when my phone rang. For a split second, relief flooded through me. Elsa.

But the caller ID said Madeline.

"Madeline!"

"Zoe, where are you?"

"I'm at LAX. I was just about to call you. Elsa's flight landed over two hours ago and I can't find her anywhere."

"That's because she wasn't on the plane."

"What do you mean she wasn't on the plane? She was supposed to—"

"Zoe, listen to me. You have forty minutes to get yourself through security for your flight. I've sent you an email with the details."

My phone pinged with an incoming message.

"What flight? What's going on? Why wasn't Elsa on the plane?"

Silence.

And then she said, "Elsa's been arrested for murder."

LAX dissolved around me, thousands of travelers blurring into meaningless shapes while their chatter compressed into static.

"What?"

"Get yourself through security, Zoe. Your flight leaves in less than an hour."

"Wait, wait. Murder? What are you talking about? Who did she supposedly murder?"

"We'll talk when you land in New York. Right now, you need to focus on getting home."

The line went dead.

I stood there in the middle of LAX, clutching my phone, travelers streaming around me, excited to be arriving in the city of dreams.

Elsa arrested for murder?

But she'd never hurt anyone. Elsa could barely kill a spider without feeling guilty.

I pulled up Madeline's email. Sure enough, there was an e-ticket for a flight to JFK departing in thirty-eight minutes.

I tried to process what was happening.

Elsa. Arrested. Murder.

Who?

And why?

I forced my legs to carry me toward security, thirty-eight minutes to catch a flight back to whatever nightmare was waiting for me in New York.

Elsa. Arrested for murder.

The words refused to make sense, no matter how many times I repeated them.

But I was about to find out exactly what they meant.

The End

About The Authors

Nolon King writes fast-paced psychological thrillers set in the glitzy world of entertainment's power players with a bold, insightful voice. He's not afraid to explore the darker side of human nature through stories featuring families torn apart by secrets and lies.

Nolon loves to write about big questions and moral quandaries. How far would you go to cover up an honest mistake? Would you destroy your career to protect your family? How much of your soul would you sell to get the life of your dreams? Would you cheat on your husband to keep your children safe? Would you give in to a stalker's demands to save your marriage?

Lauren Street has always loved a mystery. As a kid growing up in Bible Belt country she devoured every whodunit book she could get her sticky little hands on and secretly investigated all of her (seemingly) normal boring neighbors. Sometimes their pets and farm animals too. All grown up now and living in the UK with her thoroughly unsuspicious (and often unsuspecting) husband, she writes domestic psychological thrillers about families torn apart by secrets and lies. And she sometimes still peers over garden walls to check up on the neighbors.

No Return

No Stopping

No Fear

Once Upon A Crime

Once Upon A Crime

Twice Upon A Lie

Three Times a Murder

Dead For Good

Dead For Good

Left For Dead

Dead Of Night

Wake The Dead

Dead For Life

Standalone Novels

Pretty Killer

12

Blown

Miserable Lies

The Target

Secrets We Keep

Close To Home

Heat To Obsession

A Simple Kill

Tell Me No Lies

Red Carpet Black

Fade To Black

Victim

Post Partum

Also By Lauren Street

The Nanny Problem

Rock-A-Bye-Bye

Nursery Crimes

Child's Prey

The Still County Thrillers

Still Here

Still Buried

Still Burning

Still Hidden

The Bishop Smoky Mountain Thrillers

Hide Me Away

Fuel To The Flame

Closer By The Hour

A Gamble Either Way

Calling My Children Home

Too Far Gone

Here You Come Again

A Friend Like You

The Company You Keep

One By One

Come Back To Me

The Only Way Out

Replaced with Nolon King

Replaced
In Her Place
Irreplaceable

The Salazar Redwood Forest Thrillers
The Girl Who Couldn't Stop Dying
The Girl Who Couldn't Get Out
The Girl Who Couldn't Be Found

Standalone Novels
Postpartum